W9-DAY-836

The Dragon Man

THE
DRAGON
MAN

Garry Disher

Copyright © 1999 by Garry Disher

All rights reserved.

First published in Australia by Allen & Unwin

First published in the United States in 2004 by
Soho Press, Inc.
853 Broadway
New York, NY 10003

Library of Congress Cataloging-in-Publication Data
Disher, Garry
The dragon man/Garry Disher
p. cm.
ISBN-13: 978-1-56947-395-5
I. Police–Australia–Melbourne Region (Vic.)–Fiction.
2. Melbourne Region (Vic.)–Fiction.
3. Serial murders–Fiction.
4. Australia–Fiction.
I. Title.

PR9619.3.D56D73 2004
823'.914–dc22   2003067232

10   9   8   7   6   5   4   3   2

I wish to thank the CIB and uniformed officers of the Victoria Police who gave freely of their time when I sought background information for this book. Any deviations from standard police procedure are mine (the notion of a regional homicide inspector, for example).

And I owe a great debt of gratitude to my editor, Carl Harrison-Ford, for showing me how to make this a much better book.

for Helen Sargeant

The Dragon Man

PROLOGUE

Sometimes it felt as if he were prowling the roof of heaven, riding high through the night, the stars close above him, nobody about, the teeming masses with their petty concerns tucked safely into their beds. He was as restless as a fox. He seemed to have a channel through life at times like this, a path through the broad darkness that was the Old Peninsula Highway, nothing and nobody to beset him. Down he went, the whole length of the slumbering hook of land, to where it reached the ocean, and then back again, to the far easterly tip of the city, where there were lights again, and the stench of humankind, and where he lived in a loveless house. He turned at a roundabout, headed on down toward the ocean again.

He came upon her about halfway along the highway. Other cars at night were almost an affront to him, but they were always gone in a flash, just a pair of headlamps, scarcely registering. This car had stopped, parked on the gravel forecourt of a roadside fruit and vegetable outlet, a massive barn-like shape in the night. He slowed to no more than a walking pace as he passed. The car looked forlorn, its bonnet up and steam rising from the radiator. A solitary bulb high on a nearby pole cast a weak cone of grey-yellow light over a telephone box and the young woman inside it. She was speaking urgently, gesturing, but seemed to freeze when she saw him

1

passing, and stepped out to get a better look at him. He accelerated away. The image he had of her was of the loneliest figure at the loneliest spot on earth. World's end. Amen.

He turned around at the next intersection, and when he reached her again he turned in off the road, steering close to her poor, hangdog car. Good. She was alone. He drove past her car until he was adjacent to the phone box, then wound down his window. He didn't want to alarm her by opening his door and getting out.

She was hovering in the phone box. He called across to her: 'Everything okay? Phone working? Sometimes it's been vandalised.'

He sounded like a local. That would help. He saw her wrap her arms about herself. 'Fine, thanks. I rang a breakdown service. They're on their way.'

He happened to glance away from her and at her car. He stiffened, looking back at her in alarm: 'Did you have someone with you?'

She froze, began to tremble, and her voice when it came was no more than a squeak. 'What do you mean?'

'There's someone in the back of your car, behind the seat.'

She edged toward him. 'Who? I didn't see anyone.'

He opened his door, put one foot on the ground. 'I don't like it. Did you leave the car unattended at any time?'

'The station car park. It's been there all day.'

'There have been cases . . . ,' he said.

He got out then, keeping his door open. They were both eyeing her car, ready to flee. 'Look,' he said, 'you'd better hop in with me, slide across to the passenger side.'

She weighed it up. He was careful not to look at her but to let her see the anxiety on his face. Then, as she came toward him, he moved away, edging around his own car and toward hers.

Her hand went to her mouth. 'What are you doing? Come back, please come back.'

'I want to get a closer look at him. For the police.'

'No!'

Her fear seemed to communicate itself to him. 'I guess you're right.'

'Just get me away from here!'

'Okay.'

2

It was as easy as that. Inspired, really. That first one, last week, she hadn't been a challenge at all. Drunk, half-drugged, hitchhiking, she'd been too easy. At least he'd got to use his head a little tonight. His headlights probed the darkness as he carried her away, high above the rottenness that was always there under the light of the sun.

ONE

Detective Inspector Hal Challis showered with a bucket at his feet. He kept it economical, but still the bucket overflowed. He towelled himself dry, dressed, and, while the espresso pot was heating on the bench-top burner in his kitchen, poured the bucket into the washing machine. Couple more showers and he'd have enough water for a load of washing. Only 19 December but already his rainwater tanks were low and a long, dry summer had been forecast. He didn't want to buy water again, not like last summer.

The coffee was ready. As he poured he glanced at an old calendar pinned to the corkboard above his bench. He'd bought the calendar by mail order three years ago, and kept it opened at March. The vintage aeroplane for that month was a prototype of the de Havilland DH84 Dragon. Then the toaster pinged and Challis hunted for the butter and the jam and finally took his toast and coffee on to the deck at the rear of his house.

The early sun reached him through the wisteria with the promise of a hot day ahead. He felt bone-tired. A suspected abduction on the Old Peninsula Highway two nights ago—the investigation ultimately dumped into his lap. Frankston uniforms had taken the call, then referred it to the area Superintendent, who'd rung at 1 a.m. and said, 'Maybe your boy's struck a second time, Hal.' Challis had spent the next four hours at the scene, directing a preliminary search. When he'd got home again at 5 a.m. yesterday there hadn't seemed much point in going back to bed, and he'd spent the rest of the day in the car or on the phone.

A little four-stroke engine was chugging away on the bank of his neighbour's dam. Cows once drank there. Now the cows were gone and the hillside stretched back in orderly rows of vines. Challis couldn't spot his neighbour among the vines, but the man was there somewhere. He usually was, weeding, pruning, spraying, picking. Challis thought of the insecticide spray, of the wind carrying it to his roof, where the rain would wash it into his underground tank, and he tossed out his coffee.

He stepped down from the verandah and made a circuit of his boundary fence. Half a hectare, on a dirt lane west of the Old Peninsula Highway, tucked in among orchards, vineyards and a horse stud, and Challis made this walk every morning and evening as a kind of check on his feelings. Five years now, and still the place was his port in a storm.

As he collected the *Age* from his mailbox on the dirt lane at the front of his property, a voice called from the next driveway, 'Hal, have you got a minute?'

The man from the vineyard was walking toward him. Small, squint-eyed from the angling sun, about sixty. Challis waited, gazing calmly, as he did with suspects, and sure enough the man grew edgy.

Challis stopped himself. The fellow didn't deserve his CIB tricks. 'What can I do for you?'

'Look, I realise it's nothing, but you know the ornamental lake I've got, over near the house?'

'Yes.'

'Someone's been fishing in it,' the neighbour said. 'After the trout. The thing is, they're scaring the birds away.'

Ibis, herons, a black swan, moorhens. Challis had watched them for half an hour one day, from a little hide the man had constructed in the reeds. 'Do you know who?'

'Probably kids. I found a couple of tangled lines and fish-hooks, half a dozen empty Coke cans.'

Challis nodded. 'Have you informed the local station?'

'I thought, you being an inspector—'

5

'Inform the local station,' Challis said. 'They'll send a car around now and then, make their presence felt.'

'Can't you . . .'

'I'm very sorry, but it would look better if you lodged the complaint.'

Challis left soon after that. He locked the house, backed his Triumph out of the garage and turned right at his gate, taking the lane in bottom gear. In winter he negotiated potholes, mud and minor flooding; in summer, corrugations and treacherous soft edges.

He drove east, listening to the eight o'clock news. At five minutes past eight he turned on to the Old Peninsula Highway, meeting it quite near the abduction scene, and headed south, toward the town of Waterloo, hearing the screams the dying leave behind them.

He could have been more helpful to the neighbour. He wondered what the man thought of him, a detective inspector and 'New Peninsula'.

The Peninsula. People talked about it as if it were cohesive and indivisible. You only did that if you didn't know it, Challis thought. You only did that if you thought its distinctive shape—a comma of land hooking into the sea south-east of Melbourne—gave it a separate identity, or if you'd driven through it once and seen only beaches, farmland and quiet coastal towns.

Not that it covered a large area—less than an hour by road from top to bottom, and about twenty minutes across at its widest point—but to a policeman like Challis there were several Peninsulas. The old Peninsula of small farms and orchards, secluded country estates, some light industry and fishing, and sedate coastal towns populated by retirees and holidaying families, was giving way to boutique wineries, weekender farms, and back roads populated with bed-and-breakfast cottages, potteries, naturopathy clinics, reception centres, tearooms and galleries. Tourism was one of the biggest industries, and people with professions—like Challis himself—were flocking to buy rural hideaways. Some local firms made a good living from erecting American-style barns and installing pot-belly stoves, and costly four-wheel drives choked the local townships.

But although there was more money about, it wasn't necessarily going to more people. A community centre counsellor friend of Challis's had told him of the growing number of homeless, addicted kids she dealt with. Industries and businesses were closing, even as families were moving into the cheap housing developments that were spreading at the fringes of the main towns, Waterloo and Mornington. The shire council, once one of the biggest employers, was cutting expenses to the bone, using managers whose sense of humanity had been cut to the bone. The adjustments were never forewarned or carried out face to face. Challis's counsellor friend now sold home-made pickles and jams at fairs and markets. There had been a letter, telling her she was redundant, her whole unit closed down. 'Just three days' notice, Hal.'

It was happening everywhere, and the police were usually the ones to pick up the pieces.

Which didn't mean that the Peninsula wasn't a pleasant place to live in. Challis felt as if he'd come home, finally.

And the job suited him. In the old days of murder or abduction investigations he'd been sent all over the state, city and bush, with a squad of specialists, but the Commissioner had introduced a new system, intended to give local CIB officers experience in the investigation of serious crimes alongside their small-time burglaries, assaults and thefts. Now senior homicide investigators like Challis worked a specific beat. Challis's was the Peninsula. Although he had an office in regional headquarters, he spent most of his time in the various Peninsula police stations, conducting investigations with the help of the local CIB, calling in the specialists only if he got derailed or bogged down. It was a job that entailed tact, and giving as much responsibility to the local CIB as possible, or the fallout was resentment and a foot-dragging investigation.

He didn't expect that from the Waterloo CIB. He'd worked with them before.

Challis drove south for twenty kilometres. The highway ran down the eastern side of the Peninsula, giving him occasional glimpses of the bay. Then the Waterloo refinery came into view across the mangrove flats, bright oily flames on the chimneys, and glaring white tanks. There was a large tanker at anchor. The highway became a lesser road, bisecting a new housing estate, the high plank fences on either side hiding rooftops that varied greatly but were never more than a metre apart. He crossed the railway line and turned right, skirting the town, then left on to a main road that took him past timber merchants, boat yards, Peninsula Cabs, crash repairers, an aerobics centre, the Fiddlers Creek pub and a corner lot crammed with ride-on mowers and small hobby tractors.

The police station and the adjacent courthouse were on a roundabout at the end of High Street, opposite a Pizza Hut. Challis glanced down High Street as he turned. The water glittered at the far end; frosted Santas, reindeer, sleighs, candles, mangers and bells swung from lampposts and trees.

He parked in the side street opposite the main entrance to the police station, got out, and walked into trouble.

'That windscreen's not roadworthy.'

A uniformed constable, who had been about to get into a divisional van that idled outside the station with a young woman constable at the wheel, had changed his mind and was approaching Challis, flipping open his infringement book and fishing in his top pocket for a pen. He's going to book me, Challis thought.

'I've ordered a new windscreen.'

'Not good enough.'

The Triumph was low-slung. On the back roads of the Peninsula, it was always copping stones and pebbles, and one had cracked the windscreen on the passenger side.

'This your car?'

'It is.'

A snapping of fingers: 'Licence.'

Challis complied. The constable was large—tall and big-boned, but also carrying too much weight. He was young, the skin untested by time and the elements, and his hair was cut so short that his scalp showed through. Challis had an impression of acres of pink flesh.

'Quickly, quickly.'

A classic bully, Challis thought.

Then the constable saw the name on Challis's licence, but, to his credit, did not flinch. 'Challis. Inspector Challis?'

'Yes.'

'Sir, that windscreen's not roadworthy. It's also dangerous.'

'I realise that. I've ordered a new one.'

The constable watched him for a long moment, then nodded. He put his book away. 'Fair enough.'

Challis hadn't wanted to be booked, and telling the constable to follow the rules and book him would have been an embarrassment and an irritation for both of them, so he said nothing. The constable turned and made for the van. Challis watched it leave.

'A real prick, that one,' a voice said.

There was a work-dented Jeep parked outside the courthouse. The rear doors were open and a man wearing overalls was unloading air-conditioning vents. Challis glanced at the side of the Jeep: *Rhys Hartnett Air-Conditioning*.

'The bastard did me over yesterday. Hadn't been here five minutes and he booked me for a cracked tail-light. Shouted in my face, spit flying, like I was some kind of criminal.'

Challis steered the conversation away from that. 'Are you working in the police station?'

The man shook his head. 'The courthouse.'

He snapped a business card at Challis. He did it in a way that seemed automatic, and Challis had a vision of hundreds of people walking around with unwanted cards in their pockets. He glanced at it. *Rhys Hartnett, Air-Conditioning Specialist*.

'Well, I wish you were doing the police station.'

Hartnett seemed to straighten. 'You a copper?'

'Yes.'

'Just my luck. I was wasting my breath complaining to you about police tactics.'

'Not necessarily,' Challis said, turning away and crossing the road.

The police station was on two levels. The ground floor was a warren of interview rooms, offices, holding cells, a squad room, a canteen and a tearoom. The first floor was quieter: a small gym, lockers, a sick bay. It was also the location of the Displan—Disaster Plan—room, which doubled as the incident room whenever there was a major investigation.

A senior sergeant was in overall charge of the station. He had four sergeants and about twenty other ranks under him, including a handful of trainees, for Waterloo was a designated training station. The CIB itself was small, only a sergeant and three detective constables. There were also two forensic technicians—police members, and on call for the whole Peninsula—and a couple of civilian clerks. Given that over thirty people worked at the station, that shift work applied to most of them, and that the uniformed and CIB branches generally had little to do with each other, Challis wasn't surprised that the young constable hadn't recognised him from his two earlier investigations in Waterloo.

The tearoom was next to the photocopy room. Challis crossed to the cluttered sink in the corner, four young uniformed constables falling silent as he filled a cup with tap water. He looked at his watch. Time for the briefing.

He wandered upstairs and found the CIB detectives and a handful of uniformed sergeants waiting for him in the Displan room. The morning light streamed in. It was a large, airy room, but he knew that it would be stuffy by the end of the day. The room had been fitted with extra phone lines, photocopiers, computers, large-scale wall maps and a television set. Every incoming telephone call could be automatically timed and recorded on cassette, and there was a direct line to Telstra so that calls could be traced.

Challis nodded as he entered the room. There were murmured hellos in return and someone said, 'Here's the dragon man.' He crossed to a desk that sat between a whiteboard and a wall of maps. He positioned himself behind the desk, leaned both hands on the back of a chair, and said, without preamble:

'On Sunday night a young woman named Jane Gideon made an emergency call from a phone box on the Old Peninsula Highway. She hasn't been seen since, and given that another young woman, Kymbly Abbott, was found raped and murdered by the side of the highway a week ago, we're treating the circumstances as suspicious.'

He straightened his back and looked out above their heads. 'You're Jane Gideon. You work at the Odeon cinema. You catch the last train to Frankston from the city, collect your car, an old Holden, and head down the highway, your usual route home. Picture the highway at night. Almost midnight. No street lighting, cloudy moon, very few cars about, no sense of humankind out there except for a farmhouse porch light on a distant hillside. It's a hot night, the hills are steep in places, your car badly needs a tune. Eventually the radiator

10

boils over. You limp as far as the gravelled area in front of Foursquare Produce, which is a huge barn of a place, set in the middle of nowhere, but there *is* a Telstra phone box nearby. No doors on it, very little glass, mostly steel mesh painted blue-grey. Feeling exposed to the darkness, you call the VAA.'

He slipped a cassette tape into a machine and pressed the play button. They strained to listen:

'*Victorian Automobile Association. How may I help you?*'

'*Yes, my name's Jane Gideon. My car's broken down. I think it's the radiator. I'm scared to keep going in case I break something.*'

Your membership number?'

'*Er—*'

They heard a rattle of keys. '*Here it is: MP six three zero zero four slash nine six.*'

There was a pause, then: '*Sorry, we have no record of that number. Perhaps you allowed your membership to elapse?*'

'*Please, can't you still send someone?*'

'*You'll have to rejoin.*'

'Jesus Christ,' someone muttered. Challis held up his hand for quiet.

'*I don't care. Just send someone.*'

'*How would you like to pay?*'

There was a pause filled with the hiss of radio signals in the dark night. Then Jane Gideon's voice came on the line again, an edge to it.

'*Someone's coming.*'

'*You don't require assistance after all?*'

'*I mean, there's a car. It's slowed right down. Hang on.*'

There was the sound of more coins being fed into the phone. '*I'm back.*'

The operator's tone was neutral, as though she could not sense the black night, the isolated call box and the young woman's fear. '*Your address, please.*'

'*Um, there's this shed, says Foursquare Produce.*'

'*But where? Your membership number, that's the Peninsula, correct?*'

'*I'm on the Old Peninsula Highway. Oh no, he's stopping.*'

'*Where on the highway? Can you give me a reference point? A house number? An intersecting road?*'

'*It's a man. Oh God.*'

The operator's tone sharpened. '*Jane, listen, is something going on there where you are?*'

'*A car.*'

'*Is there a house nearby?*'

'No.' She was sobbing now. '*No house anywhere, just this shed.*'

'*I'll tell you what I'm going to do. You*—'

'*It's okay, he's driving away.*'

'*Jane. Get inside your car. If it's driveable, find somewhere off the road where it can't be seen. Maybe behind that shed. Then stay inside the car. Lock all the doors and wind up all the windows. Can you do that for me?*'

'*Suppose so.*'

'*Meanwhile I'll call the police, and I'll also send one of our breakdown vehicles out to you. You can rejoin the VAA on the spot. Okay? Jane? You there?*'

'*What if he comes back? I'm scared. I've never been so scared.*'

Her voice was breaking as her fear rose. The operator replied calmly, but there was no comfort in her advice: '*Get in the car, lock the doors, do not speak to anyone, even if they offer help.*'

'*I could hide.*'

Clearly the operator was torn. The Victorian Automobile Association had been taping its emergency calls ever since a member had sued them for offering wrong advice which proved costly, with the result that operators were now careful not to offer advice of any kind—but a young woman alone on a deserted road at night? She deserved wise counsel of some kind.

'*I don't know,*' the operator confessed. '*If you think it would do any good. Hide where? Hello? Hello?*'

There was the sound of a vehicle, muffled voices, a long pause, then the line went dead.

'The rest you know,' Challis said. 'The VAA operator called 000, who contacted Frankston, who sent a car down there. They found Jane Gideon's car. The phone was on the hook. No signs of a struggle. They searched around the nearby sheds and orchards in case Gideon *had* decided to hide herself, but found nothing.' He glanced at his watch. 'Uniforms started

12

searching the area at daybreak yesterday. Our first task will be a door knock.'

He paused. 'It's early days, so try not to let one case colour the other, but we can't discount the possible links between Kymbly Abbott's murder and Jane Gideon's disappearance. Since I'm already working on Abbott, I've brought her files with me. Any questions so far?'

'What are the links, boss?'

'The Old Peninsula Highway for a start,' Challis said. He turned to a wall map. It showed the city of Melbourne, and the main arteries into the rural areas. Pointing to a network of streets which marked the suburb of Frankston, on the south-eastern edge of the city, he said, 'Kymbly Abbott had been at a party here, in Frankston. The highway starts here, a few hundred metres away. Abbott was last seen walking toward it, intending to hitch a ride home.' He traced the highway down the hook of the Peninsula. 'She lived with her parents here, in Dromana. They own a shoe shop. I have her leaving the party at one o'clock in the morning, possibly drunk, possibly stoned, so her judgment would have been shot. No-one at the party gave her a lift, though I will be talking to them all again. Her body was found here, by the side of the highway, just seven kilometres south of Frankston. We're appealing for witnesses, the usual thing, did anyone see her, give her a lift, see someone else give her a lift.'

'But that suggests our man's also prowling in Frankston itself, not simply up and down the highway.'

'I know. Or he lives in the Frankston area and was just setting out somewhere, or lives down here and was on his way home. Now, other similarities. Both incidents happened late at night. Both victims are young women who were alone at the time.'

He passed out crime-scene photographs. They showed Kymbly Abbott like a cast-aside rag doll in death, her throat and her thighs swollen and cruelly bruised. 'Raped and strangled. If that was the first time for our man, he might have been on a high for a few days, eager to try again on Sunday night.'

'Slim, boss,' someone said.

'I know it's slim,' said Challis, showing some heat for the first time, 'but until we've got more to go on what can we do

13

but use our imaginations and think our way into what might have happened?' He tapped his right temple. 'Try to get a feel for this guy.'

'What about the VAA mechanic?'

'He got there after the police did. He's in the clear.'

A detective said, 'I got called to a Jane Gideon's maybe six, seven months ago? Here in Waterloo. She'd had a break-in. A flat near the jetty.'

'That's her,' Challis said. 'I checked her flat in the early hours of Monday morning to see if she'd simply been given a lift home.'

He put his hands on his hips. 'There's a lot riding on this. Waterloo's not a big place. A lot of people would have known her. They're going to be upset, edgy, wanting results in a hurry.'

He waited. When there were no more questions, he turned to a Lands Department aerial survey map on the wall behind him. 'I want two of you to take a few uniforms and conduct a door-to-door along the highway. Much of it's through farm-land, so that helps. I drove along it on my way here this morning and saw only a couple of utilities and a school bus. One 24-hour service station here, where the Mornington road cuts it. Most of the farmhouses are set back from the road, but they'll still need checking out. And certain businesses. A place called The Stables, sells antiques. A couple of wineries. A deer farm, ostrich farm, flying school, Christmas tree farm— they'll be doing increased trade at this time of the year. A pottery, a mobile mechanic—look twice at him, okay? See if he had any late calls on Sunday night and the night Kymbly Abbott was killed. Also, in addition to Foursquare Produce there are two other fruit and vegetable places with roadside stalls.'

He turned to face them again. 'That's it for now. We'll meet here again at five o'clock. Scobie, I want you to draw up a list of known sex offenders who live on the Peninsula. Ellen, come with me.'

Two

'A young uniform tried to book me for a cracked windscreen when I arrived this morning. Beefy-looking, arrogant. Know who it would be?'

As CIB sergeant at Waterloo, Ellen Destry had very little to do with the uniformed constables, but she knew who Challis was talking about. 'That would be John Tankard. They call him Tank.'

'Fitting. Built like a water tank, roll over you like an army tank.'

'There have been a few complaints,' Ellen admitted. 'Someone's been distributing leaflets about him, calling him a stormtrooper.'

She fastened her seatbelt and started the car. They were going to Jane Gideon's flat, and she eased the CIB Falcon out of the car park behind the station and down High Street, toward the jetty. She was reminded by the holly and the tinsel that she'd asked people over for drinks on Christmas morning, and still hadn't bought presents for her husband and daughter.

That brought her by degrees to thinking about Kymbly Abbott and Jane Gideon. No Christmases for them, and an awful Christmas for their families. She tried to shake it off. You could get too close. Challis had once told her that being a copper meant stepping inside the skins of other people—

victim, villain, witness—and playing roles—priest-confessor, counsellor, shoulder to cry on. But ultimately, he'd said, you were there to exact justice, and when a homicide was involved that meant exacting justice for those who had no-one else to stand up for them.

She glanced across at him, slouched in the passenger seat, one elbow on the side window ledge, his hand supporting his forehead. At the briefing he'd displayed his usual restless intelligence, but in repose there was sadness and fatigue under the thin, dark cast of his face. She knew that he looked down a long unhappiness, and she didn't suppose it would ever go away. But he was only forty, attractive in a haunted kind of way. He deserved a new start.

He said unexpectedly, 'You like living on the Peninsula?'

'Love it.'

'So do I.'

He fell silent again. She loved the Peninsula, but that didn't mean she loved life itself. Things were difficult with her husband and daughter, for a start. Alan, a senior constable with the Eastern Traffic Division, had a long drive to work each day and resented her promotion to sergeant. 'They're fast-tracking you because you're a woman,' he said. And Larrayne was a pain in the neck, fifteen years old, all hormones and hatred.

The real estate agency which managed Jane Gideon's block of flats was next to a dress shop that had gone out of business six months earlier. A sign saying 'Support Local Traders' was pasted inside the dusty glass window. Ellen double-parked the car and waited for Challis to collect the key. She watched a clutch of teenage boys on the footpath. They wore pants that dragged along the ground, over-large T-shirts on their skinny frames, narrow wrap-around sunglasses, hair gelled into por-cupine spikes. They were idly flipping skateboards into the air with their feet, and one or two were spinning around on old bicycles. 'Nerds and rednecks, Mum,' Larrayne was always saying. 'You've brought me to live among nerds and rednecks.'

Challis slipped into the car and she pulled away from the kerb. She slowed at the jetty. Water made her feel peaceful. The tide was out and she watched a fishing boat steer a course between the red and green markers in the channel. Waterloo *did* have a down-at-heel, small-town feel about it, so she could see Larrayne's point-of-view, but before that they'd lived up in the city, where Alan's asthma had been worse, and the teenagers more prone to try drugs, and Ellen had wanted to get her family out of all that.

Jane Gideon's flat was on a narrow street of plain brick veneer houses. Ellen parked and they got out. Old smells lingered in the stairwell: curry, cat piss, dope. 'Number four, top right,' Challis said.

Ellen pictured him two nights ago, the darkness, his exhaustion, the long drive down here just to knock on the door of this sad-looking flat in the hope that Jane Gideon had not been abducted but given a lift home by a friendly stranger. He turned the key. Ellen followed him inside, knowing there wouldn't be anything worth finding, only a poor mother's phone number.

Before logging on to the computer and doing a printout of sex offenders, Detective Constable Scobie Sutton signed out a Falcon from the car pool and drove to the Waterloo Childcare Centre. He'd scarcely been able to keep his feelings under control during the briefing, and drove hunched over, his knuckles white on the steering wheel.

He pulled on to the grass at the side of the cyclone fence, and watched. Morning tea. The kids were seated in circles on the grass, grouped according to their ages. There she was, in the dress she called her blue ballet, happy as Larry now, her little face absorbed under the shade of a cotton explorer hat, slurping from a plastic cup and sticking her little fist into what looked to be a tupperware container of biscuits. She turned to the kid next to her and Sutton saw her grin, and then both children leaned until their foreheads touched.

He felt the tension drain away. But that didn't change the fact that his daughter had screamed the place down when he'd dropped her off at eight o'clock. 'I don't want to go in! I want to be with you!' Six weeks earlier the shire council, hit by budget constraints, had shut down another of its childcare centres and forced an amalgamation with Waterloo. Twenty new kids, six new staff, nowhere to fit them all. Kids are conservative. They don't like upheavals in their routines. The cheery woman who'd been in charge of his daughter's room, the two-to-three-year olds, had taken a redundancy package—

17

no doubt out of anger and frustration. Now a stranger was in charge of the two-to-three room, and Roslyn threw a wobbly whenever Sutton dropped her off each morning. Was this woman slapping her on the sly? Being mean to her?

At least she was happy now. Sutton started the Falcon and wound his way back through the town to the police station.

The desk sergeant caught him at the foot of the stairs. 'Scobe, I got a woman out front. Says she's got some information about Jane Gideon.'

'What's she like?'

'A crank,' the desk sergeant said simply.

Scobie took the woman through to an interview room. She had to be humoured, like all the cranks.

'Name?'

The woman drew herself up. 'Sofia.'

'Sofia. You say you've got information about Jane Gideon's disappearance?'

The woman leaned forward and said, her voice low and rasping, her eyes like glittering stones, 'Not just a disappearance. Murder.'

'Do you have direct knowledge of this?'

'I *felt* it.'

'You felt it.'

'I am a Romany. I am a seer.'

She stared at him. Her eyes: he'd never seen such intensity. She seemed to be able to switch it off and on, too. His gaze faltered. He examined her hair, black and wild, her ears, ringed with fine gold hoops, her neck, hung with gold chains, and the tops of her brown breasts in a thin, loose, hectically coloured cotton dress. A gypsy, he thought, and wondered whether or not there were gypsies in Australia.

'You mean you kind of sensed it?'

'She died violently.'

He doodled on his pad. 'But you have no direct knowledge.'

'Water,' she said. 'That's where you'll find her.'

'You mean, the sea?'

The woman stared into vast distances. 'I don't think so. An area of still water.'

He pushed back in his chair. 'Fine, we'll certainly look into that. Thank you for coming in.'

She smiled dazzlingly and waited while he got the door. She

18

was stunning, compelling, in a creepy kind of way. The gold, the hair, the vivid dress and the soft leather, they all seemed to fit her naturally.

'You have a little girl,' she said, as she stepped out of the room.

Sutton froze. It was a rule of thumb, never let members of the public know anything about your private life. He looked at her coolly. For all he knew, she might have a kid at the childcare centre, might have seen him dropping Roslyn off in the mornings. She didn't seem to be looking for a lever to use against him, so he said simply, 'Yes.'

'She's confused by the changes in her life, but she'll come through. She's resilient.'

'Thank you,' Sutton said, and wondered why—just like that, in a flash—he believed her.

Challis returned to the abduction site that afternoon and later drove to the bayside suburb where Jane Gideon's parents lived. They had nothing to add to what they'd told him the previous day. Their daughter had moved down to the Peninsula originally because she'd met a cadet at the Navy base there, and had stayed on when he broke up with her. No, he was serving in the Gulf somewhere.

When he got back to Waterloo he found Ellen Destry standing wary guard over Tessa Kane, who was perched on the edge of a steel folding chair and smiling a smile that his sergeant was bound to find insufferable. 'Tess, how are you?' he said.

'Hal.'

'Published any scoops lately?'

'Scoops is a relative term in a *weekly* paper, Hal.'

'Boss, I said you were busy and—'

'That's okay, Ellen,' Challis said.

'She says she's got information.'

'Got it, or want it, Tess?'

Tessa Kane's voice was low and deep and faintly amused. 'Both.'

'When's your next issue?'

'Thursday. Then we miss an issue between Christmas and the New Year, and publish again on 4 January.'

Challis said. 'A lot can happen.'

19

'Hal, a lot has happened.'

Challis watched her stand and smooth her skirt over her thighs. She was shorter than Ellen Destry, always full of smiles, many of them false and dangerous, others lazy and uncomplicated. He liked her plump cheeks. Women disliked her. Challis had no opinion on the matter, beyond knowing that he had to watch what he said to her.

'This information you say you've got,' he began.

She cut him off. 'Can we do this in there?'

'The incident room? Tess, please.'

She grinned. 'Just a thought. An office, maybe, instead of here in the corridor?'

Challis turned to Ellen. 'Sergeant, let's take Miss Kane into your office, if that's okay by you?'

He saw Ellen sort out the implications. He was including her, not giving her the shove, so she said, 'Fine with me, sir.'

The office was a plasterboard and frosted-glass cubicle further along the corridor, and once they were inside it Tessa Kane turned and said, 'I was hoping—'

'This is Sergeant Destry's station, her office, her investigation—as my offsider. So, whatever it is you want to tell me, you tell her, too.'

'Suit yourself.'

They watched her take a clear plastic freezer bag from her briefcase and lay it on the desk. 'This came in the post this morning.'

A few lines of crisp type on a sheet of A4 printer paper. Challis leaned over to read through the plastic:

This is an open letter to the people of Victoria. I would be loosing faith in the Police if I were you. There running around in circles looking for me. What have they got? One body. But where's the second? Gone to a watery grave? And now there's going to be a third. She's in my sights.

'Oh, God,' Ellen said.

Are you scared yet? You ought to be.

'Envelope?' Challis said.

Tessa Kane took out a second freezer bag. He poked at it with a pencil, turning it so that he could read it. He sighed.

Block capitals. There would be no useful prints, and no saliva, for the envelope was pre-paid, with a self-sealing flap, and available at any post office. He saw the words, 'Eastern Mail Centre', but no other indication of where it had been posted.

'You got it this morning, and you waited until now to show us?'

'Hal, I was out all day. It was left on my desk and I didn't open it until a few minutes ago.'

He looked at her closely. 'Have there been any others?'

'No.' She hooked a wing of hair behind her ear. 'I think the spelling tells us a little about him.'

Ellen had been itching to say something. 'Not necessarily. He's probably trying to muddy the waters. Look at the tone, the way he uses short sentences for effect, the way his constructions are uneven, the words "a watery grave", the apostrophes. I'd say he's had a reasonable education and trying to make us think he hasn't.'

Sniff. 'You're the expert.'

Challis stepped in. 'We'll need to examine the letter, Tess.'

'No problem. I made a copy.'

'You're not going to publish, I hope.'

Her voice sharpened. 'He's talking about a *third* body, Hal. People have a right to be warned.'

'We haven't even found the second body yet,' Ellen said. 'Jane Gideon might be alive, for all we know.'

Challis backed her up. 'Your letter writer might be a crank, Tess. An opportunist. Someone with a grudge against the police.'

He regarded her carefully, and saw that she understood the implications.

'You're not holding out on me?'

'I swear it.'

'But can I say the police *think* there may be a link between the first two?'

He sighed. 'There may not be, but there probably is.'

She muttered, 'Not that quoting you does me much good if you arrest him before Thursday's issue.'

'I can't help that.'

She looked up at him. 'People are scared, Hal. This morning I had a call from a real estate agent saying he's had a couple of holiday cancellations. I checked with the caravan park and

21

the camping ground. Same story. A lot of the locals depend on summer tourists.'

'Tess, we're doing everything we can. We're following leads, checking our databases. As soon as there are any developments, I'll give you a call ahead of anyone else.'

She touched the tips of her fingers to his chest and very lightly pressed him. 'Would you? That'd be great, even if you do sound like a police spokesperson.' She stepped away from him. 'Well, Christmas soon. Season's greetings and all that.'

'You too.'

She turned to Ellen. 'Someone's been distributing leaflets about Constable Tankard. Anything you can tell me about that?'

'No.'

'Okay. Bye now.'

When Tessa Kane was gone, Ellen said, 'I hate people who say "Bye now".'

'Ah, she's okay. You just have to know how to handle her.'

'Hal, don't get in too deep.'

He frowned. 'Are you my nursemaid now?'

'I mean the police-media thing, not your private life.'

Challis was embarrassed. 'Sorry.'

'I'll get this letter off to the lab.'

'It won't tell us anything.'

'I know.'

Canteen gossip soon spread the word about John Tankard's attempt to book Challis, so he was foul company that afternoon—as if he wasn't touchy enough already, owing to that leaflet campaign against him. Pam Murphy trod delicately around him during the ground-search of the Jane Gideon abduction site. Being diverted to attend a domestic dispute with him, on their way back to the station, was the last thing she wanted. Tankard's method of policing domestics was the bellow and the clip around the earhole.

She drove through the late-afternoon heat. A week before Christmas, and four months of hot weather lay ahead of them, the heat giving a particular spin to local crime. Your burglaries increased, as people went on holiday or left windows open to catch a breeze. Cowboy water-haulage contractors stole water from the mains. Brawling increased—in the home, the pub, the street; outside pinball parlours; on the foreshore on New Year's Eve. Surfies reported thefts from their vans. Weekend farmers drove down from Toorak and Brighton in their BMWs and Range Rovers on Friday evenings and discovered that someone had emptied their sheds of ride-on mowers and whipper-snippers, or their paddocks of cattle, sheep, horses, angora goats. And now another highway murder.

'Next right,' Tankard said. He sounded keen, as if he could sense an arrest.

Pam turned the corner. The arrest rate was part of the problem. The sergeant was always urging a higher arrest rate, saying it was too low for the region. It's not as if we're in the inner suburbs, Pam thought, tackling knife gangs. Down here a quiet warning should be enough.

Still, she thought, I'm the rookie here, what do I know?

She braked the van gently about halfway along the street. There was no need to peer at house numbers: the focus of the drama was obvious, a gaggle of neighbours on the footpath. She pulled in hard against the kerb, pocketed the keys, and got to the front door of the house before Tankard could.

It was ajar. She knocked. 'Police.'

The man who came along the corridor toward them wore a bathmat of body hair on a white, sagging trunk. His feet were bare, his knees like bedknobs under threadbare shorts. Someone had scratched his plump shoulders. He'd also have a black eye by the evening. 'Look, sorry you were called out, but we've got it sorted.'

Pam said, 'I'm Constable Murphy, this is Constable Tankard. Who else is in the house, sir?'

'Just the wife, also the—'

John Tankard shouldered through. 'We need to see her, pal.'

The man retreated in alarm. 'She's—'

Pam saw worry under the weariness, the poverty and the beer. She touched Tankard's forearm warningly and said, 'Constable Tankard and I just need a quick word with your wife, sir, if you don't mind.'

The man twisted his features at her. 'Look, girlie, I—'

It had been a long day. Pam pushed her face into his and breathed shallowly. She got 'girlie' twenty times an hour at the station; she didn't need it from some civilian as well. 'Are you obstructing us in our duty, sir? Because if you are—'

A priest appeared from a back room. 'It's all right, it's all right. I'm talking to them. We're sorting it out. There's no need for police intervention.'

'See? Told ya.'

Pam hooked her finger. 'Father, could I have a minute?'

She took the priest out on to the lawn at the front of the house. Tankard scowled after her. She ignored him. 'Father, I'm as anxious as you are to avoid trouble.'

The priest nodded. 'Everything's calm now. The fellow's wife has a history, a personality condition. Sometimes, when it's been hot for a few days, things get on top of her and she snaps. That's what all the ruckus was about. She hit him, not the other way round.'

'How is she now?'

'Quiet. Ashamed. She hadn't been taking her pills.'

Pam walked with the priest back to the front door. 'Sir, we won't be taking any further action.'

Tankard was furious with her in the van. 'We should have talked to the wife.'

Pam explained. Tankard said nothing. He said nothing the whole way back to the station, not until he saw Inspector Challis outside the station, getting into his car to drive home.

'Arsehole.'

There had been a time when Challis wanted to write a book about the things he'd seen and known and done, a lot of it bad. Fiction, because who'd believe it if he tried to pass it off as fact? He'd studied with a novelist at the TAFE College in Frankston, Novel Writing, every Wednesday evening from six until ten—when he wasn't on call somewhere, staking out a house, feeling for a pulse, arresting someone who didn't want to be arrested—but soon realised that although he had plenty to say, he didn't know how to say it. It was locked inside him, in the stiff language of an official report. He couldn't find the key that would let the words sing on the page. He'd confessed all of this to the novelist, who congratulated him, saying, 'My other students either have nothing to say or never realise that they haven't got a voice, so count yourself lucky.'

Challis had smiled tiredly. 'You mean, *you* count yourself lucky you're not stuck with one more bad writer.'

The novelist laughed and invited him to the pub to say goodbye.

But one thing stuck in Challis's mind—a quote from a writers' handbook. Georges Simenon, author of the Maigret novels, had said: 'I would like to carve my novels in a piece of wood'. Challis felt like that now. As he drove away from the Waterloo police station at six o'clock that evening, he thought that he'd like to be able to stand back from this case, his life, and gauge where the shape was pleasing and where it was all wrong.

He turned right at the sign for the aerodrome and splashed the Triumph into a parking bay at the rear of the main hangar. He went in. One end had been partitioned off, and here Challis pulled on a pair of overalls, tuned in to Radio National, and went to work.

When he'd first moved to the Peninsula, he'd joined the Aero Club and learned of a Dragon Rapide lying in pieces in a barn north of Toowoomba. He'd paid ten thousand dollars to buy the wreck and a further fifteen hundred to have it trucked down to Victoria. There was a serial number, A33-8, as well as an old VH registration, but Challis knew nothing else of the particular history of his aeroplane. He knew that in 1934 de Havilland had flown the prototype at Stag Lane, in the UK, as a faster and more comfortable version of the DH84 Dragon, with Gipsy Queen 6 motors instead of the Gipsy Major 4s, but who had imported *his* Rapide, and what had she been used for?

He turned on a lathe. Several pieces of the airframe had been damaged, sections of the plywood fuselage casing were lifting away, the six passenger seats had rotted through, and both motors would need to be rebuilt. He was also attempting to find new tyres, and had asked a machinist to manufacture a number of metal parts to replace those too rusty to be restored. It could all take years. Challis was in no hurry.

A woman came in, smiling a greeting. 'The dragon man.'

'Kitty.'

Challis knew that Kitty wasn't her real name, but derived from Kittyhawk. They exchanged pleasantries, then Kitty fetched overalls from a hook on the wall and went to the other end of the partitioned space, where the fuselage of a 1943 Kittyhawk fighter sat on the concrete floor, next to an engine block. The only other restoration project in the room was a 1930 Desoutter, which was close to completion.

Challis returned to his lathe work. Behind him, Kitty began to remove the sludge from the engine block. It was companionable working with her. Challis felt some of the blackness lift away. He didn't have to account for himself here. He didn't have to apologise for, or hide, his obsession with the Dragon. Here it was as if he didn't carry his whiff of people who had died terribly or committed terrible things. He was simply Hal Challis, who liked to fly aeroplanes and was restoring a 1930s Rapide.

The moon was out when he finally drove home. The eyes of small animals gleamed in his headlights. The telephone was ringing in his hallway.

'Yes.' He never said his name.

'Hal?'

His sense of calm left him. Some of the day's badness came leaking in to take its place. He dropped onto the little stool beside the phone. 'Hello, Ange.'

She didn't speak for a while. 'An early Merry Christmas, Hal.'

'You, too.'

'I thought, I might not get an opportunity to ring you next week. Everyone here will be hogging the phones on Christmas Day, so I thought, why not call you tonight, get in early.'

'Good thinking,' Challis said. He wished he had a drink. 'Look, Ange, I'll take this in the kitchen, okay?'

'If this is a bad time I'll—'

'No, now's fine, just wait a moment while I go to the kitchen.'

He poured Scotch into a glass, stood the glass on the bench top, stared a moment at the wall phone next to the fridge, then let out his breath.

'I'm back, Ange.'

'I'm trying to picture your house.'

'It's just a house.'

A catch in her voice. 'Not that I'll ever see the inside of it.'

'Ange, I—'

'I imagine somewhere peaceful and quiet. I miss that.'

'Yes.'

'I'm not a bad person, Hal. Not deep down inside.'

26

'I know you're not.'

'Temporary madness.'

'Yes.'

'I can't really believe it all happened like that. Like a bad dream.'

'Yes.'

'You do forgive me, don't you?'

'I forgive you.'

The answers came automatically. He'd been giving them for years.

She said, in a wondering voice: 'You're an unusual man, Hal. Other husbands wouldn't forgive their wives, not for something like that.'

Challis swallowed his drink. 'So, Ange, will your mum and dad come on Christmas Day?'

'Change the subject, why don't you? Mum will, Dad won't. He doesn't want to know me.' She broke down. 'God, seven years, and he hasn't been once to see me.'

Challis let her cry herself out.

'You still there, Hal?'

'I'm here.'

The night was still and dark. The house was like an echoing shell around him.

'You don't say much.'

'Ange—'

'It's okay, Hal, I have to go anyway. My phonecard's almost used up.'

'Take it easy, Ange.'

'I shouldn't be here, Hal. I don't belong, not really.'

Challis said gently, 'I know.'

'It's not as if I did anything. Conspiracy to murder, God, how did I know he'd try it?'

'Ange—'

She sighed. 'Spilt milk, eh?'

'Spilt milk.'

'Get on with my life.'

'That's the spirit.'

'I can't believe I wanted him instead of you.'

Challis drained his glass. He said, 'Ange, I have to go now. Take it easy, okay? Keep your spirits up.'

'You're my lifeline,' his wife said.

THREE

That same night, a woman on Quarterhorse Lane jerked back her curtain and saw that her mailbox was burning. Now the pine tree was alight, streaming sparks into the night. God, was this it, some twisted way of telling her that she'd been tracked down?

She'd been briefed carefully, eighteen months ago. Never draw attention to yourself. Keep your head down. Don't break the law—not even drink driving or speeding, and especially nothing that will mean you're ever fingerprinted. Don't contact family, friends, anyone from the old days. Change all of your old habits and interests. Dress differently. Learn to *think* differently. You liked collecting china figurines in the old days, right? Went to auctions? Subscribed to magazines? Forget all of that, now. Switch to sewing, cooking, whatever. It's good to give people a box to put you in—stereotype you, in other words, so that their minds fill in the gaps in your new identity. Above all, don't go back, not even if you get word that your mum's dying. Check with us, first. It could be a trap. You make one mistake, or ignore what we've been telling you, they'll find you and they'll kill you. You've got a new ID; it's pretty foolproof; you'll do all right. You'll be lonely, but plenty of people start over again. Just be wary. Watch what you tell people. But you'll be okay. Plenty of New Zealanders in

Australia, so you won't stand out too much. Meanwhile we'll do what we can to keep you alive from our end.

That's what they'd told her. She hadn't made much of an effort. There hadn't seemed much point, because the situation had begun to unravel even before the plane that was to take her out of the country had left the ground.

She'd been in the departure lounge of Christchurch airport, eighteen months earlier, seated with the detective assigned to escort her across the water and into a new life, when two men from her old life had waltzed in and sat down nearby. The detective tensed. He knew who they were, all right.

'Terrific,' she'd said. 'They've found me already.'

'Wait here.'

She watched him walk to the desk and show his warrant card. For a while it looked like a no-go, but then the reservations clerk turned sulky at something the cop said and punched a few keys and stared at his screen.

Meanwhile one of the men had spotted her. He nudged the other, whispered in his ear, and now both were staring hard across the dismal green carpet at her. She saw hatred and hunger in their faces. One of them enacted a pantomime of what lay in store for her when they caught her: a bullet to the head, a blade slicing across her windpipe. She hauled her bag onto her lap, got to her feet.

A hand tightened on her shoulder. The cop said urgently, 'Clara, come with me.'

She pulled away. 'You must be joking. I'm pissing off.'

'No. If you leave here they'll track you and you'll be dead meat.'

'They've already tracked me down,' she said. 'Fat lot of good you people are. Look at them sitting there, large as life.'

'Coincidence,' the cop said, forcing her to go with him.

'Yeah, sure.'

'I checked. They're both getting off in Auckland.'

'But they'll know I'm going on to Australia,' she said. 'They'll come looking.'

'Australia's a big place.'

'Not big enough.'

'Look, for all they know, you're going on to Europe.'

She had glanced back. One of the two men was standing now, watching her. She saw him tap his temple, grin, and flap open a mobile phone with a neat gesture of his wrist. He was flashily dressed, like they all were from that corner of her life: shirt buttoned to the neck, no tie, expensive baggy suit, costly Italian loafers, oiled hair scraped back over his scalp.

'He's calling someone,' she said.

'Let him.'

'Where are you taking me?'

'We've got a backup seat reserved for you on another airline. It leaves in fifteen minutes.'

Six-thirty, early evening, a dinner flight, a seat in first class. Clara ate steak and salad, and palmed the knife and the fork. They weren't much, but at least in first class they were stainless steel, and they'd give her an edge if she needed it, the kind of edge she'd come to rely upon in her short life.

That had been eighteen months ago. She had herself a new life in a quiet corner of south-eastern Australia, close to the sea on a peninsula where nothing much happened. The locals accepted her. She had answers for their questions, but there weren't too many of those. Her nearest neighbour in Quarterhorse Lane was half a kilometre away, on the other side of a hill, a vineyard and a winery separating them. If she walked to the top of that hill she could see Westernport Bay, with Phillip Island around to the right. She lived on a dirt road that carried only local traffic and half a dozen extra cars to the little winery on days when it was open, the first Sunday of the month. No-one knew her. No-one much cared.

So how had she been found? Was the fire a signal? And why a signal in the first place? Why not just barge in and finish her off? Unless they wanted to wind her up first, a spot of mental cruelty. Her hands were shaking. God, she could do with some coke now, just a couple of lines, enough to ease the pressure in her head. She stared at her fingers, the raw nails. She clamped her left hand around her right wrist and dialled the number of the Waterloo police station. Above her the ceiling fan stirred the air. God it was hot; 35 and not even Christmas yet.

Danny Holsinger, twisting around in the passenger seat, peering back along Quarterhorse Lane, said, 'Burning nicely.'

Boyd Jolic felt the rear of the ute fishtail in the loose dirt. 'Baby, come and light my fire,' he sang.

30

Danny uttered his high, startling, whinnying laugh. He couldn't help it. He swigged from a can of vodka and orange, then stiffened. 'There's one, Joll.'

Jolic braked hard, just for the sensation of lost traction, then accelerated away. The mailbox outside the winery was a converted milk can, all metal, not worth chucking a match into. Not like that wooden job back down the road.

They came to an intersection. 'Left or right, old son?'

Danny considered it. 'Left, you got a couple of orchards, couple of horse studs. Right, you got another winery, a poultry place, some bloke makes pots and jugs and that, let's see, a woman does natural healing, some rich geezer's holiday place, then you got Waterloo and the cops.' He giggled again. His day job was driver of the shire's recycle truck and he knew the back roads like the back of his hand.

'Left,' Jolic decided. 'Right sounds too fucking crowded.'

He planted his foot and with some fancy work on the brake and wheel, allowed the ute to spin around full circle in the middle of the intersection, then headed left, away from Waterloo.

The first mailbox was another solid milk can, but the next two were wooden. The first didn't take, kept starving of air or something, but the second went up like it was paper. Sparks shot into the sky, spilled on to the other side of the fence. Soon they had themselves a nice little grass fire going.

'Where to now, Joll?'

Jolic blinked awake. He realised that his mouth was open, all of his nerve endings alive to the dance of the flames.

'Joll?' Danny tugged him. 'Mate, time to hotfoot it out of here.'

They climbed back into the ute, slammed away down the road just as torchlight came jerking down the gravel drive from a house tucked away behind a row of cypresses.

'Mate, where to?'

'Other side of the Peninsula,' Jolic decided. 'Well away from here. New territory.'

Danny settled back in his seat. This was ace, out with his mate, a bit of damage by night—but that's all it was. He couldn't say the same for Jolic. The bastard was pretty flame happy. Maybe it came from being a volunteer fireman for the Country Fire Authority.

The Peninsula was deceptive. There were places, like Red Hill and Main Ridge, where the earth was composed of wave after wave of deep gullies and folds and knuckles of high ground. Later on in the new year the vines on the hillsides would be encased in fine bird mesh, like long, slumbering white slugs at night. Jolic drove them to a twisting road above the bay. Suddenly pine trees swallowed the moonlight, the headlights boring into funnelling darkness as they roared down the hill toward the coast highway.

At the roundabout inland from Mornington they turned right, into a region of small farms, then right again, on to another system of back roads.

'Check this.'

A large wooden mailbox, mounted on an S-bend of welded chain, the number 9 on it in reflective enamel. Jolic slowed the ute. Glossy black paint job; small brass hinges; a sticker stipulating 'no advertising material'.

'Fucken A,' Danny said.

They got out, stood a while in the windless lane, listening. Only the engine ticking. It was a long night, and very hot, and Danny began to wonder why he was out here with this mad bastard and not slipping one to Megan Stokes, in her bed or in among the ti-trees down the beach, with a plunge into the sea to cool down after. Well, he did know: she was pissed off with him because he'd forgotten her birthday and it was going to take plenty of sweet-talking and presents to bring her around. 'Mate, let's just pack it in, call it a night.'

It always caught you unprepared, the way Jolic could explode, if explosion was the right word for a fist gathering a clump of T-shirt, choking you, and a face hissing in yours, so close you got sprayed with spit.

'You're not wimping out on me, are ya?'

Danny coughed it out: 'It's just, I've got work in the morning. Start at five. I need sleep.'

'Piss weak,' said Jolic, shaking him. Danny was small, skin and bone, and felt himself rising to the tips of his runners as Jolic absently lifted him by the bunched T-shirt. Jolic was built like a concrete power pole, slim and hard. He wore grease-stained jeans that looked as if they'd stand unaided if he stepped out of them, a red and black check shirt over a blue singlet, and oily boots. Tattoos up and down his arms, and a

32

bony skull under crewcut hair. Danny had been hanging around Jolic ever since primary school, needing—so Megan reckoned—the big cunt's approval all the time.

'Mate, I can't breathe.'

Jolic released him. 'Piker.'

Danny rubbed his neck. 'Gis the matches. I'll do it.'

He opened the little flap on the front of the mailbox, stuffed it with petrol-soaked paper towels, tossed in a match, stepped back. The flap swung down, choking the flames. They waited. Danny raised the flap again. The interior of the box was scorched, still glowing red in places, but it wasn't alight. He leaned close, blew. God, what a stink, varnish, wood preservative, whatever.

'Come on,' Jolic said. 'Better take you home to your mum.'

Home was a new estate on the outskirts of Waterloo, houses crammed together but facing in all directions because they sat on madly looping courts and avenues, not a straight road in the whole place. Danny watched Jolic leave, the ute booming to wake the dead, the brake lights flaring at the turn-off. He lit a cigarette. He didn't want to go inside yet, hear his mother yell at him.

Danny gnawed his lower lip. The last thing Jolic had said was he needed help on another break-and-enter sometime after Christmas. 'I'm waiting for word on when the owners'll be away,' he'd said. Danny laughed now, without humour. Why should Jolic care if the owners were away or not? His idea of a break-and-enter was to smash the door down and bash the occupants before tying them up and rampaging through the house. Aggravated burglary, no fun at all if the law caught up with you. Danny had been with him on two such jobs. No fun at all, but he couldn't wriggle out, not without copping a lot of aggro.

He tossed his cigarette into the darkness. His own style was more scientific. He'd stake out a street for a couple of afternoons after knocking off work, getting a feel for the surroundings. Any dogs? Any neighbours about? Any lawns in need of mowing, mail mounting up in the box, newspapers not collected? Then, having targeted a house, he'd go around it, examining the windows for alarms. That was what he was good at. Using his head. He'd steal nothing big, no bigger than a camera, say. Rings, cash, watches, brooches, credit cards,

CDs. Anything that would fit in his backpack, a fancy soft leather thing with some foreign name stamped into the black leather. He'd lifted it from a house on the outskirts of Frankston a few days ago. Almost new, lovely smell to it. He'd give it to Megan next time he saw her, tell her he was sorry he'd forgotten her birthday.

One o'clock in the morning. The bar was closing, and John Tankard had dipped out badly with that nurse, so he thought he might as well drive home.

He'd been chatting her up—not a bad sort, about a seven on the scale—and started by buying her a glass of riesling and telling her his name, 'John, John Tankard, except my mates call me Tank.' She'd looked him up and down and said, 'Built like one, too,' then her hand went to her mouth and her face went red. 'Sorry, I didn't mean you're fat or anything, I meant you're strong, you know, like you keep in shape and that.' She came out of the other side of the apology a little breathless and smiling and relieved to have turned a possible insult into a compliment, and he'd grinned at her kindly and they'd settled elbow to elbow on the bar and begun to talk.

But then came the moment. It was always there, hovering over everything he did when he was off duty:

'What do you do?'

He said flatly, 'I'm a policeman, a copper.'

Wariness and retreat were there in her eyes in an instant. An opportunity lost or failed, like hundreds over the years. Just once would he like to see approval or interest or curiosity on someone's face when he told them that he was a copper.

There was a time when he believed all of the bullshit, that he was there to protect and serve. Now he saw it as us against them, the police against the public. The public were all guilty of something, anyway, if you dug deep enough. And did they deserve his protection? They shouted 'police brutality' whenever he made a legitimate arrest. At parties they cringed comically and said, 'Don't shoot me, don't shoot me'. He'd had four malicious civil writs from people he'd arrested, just trying it on, giving him a hard time.

Over the years the hardness had grown. He was more suspicious than he used to be. The job was more violent now. You saw some ugly things, like dead people, like syringes or speed or dope on kitchen tables in full view of little kids. Tankard was full of frustration. Repeat offenders were forever getting off on a bond. Sergeant van Alphen tried to drill it into him, *Don't take the job personally. Your responsibility is simply to present the case. It's not your fault if some dropkick gets off because he's got a good lawyer or a piss-weak judge or a good sob story*—but it wasn't as easy as that.

He was no longer sure what was right and what was wrong, and nor did he care. He'd seen some pretty bent coppers in his time and some halfway decent murderers, rapists and thieves. Most people were on the take in some form or another. A nod and a favour here, a wink and a slab of cold beer or half a grand in an envelope there. Fuck 'em all.

And he felt tired all the time now, and ragged from sleep-lessness. He ate and drank too much. His back ached to the extent that he could never get comfortable in any chair, and sitting for long in the divisional van or a car was sheer hell. The insides of his cheeks were raw from where he'd chewed them. Tension. You'd think, after all this time, that he'd never let the job get to him. But it did. He was surprised at the hurt he still felt, after his name had appeared in the local paper. 'Police harassment.' What bullshit. And now someone was flooding the town with leaflets, calling him a Nazi stormtrooper. Too gutless to say it to his face.

He had a scanner in the car. He switched it on. Someone was setting fire to mailboxes. That just about summed up life, for him.

Sergeant Kees van Alphen, ashily damp from helping the Waterloo CFA unit put out the fire in the woman's pine tree, was shocked. He'd never seen anyone so distressed. First it was a job getting her to step outside and talk to him, and now she still couldn't get the words out. She was gulping, clearly terrified. He stood with her on the verandah, wanting to say, 'It's only vandals, only your mailbox,' but her fear was so acute that he put an arm around her, patted her on the back and said, 'Hush, hush,' something his mother used to say.

He felt awkward. He was no good at this sort of thing.

Then she twisted as if to get closer to him and grabbed his

free hand. He screamed. He'd burnt himself somehow. The back of his wrist.

The woman sobered. 'Are you all right?'

'Got burnt.'

She looked distractedly at the open door behind her. 'I could dress it for you.'

'I'll be fine.'

Behind him the CFA truck was turning around in her drive. With a brap of the siren it was gone. The air smelt damp and smoky. The roof of his police car gleamed wetly, and there was enough moonlight for him to see steamy smoke rising from the charred mailbox.

He sighed, fished out his notebook. 'Did you see anything? Hear anything?'

'No.'

'Name?'

'Clara will do.'

He shrugged, noted the name and put the book away. New Zealand accent. He turned to go. 'I'll make a report and see that one of our patrol cars comes by here every night for the next week or two.'

She had another attack of hysterics. 'You're not going? You're not leaving me?'

'Miss, the fire's out, it was probably kids, they won't be coming back. There's nothing more I can do here. Would you like me to contact someone for you? A neighbour? Family? Friends?'

He saw her close down, as if she were suspicious of him. Who was she? What was eating at her?

'Why would you want to contact someone? Who?'

Bewildered by her mood shift, he replied, 'Well, someone who could stay with you, look after you. Family, perhaps.'

She looked away from him. 'They're all in Darwin.'

'Darwin? From your accent I'd have said New Zealand.'

She shot him a look. 'A long time ago.'

He didn't believe her, but didn't push it. 'A neighbour?'

'Don't know them. Besides, it's late. Can't you stay for a bit? I could put a dressing on your burnt hand.'

'I'm on duty, miss.'

'Clara.'

'Clara. I'm on duty. I'll call in tomorrow, around lunchtime.'

He could smell wet ash and smoke, and see, in the moonlight, the pine-tree skeleton at the end of her driveway. He opened the door of the police car and at once she wailed, 'They're out to get me.'

'Who are? Why?'

'I don't know why. They are, that's all. It's a signal.'

'A signal.'

'They're saying: We're coming back, and next time we'll get you.'

He shut the door and walked back to her. 'Clara, it was kids.'

'I don't think so.'

'It's been on my radio. At least a dozen mailboxes torched between here and Mornington. No pattern to it, just any old mailbox on a back road somewhere. You're one of many.'

She wrapped her arms around herself. 'You're sure? You're not trying to make me feel better?'

'I swear it.'

She laughed, unclasped herself and stared at the dim form of her hands in the half-dark. 'Look at me. Can't control myself, shaking like a leaf.'

'You need a stiff drink.'

'I'll say. Scotch, vodka. You want one?'

'I'm on duty, Clara.'

She stepped closer. 'What's your name?'

He said awkwardly, 'Kees. Kees van Alphen. It's Dutch, originally. There's a few of us on the force.'

'Kees. I like it.' She grinned. 'Justice never rests with Kees on your case.'

'I'm generally called Van.'

'Which do you prefer?'

'In the force, a name sticks. I'm used to Van. The wife called me Alf or Alfie, a kind of a put-down.'

Clara touched his chest briefly. 'Not very nice of her.'

'Not real nice, no. Still, old history now.'

'Just one drink. Or at least sit with me till I stop shaking.'

He found himself warming to her, to the notion that someone wanted to touch him, that someone needed him. 'I'll have to call in and tell them I'm still here.'

'Tell them you're following up clues,' Clara said, with shaky humour.

FOUR

Seven a.m. and already some heat in the sun. Showers with a weak change forecast for later in the week. Ellen Destry poked her head around the door of her daughter's room. Larrayne lay on her back asleep, apparently peaceful, but as usual the top sheet was tangled about her slim legs and her hair was fanned over the pillow and across one cheek. She'd been a restless sleeper ever since she was little. Then Ellen returned to the kitchen and kissed her husband, putting her arms around his neck briefly as he read the paper at the kitchen table. She paused on the way out, standing at the door that opened on to the carport. No, Alan didn't look up, nothing to bid her a good day ahead.

She wound the car past holiday homes and shacks, slowing for the speed bumps. She lived in Penzance Beach, some distance south around the coast from Waterloo (for you didn't live where you worked, not if you were a copper). On an impulse, she began a sweep of some of the township's side streets on her way to the intersection with the main road. There had been an 18 per cent increase in burglaries in Penzance Beach over the past year.

Penzance. What did the 'pen' prefix mean? Penzance, Penrose, Penhaligon, Penrith, Penleigh, Penbank, Penfold, Pengilly. 'Town of . . .' maybe?

Then she saw the new uniformed constable, what was her name, Pam Murphy, waiting at the bus stop with a surfboard.

Ellen stopped the car, wound down her window. 'Morning.'

The younger woman stiffened, eyes darting warily left and right before fixing on the car itself. Cop's instincts, Ellen thought.

'Sergeant Destry. Didn't recognise you.'

'Day off?'

'Morning off. I'm on again this afternoon.'

'Surfing. Lucky you,' Ellen said. 'Where?'

Pam Murphy pointed farther south. 'Myers Point.'

They stared at each other for a moment. Ellen said, 'How are you finding things? Settling in okay?'

'Yes, thanks.'

Ellen took a chance. 'What about John Tankard? Or Sergeant van Alphen?'

She saw the wariness in Murphy's eyes. Who could you trust in this job? 'I wouldn't know, Sarge.'

'Wouldn't you?' Ellen leaned her head out a little more. 'This is off the record.'

'Off the record?'

'Yes.'

The younger woman looked away. 'They do things differently.'

'Like how?'

She swung back. 'They get people's backs up. Shouting. The odd swift clip over the ear. Pulling old people over and breathalysing them, people who've never had a drink in their lives. Always lurking to catch people speeding. Just to increase their arrest rates. They say I'm too soft. Not performing.'

Ellen mused on that, and sighed. 'I'm CIB, not uniform. There's not much I can do.'

'Will that be all, Sarge?'

'You'll have to get yourself a car,' Ellen said. 'That bus? God.'

She saw the younger woman close up and look away. What nerve had she touched? 'Well, I won't keep you.'

'Have a good one, Sarge.'

Ellen Destry skirted around the naval base and on to Waterloo. Murphy seemed lonely. She tried to imagine life as a uniformed constable again, working with a pair of thugs like van Alphen and Tankard. I could offer to take her to work in the mornings, she thought. Then again, it would only complicate things.

She parked her car at the rear of the police station. It was now seven-fifteen, her normal arrival time for a 8 a.m. start. She stretched the kinks out of her back. There was a gym upstairs. It would do her good to use it sometimes.

The air-conditioning man pulled in at the courthouse next door, his Jeep top-heavy with a roof-rack of ladders and PVC tubes. Ellen noted the name, *Rhys Hartnett*, painted on the side, and took a moment to watch Hartnett as he got out. She was doing this a lot lately, watching men, the way they moved.

He caught her at it and winked across the driveway separating the courthouse from the police station. 'Another hot one.'

'Not even January yet,' she agreed.

She watched him prop open the rear doors of his van. 'Typical,' she remarked. 'The courthouse is only used once or twice a week and gets air-conditioning fitted. We're in and out of the police station twenty-four hours a day and can't even requisition a fan.'

He stood back, began to eye the courthouse windows. He'd lost interest in her.

'Well, see you. No doubt you'll be around for a few days.'

'Couple of weeks, at least.'

On an impulse she said, 'Maybe you could give me a quote to air-condition my house.'

That got his attention. He could ignore her but not the chance to make another buck or two. 'Where do you live?'

'Penzance Beach.'

'I could drop by sometime. Got a card?'

She closed the gap between them, stepping over a line of white-painted driveway rocks and straggly low shrubs to get to him. There were leaves and pods from the flowering gums scattered over the ground. She registered the snap and buzz of summer heat in the air, and the smell of the gum trees, and the brine of the nearby sea. She proffered her card. He was very graceful, movements delicate, voice soft, and the smile was a real charmer, so no wonder all of her senses were alert.

He looked impressed. 'Sergeant. Where's your uniform?'

'I'm a detective.'

'No kidding.'

'*Boss* of detectives.'

He raised his palm to her. 'You know how it is, see a cop and immediately feel guilty about something.'

'I'm flesh and blood,' she said, to give him something to ponder upon, then tapped the card in his hand. 'I mean it about the quote. Give me a call.'

'Will do.'

She entered the station and went immediately to the uniform branch for the previous night's crime reports. A dozen mail-boxes torched, two setting off small fires. Summer's here, she thought. She flipped through the reports. Three burglaries. A tent slashed at the caravan park. An assault. Three pub brawls. Theft of a car.

Then she logged on to the grid, the Central Data Entry Bureau, a state-wide database which recorded details of crimes, who reported them, victims' names, who attended, and so on.

There was a knock on the door and Kellock, the station boss, walked in. As usual, he seemed to regard her with distaste: after all, she was plainclothes, and a woman. 'You left me a note requesting half-a-dozen more uniforms for your door-to-door on the highway.'

'That's right.'

'It's not on, Ellen. The budget won't cover it.'

'Sir, we're stretched in CIB.'

'Not my problem,' Kellock said.

Kellock was a senior sergeant, middle-aged and comfortable-looking with his uniform and his rank. 'I can stretch it to two uniforms.'

'Thank you.'

Kellock left the room. Ellen logged off and headed for the stairs, in time to hear Kellock remonstrating with Kees van Alphen about claiming overtime. 'All you had to do was get a statement from her. You can't justify a claim for three hours above your normal load last night.' Van Alphen, she noted, looked exhausted, as if all of his arrogance had been ground away by the long night, and he wore a dressing on one hand. 'You smell of smoke, Van,' Kellock said. 'Go and have a shower.'

Ellen climbed the stairs to the first floor. She glanced out over the car park. Challis wasn't in yet.

Challis woke at seven and lay listening to a conversation between kookaburras in the nature reserve opposite his house. It sounded like a dispute: sudden eruptions of name-calling, trailing off into muttered hurt feelings. Then he remembered last night, and Angela's telephone call, and that Superintendent McQuarrie was coming down to Waterloo sometime during the day to discuss the implications of the killer's letter.

His mood didn't improve when he opened his mailbox to fetch the *Age* and discovered that someone had tried to burn it down during the night.

The exterior was intact, the interior charred but serviceable. The S-bend chain-link support was blackened. Challis wiped his fingers and stood regarding the box gloomily. He lived well back from the road, but still, he was a light sleeper, so it was a wonder he hadn't heard anything. Enough had happened to him in his life to make him alert to the sound of a vehicle at night.

A voice called, 'I see they got you as well.'

It was his neighbour. He's been waiting for me, Challis thought. 'You too?'

'Mine's a milk can,' the neighbour said, 'but the bastards chucked a burning rag in it just the same. Mrs Gibbs, around the corner? She found her box in pieces out on the main road.'

'I'll have a word with the local station,' Challis said. 'See if they can send a patrol around for the next few nights.'

'Appreciated,' the neighbour said, wandering away.

Challis read the *Age* over toast and coffee. Wednesday, 20 December. A banner across the top of the front page read: 'Five shopping days until Christmas.' *News* papers don't exist any more, he thought. They've been replaced by lifestyle papers.

He locked the house and eased the Triumph over the ruts outside his driveway. He wasn't looking forward to Christmas. The world assumed that Christmas Day must be lonely for him, and so set about ensuring that it wouldn't be. Drinks at Ellen Destry's house in the morning. Lunch with his parents and siblings. Then at six in the evening, when lunch was barely digested, an early dinner with Angela's parents. There were those in his family who couldn't understand why he'd want to see his parents-in-law, couldn't understand when he explained that he liked them, and they liked him. You're surely not intending . . . ? No, Challis wasn't intending to resume his life with Angela when and if she was ever released. Then why haven't you divorced her? I'll get around to it, he told them.

He drove on. Christmas Day. With any luck, someone would find a body and free him from Christmas Day.

Challis was on the road that linked with the Old Highway when he saw them, two teenage boys carrying fishing rods, buckets, a net and tackle boxes. His neighbour's trout-dam poachers? But the trout dam was in the opposite direction. Maybe they were after the fish in someone else's dam or lake or creek. They *looked* guilty, whatever their purpose, keeping close under the roadside gums and pines, keeping their faces averted as he went by. Challis mentally flicked his fingers. Saltmarsh, that was their name. They were cousins.

He reached Waterloo at eight-fifteen. The town looked dewy and clean. He parked the Triumph at the rear of the station and climbed the stairs to the incident room.

At ten o'clock an elderly couple entered the station and said, 'Constable Murphy told us to come in.'

'Did she indeed.'

'She came by last night. She calls on us every week.'

The desk sergeant nodded. The station had a register of elderly citizens, old single men and women, and married couples, who were checked on from time to time by the uniformed constables.

'And why did Constable Murphy tell you to come into the station?'

'We've been robbed.'

When the desk sergeant had the details he took them through to an interview room to make a statement. 'It's CIB's case now,' he said. 'Someone will be with you shortly.'

The man who came in a few minutes later was tall and gangly, with protuberant eyes and long, bony hands. 'I'm Detective Constable Scobie Sutton. A woman robbed you? Can you describe her?'

The husband, his white hair badly combed, stains on his cardigan, said, 'She was New Australian.'

His wife was sharper. 'You great galoot.' She leaned toward Sutton. 'He means she looked a bit exotic. Darkish skin, wearing bright clothes, lots of gold—rings, earrings, bracelets, neck chains. But she wasn't foreign. She was Australian, judging by her accent.'

'How old, would you say?'

'Hard to tell. Forty-odd?'

'You said she came in and offered to bless your house.'

The old woman said, 'Ask him, ask the genius. He let her in. I was in the garden.'

Sutton turned to the old man, who said, 'I couldn't see the harm. She said it would bring financial reward. It's not easy, being on a pension.'

'Mad. Cracked in the head,' his wife said.

'This woman told me,' the old man continued stubbornly, 'that whatever she blessed would multiply to our advantage. She said the house was cursed. She could see black smoke coming off it, and it needed cleansing.'

'Did she ask you for payment?'

'A donation. I gave her a dollar.'

'You great galoot.'

'A dollar,' Sutton said. He looked incensed for a moment, as if he'd been asked to get a cat out of a tree. 'And then what happened?'

'The phone rang. I was at the front door, but the phone's down the passage, in the kitchen. I was only gone a minute.'

'She was alone, this woman?'

'Had a child with her. Couldn't tell if it was a boy or a girl. Cute little thing.'

Sutton nodded. The woman would engage the occupants— usually elderly men and women—while the child slipped away unnoticed to hunt out wallets, watches and jewellery. Or, while the occupants went to fetch the child something to eat or drink, the woman would rob them.

But this time the woman hadn't needed to stage a distraction. The phone had done it for her. 'And when you came back . . . ?'

'They were gone,' the old man said. 'I waited, but—'

'Fool.'

'—but they didn't come back.'

'What was taken?'

'My purse,' the old woman said. 'I always leave it on the hallstand, along with my keys, gloves and hat. Forty dollars and some loose change, my Myer charge card, Medicare card, pension card, some other odds and ends.'

Sutton scribbled down the details. 'Only the purse, or the keys as well?'

'The keys as well.'

'Better get your locks changed.'

'Oh dear.'

The old man said, 'Her eyes, that's what I remember. She knew things. She looked right through you.'

Jane Gideon was almost forty-eight hours old, and still no body. The trail was growing cold. Challis re-read the file on Kymbly Abbott, talked to the VAA operator who had taken Jane Gideon's emergency call, and began telephoning numbers from a rolodex that had been next to the telephone in Gideon's flat.

One small piece of information: at eleven o'clock he took a call from a woman who claimed that she had seen Kymbly Abbott on the night of the twelfth.

'Can you be sure of the date?'

'My wedding anniversary. My husband and I were coming home from the city.'

'Did he see her, too?'

A laugh. 'He was asleep in the car. I was driving.' Another laugh. 'But I hadn't been drinking. Or not much.'

Challis responded to the warmth in her voice. 'Can you tell me what Miss Abbott was doing when you saw her?'

'Poor thing, she was sitting in the kerb at the intersection, sticking out her thumb whenever a car went by.'

'This is the intersection at the start of the highway?'

'Yes.'

'You didn't see anyone stop for her? No vehicle that stood out in any way?'

'I'm afraid not, no.' The woman paused. There was anguish in her voice. 'I wish I'd stopped for her, seen that she was all right, but I live only a block from the intersection, and last month a pack of young girls her age mugged me at an automatic teller machine.'

'I understand,' Challis said. 'You're sure it was her?'

'I saw her quite clearly, and the clothes she was wearing match the description in the paper.'

'Is there a reason why you waited until now to contact us?'

'I didn't connect it with anything until I saw the story about the latest case.'

'All right, thank you,' Challis said. He took down her details and filed them on computer.

He worked steadily through the morning, hearing the background hum of voices and keyboards. At twelve-thirty he asked Ellen Destry to have lunch with him, aware that the encounter with Tessa Kane still rankled with her. 'Something simple,' he said.

'I know a place that does good rolls.'

'Suits me.'

They wandered down High Street. A carolling loudspeaker blasted them from the doorway of the $2 Bargains shop. All of the shop windows were frosted and hung with silver and gold tinsel. The bargains shop was very busy; the others only moderately so. Here and there Challis saw signs begging him to support his local trader, and he guessed there'd be a few closures in the new year. But not at $2 Bargains.

'Done your shopping?'

'Not yet. I know what will happen: at the last minute I'll buy Alan some T-shirts and wine, and Larrayne some T-shirts and CD vouchers. Same as last year, and the year before. It's depressing. You?'

'No. Frankly, Christmas makes me anxious. So many people have so much riding on it that you feel somehow responsible for their happiness.'

She glanced at him worriedly. 'You're still coming for drinks on Christmas morning, aren't you?'

He stopped and touched her arm. 'Sure. I didn't mean you when I said that.'

They walked on. Challis felt a sudden small surge of pleasure. The town was struggling, and there was a killer circling it, but it felt good to be walking along a sunny street with Ellen Destry and to see the shops and the people shopping for Christmas. There was a general good will in the air. 'It's strange,' he said, 'but I need to do things like this occasionally, to remind myself I'm just a working hack like everyone else, not a copper and therefore separate from them.'

She understood. She slipped her hand into the crook of his elbow and with a bounce in her step steered him past the butcher and into the health-food shop.

There were two middle-aged women waiting to be served ahead of them. Challis found himself listening to their conversation with the young woman behind the counter.

'I won't let my daughter take that road any more.'

'My niece, she takes the bus to Frankston now, in case her car breaks down.'

The shopgirl said, 'It makes you think twice about going to the pictures and that.' She shivered. 'Stay home and watch a video instead.'

'They're cowards, you know. If you're a woman and you're driving alone at night, take someone along with you. They're cowards. They won't pick on two.'

'Makes you think.'

'I'll say.'

There was no advice that Challis could offer them, so he said nothing. He'd seen women take stupid risks and pay for it. He'd seen them take extra care and still fall victim to rapists and killers. He'd seen them fall victim in public thoroughfares, where they might expect a measure of security. What good would it do for him to tell the women in the shop: 'You're right to be cautious'?

He bought a pita bread pocket stuffed with lettuce, tomato, fetta and leaky mayonnaise, Ellen a slice of quiche. They wandered down to the playground next to the public swimming pool. Some of their lightness had evaporated. 'Then something like that happens,' Challis said, knowing that Ellen would follow the trail of his thoughts, 'and I realise that I *am* different, I *am* separate from everyone else. I'm expected to be. No-one's saying, "Come in here with us", they're saying, "Stay out there and watch over us." It's a crying shame,' he said, hurling the remains of his lunch toward the seagulls, 'and nothing can be done about it.'

Ellen leaned briefly against him and said, 'Hal,' softly.

They wandered back to the station, saying little, but feeling a kind of commonality with each other, and sadness.

*

They hadn't been in the incident room for long when Ellen murmured, 'McQuarrie's here.'

The man coming toward them wore a natty suit and the alert, clipped, close-shaven look of an army officer in an old British film. 'Afternoon, everyone.'

'Superintendent.'

'Hal, have you seen one of these?'

Challis glanced at it, a leaflet headed 'Our very own stormtrooper.'

'I was aware they were around, sir.'

'The night shift found them on their cars this morning. Someone had the nerve to walk in under our noses.'

Since McQuarrie was based in Frankston and rarely visited the regional stations, Challis didn't know why he was saying *our* noses. 'I see.'

'I've talked to Mr Kellock. He's going to post a stakeout over the car park tonight.'

Challis glanced past the superintendent at Ellen Destry, in time to catch a fleeting grin. 'Good for you, sir.'

'It's the thin edge of the wedge.'

For all of his talk about the thin edge of the wedge, the superintendent was a diplomat, a man who bent with the wind. His was the face the public saw whenever the police had to explain anything. Challis knew that McQuarrie played golf with well-heeled men, and he had no trouble seeing him scurrying along behind, letting them set the agenda.

'Right, Kymbly Abbott,' McQuarrie said. 'Bring me up to speed. Any forensic joy?'

'Nothing to speak of. He used a condom. No prints, but indications of a latex glove.'

'Tyres, footprints, sightings, nothing like that?'

'Nothing, sir, except one witness, who phoned this morning. She saw Abbott on the highway the night she was murdered.'

McQuarrie spun around and regarded the wall map, his long hands on his bony hips. Challis winked at Ellen, then joined McQuarrie at the map. 'Here, sir, where it starts. Apparently she was sitting on the kerb, her feet in the gutter, holding out her thumb.'

'Pity our witness didn't pick her up.'

'Yes, sir.'

'Mad. These young girls, I don't know.'

Challis couldn't find an adequate response to that. He pointed at the map. 'And here's where Jane Gideon went missing.'

'The cases might not be related.'

'That's occurred to us.'

'She might have recognised the driver and gone off with him. Isn't aware that people are worried about her.'

Challis rubbed his forehead irritably. 'True.'

McQuarrie said, 'But doubtful. It's been too long and we can't discount that letter.'

'I agree.'

'I had Tessa Kane on the blower.'

'Yes, sir.'

'Wanted a comment. Of course, I didn't tell her anything.'

'Wise, sir.'

McQuarrie clapped his hands together. 'Right, well, keep me posted.'

FIVE

After her encounter with Sergeant Destry that morning, Pam Murphy had caught the bus for Myers Point. It had swayed along the coast road, Pam swaying with it, her surfboard upright against her knees like a broad, blank-faced, yellow extra passenger. The drivers were used to her by now. Every Wednesday morning—shift work allowing—since mid-October. The other passengers she'd never seen before: two tired-looking men in blue overalls, a raucous mother with a four-year-old who seemed to suffer clips about the ears without pain, and an elderly woman with a handbag.

The elderly woman alighted with her at Myers Point and limped toward a small weatherboard cottage. A woman watering the garden there carefully turned off the tap and embraced her visitor. Pam found that she was moved by the little incident. She had a sense of lifelong friends, who saw one another when they could and spoke on the telephone every day.

She walked around to the surfing beach. The board grew heavy and awkward. She was hot. She needed a car, but money somehow failed to stick to her. She was chronically in debt. She was barely able to scrape up thirty dollars for this morning's lesson—not that Ginger would have insisted, but he was only a kid and it wouldn't have been right.

He was waiting in the car park next to the public lavatories at the head of the dunes. Five others this morning, four women like herself and a guy in his fifties, a fit-looking character decorated with tattoos and a ponytail. Sure enough, there was a big chrome and black enamel Harley parked nearby.

Ginger flashed her a smile. She wished it was just Ginger and herself and the wide blue sea this morning—as it had been once or twice before.

The little group walked down through the gap in the dunes and came out upon flat sand opposite a mildly chopping sea. Ginger turned right and led them for some distance, staring critically at the water, the way the waves were forming and breaking. Pam admired the way he walked at an easy lope across the sand, while she and the others made hard work of it. Plenty of natural grace in that walk, nice tight muscles, long arms and legs, chin tipped back, his chopped-short, sun-bleached hair catching the sun. A wonderfully shapely face for a seventeen-year-old. No adolescent roundness, pimples or bumfluff. Cheerful. Uncomplicated. All that mattered to him were the surf and the surf school. It would be good if he had a little left over for her, she sometimes thought, even if he were jailbait—or at least cause for her to be reprimanded, maybe even dismissed, for disgraceful conduct.

The others were drawing ahead now. Pam's breathing grew laboured. Her whole body ached. Plenty of exercise, the specialist had told her, but nothing with a percussive effect. No jogging, only careful gym work, plenty of swimming, regular massage and physiotherapy. He hadn't said anything about surfing, but Pam had always loved to watch it on the box, the Bell's Beach classic, Hawaii, the swift, nifty manoeuvres. She admired the women. So much guts and careless talent. It looked to be incredible fun. So, after the accident—a three-car pile-up in pursuit of a stolen Porsche in South Yarra—and her rehab and a breakdown that left her afraid and doubting and drained of esteem, and this posting to the Peninsula, far from the badness of the past, she'd seen the surfing lessons advertised in the milk bar and had thought, Why not?

Now Ginger had seen that she was struggling. He told the others to stop and gear up, and came back for her, smiling and concerned.

'You okay?'

His wetsuit filled her eyes. She imagined his pale, slender, hard, hairless chest and stomach. 'A few aches and pains.'

Her own wetsuit hid her scars. They weren't so bad, as scars go, but no-one knew the damage and pain they stood for. Ginger's glance went to her hip and shoulder. 'Would you like me to massage you?'

She blushed. 'Ginger.'

'I mean it. I'm always massaging people who seize up in the water.'

'We'll see.'

'Keep it in mind,' he said, taking her board for her and walking with her at her pace.

She was thirty, almost twice his age. As far as she knew, he didn't have a girlfriend. But someone would turn his head eventually, someone his age. She had to keep telling herself that.

Two hours later, back at Penzance Beach to shower and change and catch the bus to work, she saw a man, no more than a skinny kid, jemmy open the side window of the house opposite her flat, and climb inside. She was waiting for him when he came out.

Clara had mixed feelings about van Alphen, not least because he was a copper and because of what had happened last night, when he'd been so sweet to her, attentive, shy and clumsy. She'd slept badly, the night wracked with dreams of masked figures tearing away their masks to reveal other masks. She hadn't drunk much of the vodka, simply curled up on the sofa with the big copper until she'd felt sleepy, but her head boomed now. She needed something to level her out. She'd sworn off coke, but what she wouldn't do for a snort right now. Trouble was, she couldn't afford to go looking for a supplier. There was no-one she could trust. Smoking dope and doing coke was the old Clara, and her enemies knew that, and that was where they'd have their feelers out, even from as far away as Christchurch.

Midday. Her house in Quarterhorse Lane stood opposite a broad paddock of rye grass. As she watched, winds pushed at the grass heads in long sweeps back and forth, like rollers pitching in an ocean. It looked lovely, but it was also a fire hazard, and she trembled again.

The patrol car crept along the dirt road toward her front gate. She watched it pause at the mailbox, then turn in. He'd come back, just like he said he would.

She hugged him briefly. He looked tired. His hair was damp. She felt shy. 'You came back.'

'Just passing. Did you sleep?'

'So-so. You?'

'Managed to snatch a couple of hours at the station.'

He'd shaved badly. She touched his jaw. 'Coffee, Van? That will blow the cobwebs away.'

'I can't stay long. We had a woman abducted three nights ago and I have to supervise another line search.'

She tugged gently on the fingers of his burnt hand. 'I won't keep you. Just a quick coffee and you can be on your way.'

But in the kitchen she found herself shaking violently and she let a cup fall to the floor. 'A woman abducted?'

He clasped her upper arms. 'Are you all right?'

'Stressed out, can't you tell?'

'Look, come and sit down.'

He cleared the newspaper off the sofa and sat with her. Their knees touched. 'An abduction,' she said. 'I just know they're out there, waiting to get me.'

'Clara, this has nothing to do with your mailbox getting burnt.'

'It feels like it does!'

'Hush, hush.'

He was huge and enveloping. They were very warm against each other, heat coming through the thin cotton, and, where her bare forearm touched his, a kind of current was passing. Her voice was muffled against his uniform. 'Van, I really need something to chill me out.'

She wasn't surprised that he misunderstood her. He began to stroke her, thinking that was what she wanted. Still, the stroking felt nice in itself. The other could wait, and would come sooner rather than later if she could soften him up over the next couple of days.

She was stroking him now, the soft skin inside his elbow. She reached up and pulled his head down to hers. The kiss started slowly, no more than a nibble, but Clara was surprised to find herself enjoying it. The line between calculation and need grew blurred.

Afterwards, drowsy and half-naked on the Moroccan floor rug, he said, 'God, I needed that.'

'Been a while?'

'I don't mean that. I mean the world's such a shitty place you forget what's good about it.'

Christ, he wasn't going to fall in love with her, was he? 'So I'm a good fuck,' she said, to keep things in perspective for him.

He was mortified. 'No! Well, yes, but in a nice way.'

She laughed. 'Only teasing.' She rolled on to her hip and lay with her cheek on the hard slab of bone and muscle that was his chest. 'Will I see you again?'

She heard the rumble in his chest wall. 'I could come again tomorrow.'

'Or I could come to your place.'

He rolled away and pulled on his underpants and trousers. 'Christ, no, don't do that.'

'Why? Ashamed of me?'

'It's better if I come here, that's all. It's quiet here. Tucked away. Nobody to see me come and go.'

It was as if everything was decided.

It was stuffy in the Displan room. Ellen Destry pinched an electric fan from the sick bay and placed it on her desk, letting the air wash over her as she opened Scobie Sutton's file of convicted sex offenders now living on the Peninsula. Twenty-two names. After a further search, she discounted eight: they were serving prison sentences. Of the remaining fourteen, five had moved interstate, two had committed suicide, and three had convictions for paedophilia. She made a printout of all the names, in case some had finished their prison sentences or moved back into the area, and printed out full criminal-file copies of the remaining four men. One, in particular, caught her eye: Lance Arthur Ledwich, born 1955, convicted in 1991 on five counts of procuring sexual penetration by fraud and three counts of rape. Released in 1995. Apparently he'd placed ads in a Geelong newspaper calling for young women to audition for a film. A producer of wedding videos by trade, he'd auditioned the women at his studio in Newtown, where his cameras, lights and props had provided the necessary verisimilitude. He'd asked each woman to undress and change into a gym tunic for the part of a schoolgirl who'd been sexually awakened after a rape. He'd managed to deceive five women into having sex with him and had raped another three. One woman also alleged that he'd punched and squeezed her windpipe when she refused to have sex with him, but this charge was later withdrawn.

Violent, devious. Was he working the highway now?

The phone rang. It was the new constable. Could someone in CIB be present at an interview of a burglary suspect? Ellen pushed Ledwich's file to one side and went downstairs.

'The time 2.30 p.m. on Wednesday, 20 December. Present in the room are the accused, Daniel Holsinger, Detective Sergeant Ellen Destry, and myself, Constable Pam Murphy. Now, Danny, this interview is being recorded. You say you waive your right to have your lawyer present?'

Danny gave a whinnying laugh. 'Her? She puts words in my mouth. Last time, she let me talk my way into a month in jail.'

Sergeant Destry stirred. 'Danny, she's not on our Christmas card list, but if she hadn't intervened that time you'd have got six months.'

Pam waited. The sergeant sat back again, indicating with a nod that it was her arrest, she should run the interview. Returning the nod, she said, 'Danny, let's start with the back-pack.'

He bristled. 'It's mine.'

'It's also Italian and worth a lot of money.'

'So?'

Sergeant Destry cut in, 'So I'd have thought a vinyl gym bag was more your style,' and Pam wanted to shoot her. Danny flushed, looked hurt and angry at the put-down, and now she would have to work hard to bring him around again. After the arrest, as they'd waited for a divisional van to collect them, she'd developed a kind of rapport with him. There was nothing vicious or bad about him, just a lack of grey matter.

Danny was pouting. 'What would you know, you bitch?'

'Danny, that's enough,' Pam said. 'Now, a lovely bag like that, weren't you worried you'd get grease on it?'

'Never been out of work since I left school,' Danny said,

55

still angry. 'You think I can't afford to spend money on nice things?'

'Let's leave the bag. What we're most interested in is what you had *inside* the bag.'

'My own gear.'

'Hardly.' Pam picked up a page from a file. 'Items found in suspect's backpack: one ladies' wristwatch, Citizen; one camera, Nikon; one Visa card in the name of Anne M. Francis; forty-five dollars in cash; a Peninsula Library Service card, also in the name of Anne Francis; amethyst earrings set in gold.'

'My girlfriend.'

'I don't think so, Danny. Mrs Francis is seventy if she's a day.'

'My grandmother.'

'Cut it out, Danny,' Pam said. 'I caught you leaving the premises by way of a window. I checked with Mrs Francis and she's never heard of you.'

'Yeah, and I bet she never heard of no backpack, neither, because it's not hers.'

'Danny, give yourself a break.'

'So I done her place over, so what.'

Sergeant Destry said, 'Were you alone in this, Danny?'

'What do you mean?'

'You hang out with Boyd Jolic, am I right?'

Danny looked hunted. 'Sometimes.'

'Do you burgle houses with him?'

Danny muttered, looking away, 'No. Look, it's hot in here. Gis a Pepsi?'

Pam glanced at Sergeant Destry, who gave her a tired smile, said, 'Interview suspended while Sergeant Destry leaves the room,' and went out.

Danny said, 'Look, miss, can't we do something here?'

'Like what?'

'I know things aren't looking real good for me. What if I had something to give you?'

'You offering me a bribe, Danny?'

Danny waved an arm. 'No, no, nothing like that. Well, kind of. I mean, I hear things from time to time, might interest you.'

'There's a lot going on, Danny. Abductions, murder.'

Danny looked shocked. 'Hey, come on. Don't know nothing about that.'

'What, then? You hang out with people who firebomb mailboxes, Danny? Or heavier people, the kind who pull aggravated burglaries?'

'Don't know nothing about no ag burgs,' Danny was muttering as Sergeant Destry entered the room.

The sergeant went very sharp and still. 'What ag burgs, Danny?'

Pam immediately turned the tape on again, saying, 'Sergeant Destry re-enters the room. Interview continues, 2.45 p.m. Danny, if you have information about a crime, now is the time to share it with us.'

'Why does it have to be here?'

'Regulations, Danny.'

The door opened and the woman who entered the room was dressed for power. She wore a costly-looking dress, an expensive haircut and plenty of gold on her neck, fingers and wrists. She was about fifty, slim and hard and fast. 'You've got no right to interview my client in my absence. Danny, you're coming with me.'

Pam was happy to let Sergeant Destry take charge. 'Marion, he waived his right to have a lawyer present.'

'Ellen, I expected better of you. What's he here for?'

'Suspected burglary.'

'Who arrested him?'

'Marion, meet Constable Murphy. Pam, this is Marion Nunn.'

'I hope you cautioned him, Constable.'

'Hello?' Danny said. 'I'm here, in the room with you all.'

'Danny, you just let me do the talking.'

And that's where it stalled. Danny was charged and bailed, and left without revealing anything. Pam was even obliged, by Marion Nunn, to return the backpack to Danny.

Mid-afternoon. Challis took the call, staring out of the Displan room windows at the carpark. 'A body, you say?'

'Dead. She's a woman.'

'Where?'

'Devil Bend Reservoir. Near the edge. There's a track to it.'

He glanced automatically at the wall map. Not so far from

where he lived, a Peninsula Water catchment reservoir. 'Your name, sir?'

Audible breathing, as though in heavy concentration. Challis was convinced that a second person was there with the caller.

'I don't want to get involved.'

'For our paperwork, sir.' *Sir*. The caller was a kid, sounded no more than fifteen.

'You're gunna trace this, right? Well, I'm getting off the line before you dob me in.'

SIX

Challis watched from the perimeter, his shadow long now that the sun was low in the west. Inside the crime-scene tape they were taking photographs of the body, and of footprints and tyre tracks. Plaster casts after that, then a sweep with a metal detector to see if anything—a ring, a weapon, a man's neck chain, a wristwatch—had been trampled beneath the mud and the muddy grasses and reeds. Meanwhile, behind Challis, and supervised by Ellen Destry, a line search of ten constables and cadets had finished tracing the tyre tracks between the body, which was at the reservoir's edge, and the gravelled surface of the Peninsula Water access track, and now were tracing footprints, two pairs, that headed west from the body toward a belt of scraggly gums. Farmland after that. Not so far away, no more than four kilometres, was Challis's house.

Challis looked across the reservoir. What a godawful place to die. Blackberry thickets, bracken, stiff, wiry grass, small, dark, knobbled trees, defeated-looking gums, a stink of primeval gases. There were waterbirds, but they were mostly silent, and rather than seeming cool and alive, the body of water sat still and heavy under a layer of algae, and Challis felt oppressed by the humidity. The mosquitos were out. One landed on his wrist. He slapped it, saw a smear of blood.

Freya Berg, the pathologist, stood and waved to him. 'Hal, you might as well come in now.'

Challis climbed over the tape and approached the body. He should have thought to pack rubber overshoes. He felt water seep into one sock.

First he tried to read the signs. The body itself could wait. 'One vehicle, quite marked tread pattern, two people on foot. Wearing gumboots?'

'Looks like it, sir,' the forensic officer said.

Challis followed the footprints with his eyes. 'They came around the reservoir, saw the body, walked around it once or twice, then headed out that way.' He pointed toward the distant gums and farmland.

'You want my job, sir?' the officer said.

Challis grinned. 'You tell me the rest.'

'No other tracks. I'd say our victim was thrown out of the rear of the vehicle. See how he's reversed in and gone out again?'

'He didn't step out of the vehicle, on to the ground?'

'No other tracks, sir, only those two.'

'A car? A van?'

'Probably something with a rear-opening door, like a station wagon or a hatchback, if it was a car, but the tyre tracks indicate a heavier vehicle than that. Minivan? Four-wheel drive? Something with inside access to the rear compartment.'

'Or a ute, and he swings over into the tray from the driver's door ledge.'

'A possibility, sir.'

Challis turned to the body. It lay on a patch of mud at the water's edge. He wondered about the absence of grass. People regularly stood there, he decided. Birdwatchers, Peninsula Water engineers, kids skipping stones across the sluggish water, blackberry pickers later on in the new year. People fishing. Anyone at all, really.

The body had been face down. Now it lay on its back. The pathologist had bagged both hands; she'd examine them later for skin samples, traces of fabric, anything that might point to the killer. She'd also take swabs of the mouth, the vagina and the anus for evidence of saliva, sperm or acid phosphatase, the cardinal signs of sexual assault. If it's the same killer, Challis thought, she'll find signs of latex condom lubricant

60

and not much else. The legs, from the bare, bruised pubis area to the Nike runners, looked grey and mottled. The upper body was clothed in a T-shirt, torn at the neck. Challis peered. Bite marks. There were also early signs of decomposition. The face was contradictory—swollen as a result of strangulation, yet curiously slack. Even so, it was clearly Jane Gideon.

Where was the lower clothing?

'Find a skirt, pants, underpants, anything like that?'

'No, boss.'

Just like Kymbly Abbott.

Ellen Destry joined them. 'We're running out of daylight, boss.'

'I know, but we're almost wrapped up here. Just make sure the wider scene is sealed off tonight so we can resume the search in the morning.'

'Will do.' She nodded at the body. 'Raped, Freya?'

Freya Berg said, 'Looks like it, but you know I can't say till I've had a proper look at her.'

'What can you say?'

'She was abducted at midnight on the seventeenth, right? I'd say she was killed and then dumped here soon after that. Over forty-eight hours ago, in the hot sun for a lot of that time, so there's some decomposition. The cause of death was strangulation, but she's also had a blow to the head.'

Unlike Kymbly Abbott, Challis thought. Then again, Kymbly Abbott had been drunk and half doped and therefore malleable. Jane Gideon had been fit and healthy and wide awake. Either she struggled or the killer thought she might, and so he'd struck her. 'What kind of blow? The old blunt instrument?'

'There's blunt and there's blunt, Hal. This one had a rounded edge.'

'Like a rock, or narrower than that?'

'Narrower. More defined. A metal bar of some kind, or a lump of wood.'

He brooded. A tool handle. A tyre iron. 'It didn't happen here in the mud. Anything you can tell me about where it might have happened?'

'That depends on what your forensic people find on her. Meanwhile I'll need a closer look at her on the table before I can say anything definite.'

Challis nodded gloomily. Jane Gideon could have been raped and strangled inside the killer's vehicle, or taken somewhere. Either way, it would have been somewhere away from the highway, for Jane Gideon had made a phone call and the killer would have been expecting someone to come for her.

'He wanted her to be found,' Challis said, 'just like he wanted Kymbly Abbott to be found.'

That was all he knew. That, and to expect another body.

Tessa Kane was at the jetty, waiting for Challis. Six o'clock, her shadow long on the water, the day winding down. She'd bought two rockling fillets for dinner that night, and while she waited she watched the fishmonger toss the day's fishheads and entrails to the gulls and the pelicans. She gasped and said, 'My God, a seal.'

The fishmonger pointed across Westernport Bay to the Nobbies, the seal colony at the western end of Phillip Island. 'He been coming in for a feed last four, five days, missus. He pretty old, I think. See the scars? Can't look after himself so good no more.'

She watched in awe. The seal thrashed in the water. Whole fish torsos disappeared. The wind was up. Sail rigging pinged against the masts of the yachts moored in the marina. She breathed the air. It was laden with sea salt and mangrove swamp, that living stew of muddied roots, cloudy water, swamp gas and crawling sea life.

'Good to be alive?'

It was Challis. She rested her palm briefly against his chest. 'You said you had something for me?'

Challis told her about the body and its discovery. He confirmed that it was Jane Gideon and detailed the comparisons with Kymbly Abbott's murder.

She scribbled in her notebook, sensing his calm eyes upon her. 'Just don't arrest anyone before midnight, okay? Or I'll miss tomorrow's issue.'

'Tess, what do you intend to do about the letter?'

'We'll see.'

'I think it would be a mistake to publish it.'

She shrugged. 'What else can you tell me? I need colour, Hal. I need the broad picture.'

'The broad picture's clear enough. There's a killer out there

62

and women would be mad to go out alone at night. They shouldn't drive alone, they shouldn't hitchhike.'

'I can quote you on that?'

'Yep.'

'It might shut him down.'

'That's the general idea.'

'Meaning you won't have anything to work on except what you've got already.'

'Tess, I can't believe you said that. You want more abductions, bodies dumped at the side of the road?'

'No, of course not. I was trying to see it from a police point of view.'

'Don't try to double guess us,' Challis said.

'I'll be reaching for links between the victims.'

'Reach away.'

She closed her notebook. 'You've never liked what I do. You like me but not what I do. That's what this hostility is about.'

As though it were an ongoing thing between them. In fact, Challis scarcely thought about Tessa Kane from one day to the next. But when he did, and when he saw her, something always shifted a little inside him, and it wasn't always unpleasant.

'I'll keep you posted.'

'I'm not finished,' she said. 'There's community concern about two of the uniformed police, John Tankard and Kees van Alphen.'

'Nothing to do with me. Ask Senior Sergeant Kellock or Superintendent McQuarrie.'

'McQuarrie. Now there's a fund of straight information. Is it true Ethical Standards might be called in?'

'McQuarrie.'

'Bugger McQuarrie,' she said.

'No thanks,' Challis said. He rubbed his face tiredly. 'Tess, do me a favour? Jane Gideon's parents still haven't been told. They've still to identify the body. Please wait a couple of days before you speak to them.'

'What do you take me for?'

They both looked up at the sound of an aero engine. She saw the lowering sun flash on the fuselage. Challis shaded his eyes. 'Desoutter II, three seater high-wing monoplane,' he said automatically. 'Found in a playground in Tasmania four years ago.'

'Is that a fact.'

He grinned shyly, as if caught out in something. 'I helped to restore it.'

Her gaze settled on him.

When Ellen got back to the station car park, she checked that her initials, and those of the forensic technician, were etched into the plaster tyre and footprint casts, and was unloading them from the rear of the forensic van when Rhys Hartnett said, behind her, 'Sergeant Destry?'

She pulled bin liners over the casts hastily and turned around to face him. He was standing there, the setting sun behind him, coiling electrical flex between elbow and hand. It was an automatic but neatly articulated process, and it got under her skin. There was something about men who worked with their hands. She seemed to float on her toes. 'Call me Ellen.'

He bobbed his neat head shyly. 'Call me Rhys. Look, I could come to inspect your house on Saturday, if you like.'

'Are you sure? That's only two days before Christmas.'

'I'm sure. I'm working right through, apart from Christmas Day and New Year's Day. I take my summer break in February, when the schools go back.'

'Wise man,' Ellen said. 'How about late morning, around twelve?'

'Fine.'

Danny Holsinger waited until seven-thirty in the evening before going to the police station. The chick who'd arrested him said she was on duty until eight, and he didn't want to talk to anyone else about Boyd Jolic. She was nice. But first he had a pizza, extra thick, in Pizza Hut, sitting in the window where he could watch the cops come and go on the other side of the roundabout. He felt jumpy. After that Nunn bitch had taken him home earlier, calling him a moron, he'd gone straight around to Megan's place and given her the backpack. Sort of getting rid of evidence, even though the backpack hadn't been lifted from the old lady's house but from a house he'd robbed last week. 'Happy birthday, Meeg,' he'd said.

'Sorry it's so late,' and she'd smelt the leather and gone all soppy over him and they'd had a quick one on her bed, so that was all right.

But then he'd gone home again and Boyd Jolic had rung, reminding him that his help was expected on a break-and-enter soon. 'I don't want you forgetting, Danny, or pissing off on me.' Danny's position now was, he needed help of his own.

He gathered himself, walked across the road, reached the door and chickened out. Boyd Jolic had a longer reach than the law did. Even if the law put Jolic away, he had mates who knew where Danny lived.

SEVEN

The next morning, Challis read the *Progress* while Scobie Sutton drove. Tessa Kane had splashed the killer's letter all over the front page. Soon the metropolitan dailies would pick up the story, and meanwhile McQuarrie had left messages, asking for an explanation. All this on top of a bad night for Challis, the image of Jane Gideon's parents staying with him through the long hours. Better to spend the morning away from the station. 'She says to me, "Eat your munch, Daddy. Sit up prop-ly and eat your munch."'

Challis worked a smile onto his face. '"Munch." I like that.'

'But where did she get it from, boss? Not me and Beth. Childcare, that's where.'

'I expect you're right.'

'I mean, they're like a sponge, that age. Absorb everything.' Scobie fell gloomy. 'The good and the bad.'

'I suppose it's up to the parents to provide most of the good and counteract the bad,' Challis said, for something to say, but wondering if he believed it. Look at his own wife. Fine, upright family background, and look what happens. She falls in *lust*—her explanation. 'Hal, I fell in lust, I couldn't help it, I had to have him and he had to have me.' Sure, but you didn't have to kill me to achieve it.

'Which way, boss?'

66

Challis blinked. 'Quite a way yet. Up near where I live.'

'How long you been there now?'

'A few years. You've got a place in Mornington, right?'

Sutton nodded. 'But thinking of moving. With all the new housing, you know, house-and-land packages, cheap deals, newlyweds and welfare cheats and what have you living in each other's pockets, the place is changing. No way I'll send my kid to the local primary schools. You don't know of any Montessori schools?'

'Sorry, no.'

'I forgot, you didn't have kids,' Sutton said, then fell silent, embarrassed.

He's heard the stories, Challis thought. 'How's your daughter coping with creche? Still kicking up a fuss in the mornings?'

Sutton shrugged. 'So-so. But tomorrow's the last day for the year, and they're having a party at the Centre, so she's looking forward to that.'

The days were sweeping by. Tomorrow was the twenty-second. Christmas day was Monday. Challis squirmed in his seat. He wasn't ready.

He spotted the turn off. 'Next left, then follow the road for about two k's.'

Sutton took them on to a badly corrugated dirt road, then over a one-lane wooden bridge. 'Sheepwash Creek,' he read aloud. 'God, the names.'

Challis was fond of the old names. They were a map of the Peninsula in the nineteenth century. Blacks Camp Road. Tarpot Corner. He said, 'They washed sheep here in the old days, to prepare them for shearing.'

'No kidding,' Sutton said absently, and Challis knew that the man was thinking of his daughter again. It was as if having a child destroyed your sense of time's continuum. Time was reduced to the present and nothing else.

'Somewhere along here,' he said. 'Look for the name Saltmarsh on a mailbox or fence railing.'

They drove for a further kilometre before they found it, a mailbox hand-lettered with the words M. Saltmarsh. They turned in and saw a small red-brick veneer house with a tiled roof. Behind it sat a modern barn, the doors open, revealing a tractor, a battered Land Cruiser, coils of rope, bike parts, wooden pallets, machinery tools and dusty crates crammed with one-day useful bits and pieces—chain links, cogs, pulley wheels, radiator hoses and clamps. A rusted truck chassis sat in long grass next to the barn. Hens pecked in the dust beneath a row of peppercorns. The apples in the adjacent orchard were still small and green. A dog barked, and beat its tail in the oily dirt, but failed to get up for them.

'She's a bit on the tired side,' Sutton said, meaning the farm and whoever farmed it.

'The Saltmarshs are old Peninsula,' Challis explained. 'Been here for generations, scratching a living out of a few acres of old apple trees. Two brothers and their families, on adjoining farms. Both brothers have other jobs to get by. Ken here works part time for the steel fabricator in Waterloo. Mike next door drives a school bus.'

'Poor white trash.'

Challis thought of the two teenage boys, Saltmarsh cousins, whom he'd seen walking along with their fishing rods the previous morning. How far was that image from the poor South of American film and literature? He finally said, 'No, not poor white trash. Poor, but steady, and decent.'

Maureen Saltmarsh came to the door. She was large, sun-dried and floury, smelling of the kitchen and the morning's early heat. She wasn't inclined to suspect them of anything, but smiled and said immediately, 'Me husband's not home. Did in the big end on his truck.' The smile disappeared. 'You're that inspector.'

'Hal Challis, Mrs Saltmarsh. And this is Detective Constable Sutton. We want to talk to your oldest boy, and his cousin.'

'Brett and Luke? Why, what they done?'

'I just need to talk to them. I'm more than happy for you to be present.'

She was losing a little of her control. Her hand went to her throat. 'They're in watching TV. You know, school holidays.'

'Bring them into the kitchen, would you, please? There's nothing to worry about. They're not suspects in anything. We're not going to arrest them, only question them about something.'

She ushered Challis and Sutton into the kitchen, cleaned breakfast dishes from the table and asked them to sit. While she was out of the room, Challis took stock: 1970s burnt-orange wall tiles above the benches, a clashing brown and green vinyl linoleum floor, chrome and vinyl chairs, a laminex and chrome table, a small television set, tuned to a chat show, the sound turned down, dishes in the sink, a vast bowl of dough next to a floury rolling pin and greased scone tray.

The Saltmarsh cousins could have been brothers. They were about sixteen, large and awkward, both mouth-breathers with slack, slow-to-comprehend faces. Challis had an impression of softness and clumsy angles, of pimples and sparse whiskers, of ordinary teenage stubbornness and stupidity, but not mean-ness or calculation. They seemed to fill the little kitchen. When they spoke, it was in gobbled snatches, as if they didn't trust speech and hadn't much use for it.

'You boys were at Devil Bend Reservoir yesterday, correct?'

'Us? No way.'

Challis gazed at them for a moment. 'But you both like to fish?'

'Fish?'

Scobie Sutton was impatient. 'With fishing lines and rods and hooks and bait. You like to go fishing.'

'Haven't got a boat.'

It was Brett, Maureen Saltmarsh's son. Challis leaned over the table toward him. 'I recently saw you and your cousin, on foot, all geared up to go fishing. You were climbing a fence and crossing a paddock. Not two kilometres from here.'

'So what?'

'Well, you weren't out blackberrying. Now why don't you tell us about Devil Bend Reservoir.'

Brett stared at the table. His mother said, 'Brett? What have you boys been up to?'

'Nothing, Mum.'

Challis said, 'We've had reports of poachers in the district, dams and lakes fished for trout.'

'Not us.'

'I'm sorry, but I have no alternative but to charge you with—'

'You said they hadn't done anything!'

'Mrs Saltmarsh, please . . .'

'You can't charge them if they haven't done anything.'

Challis hated what he was doing. He said, 'Brett, look at me. I don't care about the illegal fishing, the trespassing. I don't even intend to report your names to the local station.

But unless you tell me what you saw at the reservoir yesterday, I will have you arrested and charged, believe me I will.'

Brett shot a look at his cousin. The cousin said, 'We never done nothing. We just found her, that's all.'

Challis sighed and sat back. 'You went there to fish?'

'Might have.'

'Okay, okay, forget the fishing. You were out for a stroll. You were skirting the reservoir and came upon a body.'

They looked doubtful about the word skirting. Did it mean he suspected them of doing something unspeakable at the reservoir? But Brett muttered, 'Yeah, we found her.'

'What did you do?'

'Nothing! We didn't kill her! She was already like that!'

'Did you touch her?'

'No way.'

'Did you take anything?'

'Rob a dead body? No way.'

'Did you remove anything from the vicinity of the body?'

'What?'

'I'll rephrase the question: Was there anything on the ground near the body? If so, did you take it away with you?'

'Nothing.'

'We wouldn't charge you with theft,' Scobie Sutton said. 'We just need to know.'

'There was nothing there.'

Challis said, 'Did you see anyone?'

'No. Only her.'

Luke said, 'She the one what was grabbed when her car broke down?'

Challis thought about it. He wanted to give something back to the boys. 'Yes.'

'Cool.'

'What time did you find her?'

'Dunno. Pretty early.'

Mrs Saltmarsh said, 'A school morning, you can't get the buggers out of bed. School holidays and they're up at the crack of dawn.'

Scobie Sutton asked, 'Why did you wait before phoning the police?'

The boys looked at each other. Mrs Saltmarsh eyed them suspiciously. 'They was waiting for me to go out shopping.'

'Is that right?'

Brett scratched at a burn mark in the laminex with a grimy fingernail. 'Suppose so.'

'Your mother left the house when?'

'About two,' Mrs Saltmarsh said.

Challis had logged the call at 2.45.

'You'd have saved us a lot of trouble if you'd given us your names, and rung earlier,' Sutton said.

'Didn't take you long to find us anyway,' Luke muttered grudgingly.

'We'll need your gumboots,' Challis said.

Mrs Saltmarsh narrowed her eyes. 'What for, if they've done nothing?'

'To check their footprints against those found at the scene.'

'To eliminate them,' Sutton explained.

Both boys looked alarmed, as though elimination meant something damaging and final.

'I'll get them,' Mrs Saltmarsh said.

'Pop them in a supermarket bag,' Sutton called, to her departing back.

The boys looked frightened now. Challis got to his feet. 'No more sneaking around fishing from the neighbours, okay? Someone could take a shotgun to you, then I'd have another murder inquiry on my hands.'

They went white. 'Joke, fellas,' Sutton said.

Their grins were shaky.

On the way out, Challis said suddenly, 'We're forgetting something.'

'Maureen, Mrs Saltmarsh,' he said, when she opened the door to him again, 'a quick question. What vehicles do you have on the place?'

She understood, and flushed sullenly. 'Tractor, Land Cruiser, truck, Holden.'

'The Holden—a sedan or a station wagon?'

'Sedan.'

'The truck. Is—'

'I told you, he done the big end in a few days ago.'

'Maureen, if you don't mind, I've got a camera in the car. Couple of quick shots of the Land Cruiser's tyres and we'll be on our way.'

'It hasn't been out for days.'

He smiled, ignoring her. 'Do the boys know how to drive?'

'They're too young to have their licences.'

'But they know how to drive?'

'Suppose so.'

'Just a quick snap of the tyres and we'll be gone,' Challis said again.

'In the bloody shed,' Maureen Saltmarsh said, closing the door on them.

'Really laid one on last night, Murph.'

'Wacky doo,' Pam said, stopping at the roundabout for a station wagon that had begun to nose uncertainly around it, as though lost. A rack of suitcases on the roof, a hint of bedding, buckets, spades and foam surfboards in the rear, children staring through the side windows, a woman driving, a man next to her, cocking his head at a map and waving one arm at her. Maybe, Pam thought, they'll be next door to me in Penzance Beach when I knock off work tonight, ensconced like kings until school goes back in late January.

'How come we never see *you* down the pub?' Tankard demanded.

'Got better things to do.'

'Like what? Don't tell me you've got a love life.'

That hurt. She took her attention from the road to flash him a look. 'Why wouldn't I have a love life?'

'Don't get me wrong, I've got nothing against it.'

'Against what?'

'If you prefer women to blokes that's no skin off my nose.'

Pam rubbed her cheek wearily. 'Give it a rest, Tank. You wouldn't know the first thing about me.' She braked for the pedestrian lights outside the post office.

'Like hell.' He yawned. 'Where'd you say we were going?'

'The photo shop. The manager wants us to check out a roll of film he developed this morning.'

Tankard looked disgusted. 'Who cares? You get all kinds of stuff now, no-one turns a hair. Holiday snaps in the nuddy, pregnancies, sheilas giving birth. No-one's stupid enough to drop hard-core stuff off for developing.'

Pam wished that Tankard would shut up. 'All I know is, the manager called the station, asked for Scobie Sutton, he's busy, so he gave it to us.'

Pam turned left into the shopping centre, looking for Kwiksnap. Tankard glanced at her keenly, with a touch of not-unkind humour. 'You'd rather be plain-clothes than driving around in the divvie van, wouldn't you?'

She shrugged. 'I don't want to be in uniform all my life.'

Tankard barked a laugh. 'You'll see a shitty side of human nature whatever you wear in this job. If the uniform work makes you suspicious of your fellow man, plain-clothes work only confirms it.'

Pam remembered: he'd been a detective for a while, at his last station.

He pointed. 'Parking spot.'

'I see it.' She braked and parked.

There were bridal photos in one window of Kwiksnap, an automatic developing machine in the other, a young woman seated next to it, pushing buttons. Inside the shop were racks of film canisters, display cases of cameras and picture frames, and a booth set aside for passport photographs. The manager twitched aside a curtain and said, 'I asked for Scobie.'

'Constable Sutton's tied up at the moment,' Pam said. She introduced herself, then Tankard, and said, 'You're Mr Jackson?'

'Yes.' The manager glanced at Tankard. 'And I know who he is.'

Tankard bristled. Pam said hurriedly, 'You called about some suspicious photographs.'

The manager looked agitatedly at the door. 'Yes. Look, she's picking them up any time soon.'

'Who is?'

'The customer. She dropped the roll in for developing at five yesterday, pick up at ten this morning. That's—' he looked at his watch '—ten minutes ago.'

'Let's see these snaps, shall we?'

The manager hunted around in a shoebox for a Kodak envelope, then took out the photographs and laid them out on the counter top as though dealing cards in a game of patience. Pam peered at them. Exterior and interior shots of a huge house set in a vast lawn. White fence railings, a suggestion of outbuildings. The interior shots, she noticed, seemed to move from the general to the particular: a room, then what

73

was in that room. Paintings in one photograph, a display case of silver snuffboxes in another. A vase. An antique mantel clock. She began to make scratch notes in her notebook.

But John Tankard was unimpressed. He pushed the photographs aside. 'So what?'

The manager swallowed. 'Well, see for yourself.'

'I see sentimental snapshots,' Tankard said. 'Or maybe snaps taken for insurance purposes. Maybe the owners are scared a bushfire will destroy everything, so they're keeping a record.'

'Look at these two, John,' Pam said. 'The alarm system.'

'See?' the manager said.

'If an alarm system set me back a few thousand bucks,' Tankard said, 'I'd want photos of it, in case the place burned down.'

Pam stared at him. Everything about him was contestable: his attitudes, his approach to the job, his day to day relations with people. She turned to the manager. 'Let's see who left these to be developed, shall we, sir?'

She tried to read the handwriting. 'Marion Something.'

'Marion Nunn,' the manager said.

Tankard laughed. 'Marion Nunn? Every policeman's friend. Plus being a lawyer,' he said, leaning his face close to Pam's, 'she deals in *real estate*. Hence the pictures. Live and learn, Pammy. You'll run into the lovely Mrs Nunn sooner or later.'

Pam pushed the photographs away. 'I already have.'

Ellen Destry fielded phone calls from journalists and worked on the sex offenders file again. She'd left it too long; it was clear that Lance Ledwich deserved a closer look. She picked up the phone. She'd try his employer first, then his home number.

By the time Sutton had returned to the station, she was ready to roll. She had the CIB Falcon waiting, a forensic technician in the back seat. 'Don't get too comfortable, Scobie. You're coming with me.'

Ledwich lived on a new estate near the racecourse on the northern edge of Waterloo, and they came to his house along a narrow court, creeping over speedbumps to get to it. The area depressed Ellen. A stained pine fence and a metre of air were all that separated the houses from one another on this estate. There were no trees to speak of. The nature strips looked raw, still to recover from trench-digging equipment and the summer's dryness. There was a steel lockup garage at the end of Ledwich's driveway, the door closed. A well-kept Volvo station wagon was parked in front of the garage, near a ragged patch of oil drips. The forensic technician went immediately for the Volvo.

As Ellen and Sutton approached the front door, a man slipped out of the metal side door of the garage and padlocked it hurriedly before coming toward them, wiping his palms on his trousers. Ellen recognised him from the photograph in his file.

'Mr Ledwich? We're—'

'You don't have to tell me who you are,' Ledwich said.

'Don't we?'

There was something oily about Ledwich. Oily hair, an air of surreptitious oozing. 'You bastards ever going to leave me alone?'

'That depends, Lance,' Sutton said.

Ledwich stared angrily at the forensic technician, who was taking photographs of the Volvo's tyres. 'What's that arsehole doing?'

'Why don't we come inside, Lance?' Ellen said, moving to usher Ledwich to the front door.

Ledwich twisted away from her. 'Whatever it is, we do it out here. I don't want the wife—'

'Fair enough, Lance. I can understand that. Why don't we move over here, let the technician do his job.'

They took Ledwich to the CIB Falcon. Ellen sat in the driver's seat, Ledwich beside her, Sutton in the rear. 'You're all the fucking same,' Ledwich said. 'A bloke goes straight, and you lean on him, hoping he'll fuck up so you can put him away again.'

'*Are* you going straight, Lance?'

'I'm a storeman.'

'Irregular hours, some night shift work, right?'

'So what? What's it to do with you? That other business, that was years ago.'

'Not that long ago,' Sutton said.

Ellen leaned confidingly toward Ledwich. 'About your Volvo, Lance.'

His eyes shifted. 'What about it?'

'Nice set of wheels,' Sutton remarked.

Ledwich was obliged to swivel his head, from Ellen and then around to Sutton and back again. 'I look after it, yeah.'

'How did you afford to buy it, Lance?' Ellen said.

'Christ, it's twelve years old. It's not worth all that much.'

'How long have you owned it?'

'Few years.'

'Why a Volvo?' Sutton asked. 'Why not a Ford or a Holden, like everyone else?'

Ellen leaned closer. 'Is it so people will think you're an ordinary bloke, Lance, rather than a pervert?'

He flushed. 'It's the wife's car, all right?'

'How about tyres, Lance, between you and the road. You'd want to fit pretty good ones, yeah?'

Ledwich narrowed his eyes. 'I wouldn't know what brand they are. What's this about?'

'Do you own any other vehicles?'

Ledwich looked away, out at the forensic technician. 'Nup.'

'We can check with the Department of Motor Vehicles.'

'Check all you like,' Ledwich said. He turned back to them. 'You going to tell me what this is about?'

'You're well set up, aren't you, Lance? Roomy set of wheels, the freedom to move around at night.'

Ledwich muttered, 'Lost my licence a while back.'

'That doesn't stop you from driving, though.'

Ledwich folded his arms. 'I suppose if I sit here long enough you'll tell me what this is all about.'

Ellen said softly, into his face, 'Abduction, rape and murder.'

He jerked back. 'Me? No way.'

'You can't get sex the normal way, you have to con women and force yourself on them. We know that. It's a matter of record. But you began to get more violent toward the end, didn't you? You started to use your fists.'

'That charge was dropped.'

'So what? Doesn't mean you didn't do it.'

'You know what we think, Lance?' Sutton said. 'We think you've graduated. We think you now realise what hard work it is conning women to get a root. Much easier just to use force.'

'Subdue them,' Ellen said, 'drag them into the rear of your station wagon, rape and strangle them.'

Ledwich swallowed. 'I'm not into that. I'm married now.'

'Poor woman,' Ellen said.

That, more than the badgering, seemed to anger Ledwich the most. 'You lousy slag. I'll get you for that. Somewhere dark, no backup to look after you, then we'll see how tough you are.'

'You're threatening me, Lance? Or is that an admission of how you operate? A woman alone at night, defenceless . . .'

'You're putting words in my mouth.'

'Kymbly Abbott,' Sutton said, 'Jane Gideon. You forced them into the rear compartment of your Volvo, raped and killed them, then dumped their bodies.'

'I bet I was working. Check with my boss.'

'I did, Lance.' Ellen numbered her fingers: 'Late to work, finishing early, slipping away sometimes for an hour or more at a time. You aren't up for Employee of the Year, Lance.'

Ledwich looked hunted. 'I never fucking killed no-one. Prove I did.'

'We will.'

'I've put the sex stuff behind me.'

'Lance,' Ellen said, examining his perspiring face, smelling the fear, 'you were sick back in 1991, you're sick now, you'll always be sick.'

'Two days in a row,' Clara told him. 'That's nice.' She held him tight on the doorstep, then led him into the house. Incense, already lit. Curtains already drawn.

'Just passing,' Kees van Alphen said.

'Yeah, sure.'

She unbuckled his belt. He groaned. He was so hungry for her. Afterwards he said, 'Did you sleep all right last night?'

It was the question she needed. 'No,' she said, with a laugh of real pain. 'It's been awful, just awful.'

'You should get something to help you sleep.'

'Having you there would help me sleep, big boy.'

He was pleased and embarrassed. 'Maybe soon. I'm on nights a lot at this time of the year. What about sleeping pills?'

'They make me hazy in the head the next day. Look, don't be upset with me, but the only thing that would relax me is dope or coke.' She stopped. 'Now you're disappointed. Sorry, I shouldn't have said anything.'

He'd gone tense in her arms. She held on, willing him to relax.

'Sorry, I've clearly said the wrong thing.'

'It's all right. It's just, I don't understand it, that's all. I don't mind so much if people are private users, it's the scumbags who traffic in the stuff, to schoolkids, that really gets to me.'

'I know. I'm sorry, I shouldn't have brought it up.'

She turned away from him and began to get dressed. She was cutting him out, and she saw that it scared him a little. He pulled her back down to him. 'Look, when you're in the job you forget that most people are basically okay. You must've thought I was judging you. I wasn't.'

'It's just my nerves at the moment,' she said. 'I'm not what you'd call a user. I used to smoke a bit of dope, do a line or two of coke, but that was years ago. I was hardly twenty. I'm clean now. It's just, I'm so jittery, so bloody scared at night, if I had some dope or coke I think it would help straighten out my nerves.'

He was silent. She began to trace circles on his stomach with her tongue. He was so sensitive! She heard him groan as she took him in her mouth. She knew what she was doing, but even so there was a part of her that was immersing herself in physical pleasure and comfort. She lost herself for a while.

When he was finished, she wriggled to get close to his body, working her mouth to clear the thick saltiness away.

She heard the rumble of his voice in her ear: 'I could get you what you want.'

She was very still. 'Come again?'

'Some grass, if that's what you want. A couple of grams of coke maybe.'

She sat up and said earnestly, 'That's really all I want, Van. I don't need much. How—'

'Don't ask. And if you repeat any of this, I'll deny it.'

She moved away from him. 'Don't be like that. Don't get angry with me.'

He pulled her against him. 'Sorry.'

'I'd never dob you in.'

'Sorry, Clara, honestly, forget I said it.'

'I mean, we'd both go down, Van. Ruin both our lives.'

'Exactly.'

'When?' she said. 'When can you get the stuff?'

'I'll come around some time tonight.'

'What about your wife?'

'Her?' He laughed. 'We separated long ago.'

She realised that she knew nothing about him. 'Kids?'

'One. I don't see her any more.'

McQuarrie turned up that afternoon. 'This letter, Hal. Any joy?'

'We're looking for a Canon printer, but the technicians doubt that the *actual* printer can be identified.'

McQuarrie swivelled in his chair. He seemed to be mulling over the dimensions of the incident room and the aptitude of Challis and his detectives. Wall map, half-a-dozen desks, files, telephones, computers, and three officers, heads well down because the super was in the room.

'Two murders, with the likelihood of a third to come.'

'More than two, sir, if he's not a local and done this kind of thing before. There's a series up around Newcastle we're looking at.'

'I'm tempted to bring in the Homicide Squad, Hal.'

There were times when Challis used McQuarrie's first name. Usually during social occasions. This wasn't a social occasion, but McQuarrie's voice had been tinged with doubt, as if he saw the case ballooning out of control—Challis's, his, the force's in general. He was a politician, essentially. He wanted reassurance, so Challis said, confidently, 'That's not strictly necessary at this stage, Mark.'

McQuarrie looked around helplessly. 'You've got enough support?'

'No. I could do with more detectives. See if you can get them assigned from two or three different stations so that no-one's left short-staffed. I've already requisitioned more desks, phones and computers.'

McQuarrie sighed. 'Fair enough. But the minute—'

'The minute it threatens to fall apart, I'll let you know.'

'I mean, this isn't exactly a case of a husband doing in his wife, Hal. This is different. This is big. I had the London *Daily Telegraph* on the line last night.'

Challis, to amuse himself, said, 'What did you tell them?'

'Oh, it was well under control, and nothing like the Belanglo Forest killings. I hope I said the right thing.'

'Sir, we've got some solid forensic evidence with Jane Gideon. Tyre tracks in the mud, so we have some idea of the kind of vehicle we're looking for. Apart from the blow to the head, her death resembles Kymbly Abbott's. I think we can rule out coincidence. We're putting warnings over the media. With any luck, our man's supply will run out.'

McQuarrie screwed his mouth up. 'Nice way of putting it.'

'To him, sir, young women are a source of supply, they're not real.'

'Point taken.'

'Anything else?'

'Yes.' McQuarrie got to his feet. He tilted back his head. 'Listen up, everybody.'

Ellen Destry threw down her pen. What did the fool want now? She had work to do. Ledwich had taken up most of the morning, and she was still waiting for the forensic technicians to identify the brand of tyre from the plaster casts they'd taken. So far, all they could tell her was that it was an off-road tyre, only slightly worn—ten, maybe fifteen thousand k's—and distinctive because it had a round shoulder and a very deep tread. No other distinguishing marks, such as chips, burrs or uneven wear in the rubber. 'But find me the tyre, and I'll see if I can match it,' the technicians said. 'Yeah, sure, piece of cake,' she'd told them. As for the cast matching the tyres on Lance Ledwich's Volvo, that seemed very unlikely, even to her untrained eye. Quite a different 'footprint', as the technicians put it. She really was not inclined to listen to some crap or other from McQuarrie.

She looked up to see that McQuarrie was watching her, waiting for her to pay attention. 'First, I want to say that I think you're doing a fine job under difficult circumstances. For that reason, I will arrange for extra detectives to be assigned to the case from Rosebud and Mornington. Sergeant Destry, you will continue to be in charge on the ground, answerable to Inspector Challis.'

She gave him a tight little smile. He washed his palms together. 'Now, clearly this is the work of one man. Our priorities are to find him before he kills again. Equally, we need to provide a safe environment here on the Peninsula. We also need to find the vehicle used to dump Jane Gideon's body.

Finally, we need to think about the mindset of the person behind these killings.'

Mindset, Ellen thought. God.

'Similarities between the victims,' McQuarrie went on. 'Differences. Did they know one another.'

Now he's telling us how to do our job, Ellen thought.

'Kymbly Abbott, Jane Gideon,' McQuarrie went on. He shook his head and laughed, and it was a laugh that went wrong, even as he uttered it and said, 'Kymbly. Where do these people get their names from?'

No-one shared the laughter. He was speaking ill of the dead. Meanwhile Ellen Destry felt herself blush, for she'd named her daughter Larrayne, not Lorraine, so what did that say about her? McQuarrie was a prick.

It was with relief that she went to her car at the end of the day and was able to snatch a moment with Rhys Hartnett. She wasn't sure, but there was something there, in the way he looked at her. 'Are we still on for twelve o'clock Saturday?'

'I'll be there.'

'If you like, stay on and have some lunch with us,' she said.

Challis worked until six-thirty that evening. As he was leaving the station, the prison called. Apparently his wife had tried to saw across her wrists with a plastic knife and had written a note that said, 'Forgive me.' They'd assumed that the note was for him. Maybe it was. Challis had long forgiven her, he was past making judgments about her, and had even told himself that she wasn't his responsibility any more, but it was always him they called whenever she went off the rails. The call depressed him. He slumped back in his chair and stared at the wall maps.

Then the front desk buzzed him. 'Tessa Kane to see you, sir.'

He put his hand to his forehead briefly. 'Show her up.'

He stepped into the corridor and waited. He was alone on the first floor. When Tessa appeared with a young constable, he sent the constable back downstairs. Tessa's eyes were bright and searching. She was pleased with herself, but also gauging what he thought of her now. 'Hal, don't be mad at me.'

'I thought you agreed you wouldn't publish.'

'No, I said I'd *consider* not publishing. Your finding Jane

81

Gideon made it imperative, Hal. This was a scoop. It meant a lot to me, and I think it was in the public interest.'

'I've never heard a more cynical—'

'Hal,' she said, and reached up and kissed him. He closed his eyes.

In her low voice, she said, 'I've been wanting to do that for ages.'

He was surprised to find that his anger was gone, and made a sound in his throat that might have been assent and pleasure.

'Hal, would you have dinner with me tonight?'

Challis thought about it. He felt better about Tessa Kane, but doubted that he had energy and selflessness enough to be pleasant company for her. All he wanted to do was drive to the aerodrome and work on the Dragon.

'Not tonight. Tomorrow?'

'Fine.'

'Somewhere out of the public eye,' he said.

'That's easy.'

When he let himself into the hangar, twenty minutes later, he saw that Kitty had left the new issue of *Vintage Aircraft* on his tailplane, open at the centre spread. It showed a restored Dragon at Bankstown airport, full colour, the red and silver livery of an airline that had folded in 1936. Challis didn't think he'd ever seen a more beautiful aeroplane. The rounded nose reminded him of a tentative, questing snake, but in all other respects the Dragon Rapide was nothing like a snake. An insect? It suggested delicacy, restraint, grace, and the atmosphere of England-to-Australia races and records as the world came out of the 1930s Great Depression, before it all went wrong again.

He turned the pages to the 'Help Wanted' column. His letter was there. Somewhere in the world there might be a man or a woman who knew a little of the history of his aeroplane.

Kees van Alphen sat in the window of Pizza Hut. They were used to him in there; he often ate there. He saw Tessa Kane leave the station. At seven-fifteen, Challis's car pulled out of the station car park. Van Alphen waited for the 8 p.m. shift to get under way before he walked back across the road and into the station.

Thursday night, a bit of action in town, what with people

spending their pay cheques and gearing up for Christmas and the summer break. But quiet in the station itself. Van Alphen prowled about the building, opening and closing doors, chatting to the young constable on the front desk, the probationers in the tearoom, a couple of other sergeants writing up reports. In effect, he was mentally mapping the station, placing everyone, anticipating where they might accidentally wander. When he was satisfied, he walked into the office of Senior Sergeant Kellock—he who said his door was always open—and located the key to the evidence safe.

The drugs were on the top shelf, just a handful of small plastic sealables of coke and hashish, some pill bottles of ecstasy, some amphetamines from a garden-shed laboratory in a twist of paper. Van Alphen substituted two of the cocaine baggies for baggies of castor sugar, double checked the paperwork—they'd not be needed in trial for another six weeks yet—and left the office, locking the safe behind him.

'I'll be out for a couple of hours,' he told the constable on the front desk.

'Okay, Sarge.'

'Our pyromaniacs might decide on return visits.'

'Good one, boss.'

The constable seemed to be assessing him.

'What are you looking at, Sunshine?'

'Sorry, nothing, Sarge. I mean, you're not on night shift tonight.'

'Things hot up before Christmas, you know that. Plus we got members down with a stomach bug. I like to keep on top of things. It's what makes a cop, that little bit extra.'

'Yes, Sarge.'

'All right then.'

Van Alphen took an unmarked Commodore from the car pool and drove to Clara's house with the radio dispatcher's voice scratching in the darkness and all of his heartaches on his mind. Fucking Tessa Kane and her editorials. What was she doing at the station? Trying to get more dirt?

Three strikes and you're out. He'd been warned for over-enthusiastic policing in his previous two districts, and now it was happening again. No-one understood that you had to start hard and carry through on it, or the scumbags won. But the top brass were hypersensitive to the image the press gave the force, and the civil libertarians were always making a noise about police brutality. Fuck them. He knew his methods got results. He'd had the highest arrest record in each of his districts, which proved that crime was always there, under the surface, and had been allowed to tick over unchecked.

It was a pity the women in his life hadn't been able to hack it. His wife and daughter had walked out, finally, saying they couldn't stand the stares, the whispers, the aggravation. He felt sorry they'd had to suffer, but the fact that they hadn't stuck by him left a sour taste in his mouth.

Then Clara wrapped herself around him like a cat, and his cares flew out of the window.

EIGHT

Challis rose at six on Friday morning and, dressed in trousers, shirt and tie, sat on the decking at the rear of his house to watch the lightening sky and the swallows as they caught mosquitoes and other insects on the wing. The garden, such as it was, showed signs of cracked soil: even the weeds were dying. We were lucky to get that tyre track, he thought. The rest of the Peninsula is bone dry. But the tyre was all they had. No semen traces, for the killer had used a condom. No prints, for he'd worn gloves. What he'd left on his victims were *absences*, including the absence of life.

So, what did his victims leave on him?

Challis was expecting the additional detectives from Rosebud and Mornington to be at the early briefing. He drained the dregs of his coffee and walked the boundary again. Just as he reached the road gate, the council garbage truck slowed, saw that Challis had forgotten to wheel out his bin, and accelerated away again, leaving Challis a taste of dust and diesel exhaust. That's what happened during the long cases— Challis forgot his life.

He stopped for petrol on the outskirts of Waterloo. A car towing a caravan was parked clear of the pumps, a disgruntled family watching a mechanic on his back beneath the rear of the car. Queensland plates. Challis imagined the oppressive summer heat of Queensland, the family driving to the same beach shack or caravan spot down here on the Peninsula year after year in search of a balmier sun.

Would they read the *Progress* and become fearful, and head back the way they'd come?

When he parked at the rear of the police station in Waterloo, he saw Ellen Destry getting out of her car, keys gripped neatly in her teeth, a briefcase and bundled folders in her arms. She hitched and hoisted this load and then, composed, bent swiftly to lock her car and check her reflection in the wing mirror. Wings of glossy brown hair swung about her cheeks. She was neatly packaged, Challis decided, and allowed himself a moment to watch her. She was a good detective, but saddled with irritations at home, and that made her like 90 per cent of the population. He saw her wave to the air-conditioning man, who'd been working at the rear of his Jeep. They drew close, and talked animatedly. Challis suspected everybody of something, these days. He didn't make judgments, he simply observed.

Rhys Hartnett had been waiting for her. She was sure of it. She'd seen him idling at the rear of his van as she drove in, and he called her name as she locked her car. She didn't want to seem too eager, and was pleased when it was he who moved first, stepping over the line of driveway shrubs and toward her.

'Another early start?'

'No rest for the wicked,' she said, feeling immediately that she'd said something inane.

They chatted for a while. Then he fished for a square of paper that had been folded into his overalls and shook it out. 'This was on my windscreen when I knocked off yesterday.'

She hadn't seen this particular one before: BEEN HASSLED BY TANKARD AND VAN ALPHEN? DON'T LET THE FASCISTS GET AWAY WITH IT. REGISTER A COMPLAINT. DO IT NOW.

She passed it back. 'Nothing to worry about.'

'What's it about?'

You were loyal to the job, your fellow members. Ellen Destry didn't particularly like Tankard and van Alphen, but still, she didn't know Rhys Hartnett, even if she did find him nice to look at and think about, so she said, 'The world's full of aggrieved people.'

He said darkly, 'There's a youngish bloke, big beer gut. He pulled me over when I first come here, did the full roadworthy on the van. Treated me like I was scum.'

'Let's just say a couple of my colleagues are a bit over-enthusiastic,' Ellen said.

Rhys waved the leaflet. 'Sounds like they're getting people's backs up.'

'Rhys, about tomorrow. I should give you directions. Penzance Beach is a bit of a maze.'

And she rattled off directions, as you tend to do, even as he said he knew the Peninsula, and had a street directory.

He grinned, not listening, until she'd finished. 'Look forward to it.'

She went in and found an envelope on her desk. Preliminary report on the tyre cast.

Challis stood before the wall map and said, 'I'd like to welcome officers from Mornington and Rosebud. It's good to have you on board. Most of you know one another already. If you see someone you don't know, introduce yourselves after the briefing.

'Now, to recapitulate. Two young women murdered, and a letter, which we think is genuine, promising another. Kymbly Abbott left a party in Frankston on the night of 12 December, was seen hitchhiking at the start of the Old Peninsula Highway, and was found raped and strangled by the side of the road early the next morning. Just under a week later, on the night of 17 December, the VAA recorded a call from a Jane Gideon, whose car had broken down outside a produce stall on the Old Peninsula Highway. The tape indicated the presence of someone else, Gideon was not there when police and the VAA mechanic arrived, and her body was found on Wednesday, dumped by the edge of the Devil Bend reservoir.'

Challis paused to sip from his coffee. He let his gaze take in Ellen Destry's detectives and each of the new officers. He gazed at them calmly. He had no idea what they thought of him. He didn't care. But he wanted them to know that the investigation was his, and that they were all equal in his eyes.

'What have we got to go on? Very little. Indications that

our man wears gloves, probably latex, the kind used by people who handle food, and therefore easily obtainable and that he uses condoms.

'We've found traces of cotton and other fabrics on Abbott and Gideon, but some of those are likely to be innocent, and those that aren't innocent are no good to us if our man burnt his clothing after each murder. His caution in other regards suggests that he might.

'Abbott and Gideon were dumped. We don't know what traces from the murder scene may have been transferred with their bodies because we don't know if our man kills inside a house or a vehicle or somewhere else. But we do know they weren't killed where they were abducted, out in the open, for the only signs of dirt or grass found on the bodies came from where they were found.

'Now, the victims. They have in common that they were young, unaccompanied women, and abducted on the Old Peninsula Highway at night. We've found nothing to suggest that they knew each other, and I think we can say that they didn't know their killer.'

He paused. 'All we have is a set of off-road tyre tracks from the vehicle that must have dumped Jane Gideon. Ellen can tell us more.'

He saw her cough, as though he'd caught her with her attention wandering. 'We found identical twin tracks—from the rear tyres if he backed in, and presumably he did to make dumping the body easier—and they've been identified as Coopers, an American tyre, this particular one an off-road tyre, quite distinctive, and rather uncommon in this country.'

A Rosebud detective said, 'Ellen, I've seen utes with off-road tyres.'

Others murmured their agreement.

Challis stepped in. 'But try to think your way inside his skin. He snatches a young woman, subdues her, and needs to hide her. He's not going to hide her on the front or rear seats. Too risky. And if he were driving a utility, would he risk putting her in the tray, under the tarp or a blanket or a few old bags? I can't see it, myself.'

'A ute with canvas sides and roof,' someone said.

'Yes, possibly,' Challis said, 'but that would entail getting out of the cab and walking around to the rear, and when he

88

dumped Gideon he didn't leave footprints. The only footprints we found at the scene belong to the kids who found her. My gut feeling is, our man tossed the body out from the rear of his vehicle, and did it without alighting from the vehicle itself, suggesting a four-wheel drive or similar, with rear-opening doors.

'But keep an open mind,' he went on. 'Now, prevention. You've probably observed lately that a mild panic has settled over the community. Many women are scared, and who can blame them? That's going to make it more difficult for our man to operate. Maybe he'll shut down, maybe he'll move to another part of the Peninsula—but everyone's wary, not just here in Waterloo. Maybe he'll move interstate and become someone else's headache, but that doesn't mean we stop investigating what he's been getting up to here. I've found similar cases interstate, so maybe he's been active before, but we're going back ten years or so, and the details are sketchy and it's hard to recognise a pattern unless you're looking for one.

'Any questions?'

Scobie Sutton had been tapping his long teeth with a pen. 'That Land Cruiser we saw at the Saltmarsh house.'

Challis turned to Ellen Destry, who shook her head, saying, 'Different brand, different rim size. The Cooper we want fits a 235-75-15 rim, meaning a smaller vehicle, like a Jackaroo or a Pajero.'

'And not a Volvo station wagon?'

'No. Ledwich's in the clear.'

'And we have to ask ourselves,' Challis put in, 'whether or not a man like Ledwich—essentially a coward who relies on knock-out drugs and deception—is capable of graduating to the kind of violence and risk-taking needed to snatch young women from a public highway.'

Sutton slumped. They all did, a little.

Danny Holsinger finished work at 1 p.m., went home, pulled off his T-shirt and jeans, which were dusty and damp from his morning on the recycling truck, and stood under the shower for ten minutes. Just the thought of Megan Stokes made him tug on his tackle, his mother on the other side of the door, screaming, 'You going to be in there all day?'

'Ah, get stuffed, you old bitch.'

'Don't you talk to me like that.'

He waited. Nothing more. His mother slagged off at him just to keep in practice. He towelled himself dry and pulled on shorts, a T-shirt and sandals. Poofter gear, yuppie gear, he privately thought, but it was humid out and Megan had given him the gear as a present a few weeks earlier and he needed to keep in her good books.

He found her in a shifty mood. Wouldn't look him in the eye, half-ducked away from his kiss. 'Check out the shorts, Meeg,' he said.

'You look good in them,' she said absently.

'How's the backpack?'

'Oh, good.'

'Your enthusiasm overwhelms me,' Danny said, immediately pleased with the way the words had come out. 'Your mum in?'

'Gone to see Gran.'

Danny jerked his head toward the bedroom. 'You on?'

'Suppose so.'

She was like a damp rag. She just lay there, saying things like, 'Ow, that hurt,' or not saying anything at all.

'Got your period?'

'Yeah.'

'Fair enough. But you could wank me, suck me off. Doesn't mean we have to stop.'

'I don't feel right.'

Danny opened his mouth to complain, then flopped onto his back next to her magnanimously, and eyed her room: a poster of Hutchence, screaming into a microphone; Lady Di; a cat with huge, soulful eyes; scarves hanging from her dressing-table mirror; an impression of smudged make-up on the mirror.

'Where's the backpack?'

He'd seen her hang it on the back of her door yesterday.

She burst into tears. 'That fucking cow.'

'Who?'

'Mum.'

'Why?'

'She let it get stolen, that's why.'

'Stolen? I only gave it to you yesterday.'

'This lady come round with a kid. Said she was going to

bless the house. Mum lets her in, the stupid cow, and when her back's turned they nick her purse, the cordless phone, Dad's watch, stuff like that. I didn't realise till later they'd also nicked the bag. Dan, I'm really sorry. I'll make it up to you.'

That bag's getting around, Danny thought. Maybe I can pick something else up for Megan, this job Jolic's got lined up for us.

'Don't hit me, please.'

He stared at her. 'Hitcha? What do you take me for?'

'You'd have a right,' Megan said, 'that beautiful bag.'

The daily postal deliveries were arriving later and later in the lead-up to Christmas. Jolic wasn't even sure that the package would arrive before the weekend. But it was there, waiting for him in his letterbox when he came back from the pub at five o'clock. He walked through knee-high weeds to his backyard, punching a mobile phone number into his own mobile. 'The stuff arrived.'

'You can mock up a floor plan from it?'

'No problem.'

'The owners are going away after Christmas, two weeks in Bali, so you won't be obliged to bash anyone this time.'

'Oh, thanks a lot,' he said. 'You're a funny woman.'

'Take only the stuff on the list. If there's any spare cash lying around, it's yours, but don't get greedy. Don't stay too long and get caught, in other words.'

'If I go down, you go down with me.'

'I'll ignore that. Is Danny all right on this?'

'I can handle Danny. He does what I tell him.'

'As long as he stays in the dark.'

Jolic laughed. 'Danny's always in the dark, O Beautiful One.'

'How come whenever you say something that's the least bit nice about me, it's in a mocking voice?'

Jolic registered the shift in her tone. He knew how to mend the situation. Working a shy, tentative note into his own voice, he said, 'I'm not laughing at you, I'm laughing at *me*, if you want to know, in case you think I'm coming on too strong, you know, saying things you don't want to hear.'

Phew.

He heard her voice shift again. 'Boyd, I'm not so hard that I don't want a touch of romance now and then.'

Challis arrived home at seven. He was due at Tessa Kane's house at seven-thirty, and he almost called to say he wouldn't be coming. He didn't want to rush but to sit and watch the sun go down with a glass of red. Read a book. Microwave something from the freezer. Let the day ebb, in other words, his cares dropping away as the light faded in the west.

But he hadn't had a dinner date—if this could be called a dinner date—for some time. His invitations to dine with police colleagues had declined in the past six years. Part of it was his single status. An unattached person at the dinner table was a reproach to coupledom. And Challis wondered if those husbands and wives saw him as jinxed, an unhappy ghost or shell of a man.

He stripped and stepped into the shower. There was a shower head over his bath, but Challis preferred the shower cubicle inside his back door, next to the laundry. He thanked the foresight of the people who'd built the house. He liked being able to step in from an hour's gardening or walking and dump his clothes in the basket and step into a box of steaming air and water.

He worked shampoo into his hair and left it there while he soaped his body. Slowly the bucket at his feet filled with sudsy water.

Then there was no water hitting his head and shoulders and he hadn't rinsed the shampoo away and he knew that the electric water pump above the underground tank would be screaming, sucking air.

Challis burst naked through his back door and switched off the pump. He needed to rinse his hair. He filled a saucepan with water from the corrugated iron tank attached to his garage and poured it over his head. It was like ice. He did it again, then worried that he was being wasteful. The third time he tried to stick his head in the saucepan and swish the water through his hair. He looked at the result. The water was mildly soapy. He poured it at the base of an old and possibly dying lemon tree. He wasn't convinced that his hair was free of shampoo.

Finally he dressed, dragged a comb across his itchy scalp

and went back outside. Clearly he'd need to buy water, but no carrier would come at this hour and possibly not for several days, if there was a rush on in the district. Challis found three lengths of hose in his garage and joined them together. He attached one end to the tap at the bottom of the iron tank, fed the other into the overflow of his underground tank, and turned on the tap. He'd let the water drain over several hours. He reminded himself to prime the pump.

The phone was ringing inside.

'Hal, it's almost eight thirty.'

She was trying not to sound hurt or let down. Challis glanced at his watch: eight fifteen. 'Sorry, Tess. A small emergency here.'

'Police wives must feel like this. Hal, you hadn't forgotten?'

'Coming now.'

He left, feeling scummed and scaly, and more jittery than at any time he could remember in his puzzling life.

John Tankard and Pam Murphy were assigned to the night shift for the Christmas weekend, routine patrol, Tankard behind the wheel of the divisional van for a change, figuring that driving would keep his mind off the pain in his lower back. He found the scratchy murmurs of the police band comforting.

They rode around in silence, lit greenly by the instrument panel. Nine p.m.. Ten. Eleven.

Then Murph the Surf had to break in. 'Not much happening.'

'Wait till New Year's Eve. On for young and old, parties all over the joint.'

She nodded. 'The town's gradually filling up, have you noticed? More traffic during the day down where I live. People arriving for their holidays.'

Tankard grunted.

Silence. Then: 'You should see a physio, or a chiropractor.'

Tankard blinked. What was she crapping on about now? 'What?'

'You look like you're in pain, Tank. Is it your back?'

'I'm all right.'

'It's all the gear we have to lug around on our waists. Heavy belt, handcuffs, baton, capsicum spray, holster, gun. Puts a strain on the lower back. Plus the weight's not evenly distributed.'

He glanced at her. To his mind, she was as ugly as a hatful of arseholes. 'You don't say.'

'A sports medicine clinic should be able to help you.'

'I'm fine.'

'No, you're not. It's not weak to admit your back needs adjusting.'

'Look, Murph, why don't you just rack off, okay?'

He saw her slump against her door. 'Suit yourself.'

A car shot out of a side street, BMW sports, going like a bat out of hell.

Tankard chortled. 'Okay, dickrash, let's see how you like this,' and he activated the siren and planted his foot.

As they drew closer, a lazy hand appeared, giving them the finger, and the BMW twitched under heavy acceleration and drew rapidly away.

'Oh, mate, will I have you for breakfast.'

Beside him, Pam Murphy was sitting intensely, peering ahead, her hands on the dash. 'Careful, Tank.'

'Careful? You don't chase someone carefully.'

'Just watch where you're going.'

The BMW sped away from Waterloo, heading south-west, inland from the coast. Tankard didn't want to lose him. The Peninsula was stitched together with narrow roads and lanes, where there was no lighting, only shadowy driveways and screening trees and hundreds of access gates.

Then they did lose him. They were on Tubbarubba Road when the BMW vanished. 'Slow down,' Pam Murphy said. 'I saw something.'

'What? Where?'

'Behind that funny building on the corner.'

'Automatic telephone exchange,' Tankard said. 'What did you see?'

'A light, like someone opened the door of a car.'

Tankard reversed so hard and fast that the engine howled and the van snaked, leaving rubber on the road. 'Spot on. There he is, the cunt.'

He parked, switched off, got out. 'You wait here. Call the plate in, see if the car's stolen.'

He could see that she didn't like it, but she did as she was told. He approached the BMW, which was parked in long grass next to a cyclone fence, and shone his torch at the driver's door. 'Step out of the car, please, sir.'

It was a woman. She was young, and inclined to totter and giggle. Plenty of blonde hair, including a rope of it that she was chewing while she looked him over. Legs up to her arse and showing a bit of tit, too. John Tankard had an image of wealth and privilege disporting itself while the workers were slogging away. He called, 'Murph, come here a minute?'

He didn't take his eyes off the girl. When Pam Murphy was standing next to him he said, 'This young lady got out of the driver's seat.'

'Impossible.'

'Exactly.'

The blonde screwed a look of bafflement on to her face. 'What do you mean?'

'Miss, is there someone with you?'

'You mean my boyfriend?'

Tankard tipped back his head and called, 'Sir, would you get out of the car, please?'

Pam Murphy edged away, and now she was staring along the flank of the car, at the passenger seat. She had her hand on her gun. 'We don't want any trouble now, sir.'

'God, lighten up, why don't you?' the blonde said.

They watched the door open. A young man emerged from the car. 'Why the strongarm act?' he asked.

Pam said, 'Sir, are you the owner of this car?'

'So?'

'Were you driving it?'

'No way.'

'We have reason to believe that you swapped places with your lady friend.'

'Are you for real?'

Tankard said, 'Sir, we have reason to believe that you were driving this car. You were driving above the speed limit and we'll be breathalysing you to see if you were driving while under the influence of alcohol. We also believe that you changed places with your friend in an effort to escape possible prosecution. I'd like to see your licence, please, sir, and yours, young lady, and ask you both to submit to a breath test.'

'Come off it! You bloody coppers don't know who you're dealing with. You've made a big mistake this time.'

They ignored him. They separated the couple and took them one at a time to the van for a breath test. When Tankard had the woman alone he said, 'You could make it easy on yourself.'

'How do you mean?'

'You give me something, I give you something.'

She said nothing, but her eyes narrowed, waiting for more.

'What's your name?'

'Cindy Price.'

'Cindy. Well, Cindy, do you really want to be booked for drunken driving and making a false statement to police?' Tankard jerked his head. 'Just to protect some arsehole? Your boyfriend, is he?'

'Sort of.'

'Sort of. So you don't feel too strongly. That's good. Well, Cindy, we're going to have to chuck the book at someone, so why don't you go easy on yourself. Tell us what really happened, how he asked you to swap places with him, and I'll see you don't get charged with anything.'

'And?'

'And what?'

'Is that all?'

They were closing in on it now. They were on the same wavelength. 'If you wanted a watertight assurance, Cindy, you'd have to do one more thing for me.'

She said challengingly, 'Try me.'

He waited a beat. 'I intend to.' He fished out his notebook. 'What was the address?'

These days, his only way of pulling a bird. They rejoined the others.

'You'll be sorry about this,' the boyfriend said.

He was like the girl, young, drunk, stamped with privilege. 'I'll punch you out in a minute, you don't shut up,' Tankard said.

'You don't know who you're dealing with here.'

Tankard said to Pam Murphy, 'There's this joke, only it's about Porsches, not BMWs, but it still applies. What's the difference between a Porsche and a cactus?'

'With a Porsche, the pricks are on the inside,' Pam said.

NINE

'What are you doing?'

Challis had thought she was asleep. He himself had been asleep, but then he'd awoken, and the strangeness of the bed, the house and the situation had swamped him suddenly, there in the darkness lit only by the digital display of her bedside clock and a glimmer of moonlight from behind the curtain that he remembered was heavy, too heavy for the room, and he'd been dragging on his clothes, and was hunting for his shoes, ready to leave, but she'd caught him.

He stretched across the bed and kissed her. 'I have to go, Tess.'

She stared at him, then looked away. 'I'd thought we'd have breakfast together.'

He sat for a while, one hand cupping her neck until the tendons there told him that she was unrelaxed. He removed the hand. 'I couldn't sleep.'

She rolled away from him. 'Fine. I'll see you around.'

'Tess—'

She turned back to him. 'Hal, it's okay. I'm not angry. You feel strange, I understand, so you should go.'

'I'll see you again.'

She kissed him and collapsed onto her pillow. 'No talking. I'm tired. See you around.'

*

Ginger taught two classes on Saturday mornings. He was able to fit Pam into his ten o'clock. She almost didn't pack the Bolle sunglasses she'd bought him, thinking not to make a fool of herself, but he seemed to pay special attention to her, so she presented them with a shy flourish at the end of the lesson, when the others were getting changed and driving off.

'Christmas present for you.'

He blushed. 'I didn't get you anything.'

'I wouldn't have expected you to.'

'I wanted to,' he said.

'Did you?'

'I thought you'd take it the wrong way.'

'No,' she said.

The colours of the sky and the water were pink and grey, a typical soft Peninsula beach day. Pam went home in a pleasant muddle, a tingle on the surface of her skin, but that soon evaporated. The button was flashing on her answering machine. Sergeant Kellock wanted her at the station at two o'clock and she'd better not be late, if she knew what was good for her.

Rhys Hartnett arrived ten minutes early, just as Ellen was getting back from the shops with lunch things and the Saturday papers. She dumped everything in the kitchen and began to show him around the house, apologising for its faults. Alan trailed suspiciously behind them, asking what was the best way of cooling it *without* air-conditioning. Ellen knew what that was about: he wanted to see if Rhys was prepared to give them neutral advice.

'Insulation, for a start.'

'It's already insulated,' Alan said.

'Have you thought of ceiling fans?'

'They're no good if the air's already hot.'

'Blinds? Shutters? Grapevine on a trellis?'

Ellen said, 'We're clutching at straws, Rhys, that's obvious. So why don't you finish looking around and give us a quote.'

'We can't afford it,' Alan said.

Rhys looked inquiringly at Ellen, who said, 'It can't hurt to get a quote.'

'Noisy bloody things.'

'It's possible to station the main unit some distance away

98

from your living areas,' Rhys said. 'You won't really hear anything.'

They came to Larrayne's bedroom. She was on her bed, reading, dressed in skimpy shorts and a singlet top. A small desk fan ruffled her lank hair. Rhys Hartnett flashed her a grin and said, 'Hi there. Hot enough for you?'

Ellen felt a twinge of pure jealousy. It surprised her. She watched for her daughter's reaction to Hartnett and was pleased to see a customary scowl. Larrayne flounced out, saying, 'So much for privacy in this house.'

Ellen rolled her eyes. 'Sorry, Rhys. She can be very rude sometimes.'

'Rude? That? Nah. I've done quotes on tax-dodge farms for Brighton society cows who could show your daughter a thing or two about rude.'

Challis had rung the state distributor of Cooper tyres, who'd said: 'I used to be the only distributor, but these days there's a rip-off merchant selling them in your neck of the woods,' and now he was driving along a side street in Rosebud. Tyre City covered half a block, an eyesore of stacked tyres, grimy sheds, oily dirt and dead grass caught in the cyclone perimeter fence. CHEAP TYRES in letters taller than a man covered the front wall of the main building. When Challis drove in, and parked to one side, and showed himself, half of the workforce seemed to melt away into the shadows while the other half stared hostilely at him. Challis knew that he smelt like a cop. All cops do—to those who have reason to be sniffing for one. Meanwhile the din—rock music, pressurised air escaping, the hammering of hand tools—was stupefying.

He showed his ID to the man who emerged from a small, glassed-off office. 'Are you the boss?'

The man nodded. 'You're talking to him.'

'You sell a brand of tyre called Cooper?'

A cigarette bobbed in the man's mouth. 'Might do.'

'Either you do or you don't.'

'All right, I do. So what?'

'Not a common tyre,'

'Not real common, no.'

'Not many sales?'

The man shrugged. 'People buy 'em.'

'You'd remember it if someone wanted to fit a set of Coopers?'

The man seemed to have oil and grease deposits on his face, hands and clothing. He was small, shaped like a barrel, and wore a permanent scowl. 'Probably not.'

'Come on. A deal like that would stand out in a business like this.'

The man squared his jaw. 'Meaning what, exactly?'

'Meaning most of your business consists of selling barely roadworthy tyres to people who drive rustbuckets,' said Challis harshly. 'I want your undivided attention for a minute.'

'Mate, I sell all kinds of tyres and buy all kinds. Blokes in Jags come here, blokes in VWs. I sell truck tyres. I got tractor tyres out the back. I buy job lots at auction and I buy single tyres. I buy from other dealers. I buy bankrupt stock. I'm an acknowledged dealer for most of the main brands.'

'Point taken, point taken,' Challis said. 'So the only way we can investigate your sales of Cooper tyres is if we look at your books, is that it? You'd have them recorded, wouldn't you? I'm sure you're the type of bloke who does the right thing by the tax man.'

The man shifted uneasily. 'Bit behind in me paperwork this month. Take a bit of finding, the office is in a bit of a mess. Plus, I wouldn't necessarily have the customers' names written on the invoices.'

'What about car registration numbers? Surely you'd record them on the invoices?'

The man scratched his head. 'Not always.'

An hour later, defeated by the man's office chaos, Challis returned to Waterloo. As he drove into the car park at the police station he recognised McQuarrie's car in the visitor's slot and was tempted to turn around and go out again. He needed a haircut, he hadn't walked on the beach for weeks, he had Christmas shopping to do.

The phone was ringing when he got upstairs. There was no-one else to answer it.

He recognised the caller's voice. 'It's Hal Challis, Mrs Gideon.'

Her voice was low and tired. 'Have your men found anything, Mr Challis?'

He said carefully, 'We're running down several leads. We

have a clear idea what sort of vehicle your daughter was taken away in.'

'And what sort would that be?'

'A four-wheel drive of some kind.'

She was silent.

'Mrs Gideon?'

'Thank you.'

And the line went dead.

Pam Murphy reported to the conference room, a room chosen to intimidate her, she thought, with its huge table and flattening ceiling and all but two of the chairs empty and accusatory. She sat in a third chair and watched Superintendent McQuarrie steeple his fingers beneath his chin and gaze at her. She felt sick. Why was *he* sticking his oar in? She glanced across at Senior Sergeant Kellock, who wouldn't look at her.

'Sir, we did everything by the book.'

'Lady Bastian says otherwise,' McQuarrie said.

'Sir, with respect, she wasn't there.'

'A young man from a good family, never been in trouble before.'

'That's not true, sir. Two traffic offences and—'

'Small potatoes,' the superintendent said. 'We have a young man from a good family, and two police officers at the end of a long shift at one of the busiest periods of the year, namely Christmas. It's late, very dark out. No independent witnesses. One constable is well known for his aggressive policing. In fact, he's the focus of community concern, and I've had to talk long and hard to persuade Ethical Standards that they need not send a team in to investigate.'

Tank had told her that might happen. If enough people complained about him, Ethical Standards might be obliged to take a look.

'Perhaps you're not aware, Constable Murphy,' Kellock put in, 'exactly what an Ethical Standards visit can mean. If they find against you then not only does your station undergo random behavioural management audits, but the officers under scrutiny would be forced to undergo extra behaviour and leadership courses at the Academy. Is that what you want?'

'No, sir.'

'Fortunately the Superintendent and I are confident that Mr

101

Bastian's complaint falls within the resolution process. There's no need for further examination from outside.'

'Complaint, sir?'

'Harassment.'

Pam shook her head, thinking, I don't believe this.

McQuarrie leaned forward. 'Constable Murphy, isn't it possible there was something unsound about the arrest? Isn't it possible that Constable Tankard overreacted?'

'No, sir.'

'You were with him at all times?'

'Sir, it's procedure to separate witnesses and offenders during questioning. Constable Tankard took the girl aside for questioning and I questioned Mr Bastian. Standard procedure. We didn't want to give them more of a chance to agree on the story they'd cooked up for us.'

'Miss Price claims she was driving the car.'

'That's a lie, sir. We both saw the driver at the start of the pursuit. It was a man.'

'Saw him clearly?'

'Fairly clearly. A man's arm.'

'Perhaps she was wearing his jacket.'

'It was a warm night, sir. Neither was wearing a jacket.'

'Do you see what I'm getting at, Constable Murphy? This could mean egg on our faces—*your* face.'

The man was a bully. He was clean, alert, neat, and as slippery and nasty as a snake. And piss weak, a man more inclined to suck up to a wealthy family than protect the interests of his officers.

'Doubt, Constable Murphy. Doubt is creeping in.'

'I stand by my statement, sir.'

McQuarrie leaned his sharp head close to the file before him. 'Miss Price also says, and I quote: "The male police officer tried to put the hard word on me. He asked for sex and for me to admit I was not the driver, or I'd go to jail." Did you hear that conversation, Constable?'

'No, sir.'

'But it *sounds* right, wouldn't you say? It's the sort of thing Constable Tankard is capable of?'

'He strikes me as a competent officer, sir. Professional.'

In reply, McQuarrie stared at her. He seemed to be making

mental calculations, about her, or Tankard, or the case itself, she didn't know.

John Tankard saw her coming out of the conference room. 'Pam. How you doin', mate?'

'Not bad, Tank, considering.'

'Holding up okay?'

'Trying to.'

'Don't let the bastards grind you down.'

'I won't.'

He took her arm and pulled her into a corner, where he muttered, 'Look, Pam, what did they say about me?'

The door to the conference room opened. Kellock poked his head out. 'Constable Tankard, we're ready for you now.'

Three o'clock, the station very quiet, everyone gone home or doing Christmas shopping or playing cricket or tennis, so Scobie Sutton was relieved to see John Tankard coming out of the conference room. 'Tank, you busy?'

Tankard looked bleak and cold. 'I'm not on duty for another hour.'

Sutton glanced at the conference room. 'What's going on?'

'Nothing.'

Sutton let it drop. 'You'd be doing me a favour.'

'Like what?'

'I need to talk to some gypsies.'

Tankard broke into a grin finally. 'Gypsies? You're having me on. What, they crossed your palm, told you to sink all your savings on a slow horse? All right, I've got nothing better to do.'

Sutton explained while Tankard drove. 'I didn't put it together until last night, when I was reading my kid a story. She asked me what a gypsy was. A few days ago I interviewed an elderly couple who'd had a woman come to the door, offering to bless the house or any spare change they might have lying around, except when the old dears turned their backs she tossed the joint. And a few days before that a woman came into the station, reckoned she was a "Romany seer", telling me we'd find Jane Gideon's body near water.'

'No shit.'

Sutton pursed his lips, staring ahead through the windscreen, remembering what this Sofia had said about his daughter. How had she known it? Next to him, Tankard said, 'Scobe? You awake in there?'

'Pardon?'

'Jane Gideon.'

Sutton waved his arm. 'Oh, the information was too vague. The point is, I checked the daily crime reports. If it's the same woman, she's robbed half-a-dozen people.'

Tankard slowed for a level crossing. The tyres slapped over the rails and then he accelerated again. 'You could bring her in, put her in a line-up, see if anyone identifies her.'

'The boss would never okay it. This is just a hunch,' Sutton said. 'But a photograph, now that's a different matter.'

He reached back between the seats to a camera and dumped it in Tankard's lap. It was a Canon fitted with a telephoto lens.

'I hope you know how to use it,' Sutton said.

'No problem. Just keep her talking where I can get a clear shot at her.'

They came to the Tidal River Caravan Park, a depressing patch of stunted ti-tree, dirty sand and stagnant, mosquito-infested water that wasn't a river and hadn't seen a tide in a long time. The main area consisted of toilet blocks, a laundry, the main office and early summer holidaymakers in large caravans with tent annexes. The margins of the park, nearest the main road and poorly sheltered from dust, noise, wind and sun, had been set aside for longer term tenants in caravans, recreation vehicles and plywood or aluminium portable homes.

'Gypsies?' the park manager said.

'A woman calling herself Sofia. Tells fortunes,' Sutton said.

'Oh, her. A gypsy? Didn't know we had any. I just thought she was a wog. Goes to show.'

'If you'd point it out on the map?' Sutton said.

The map was rain-stained and sun-faded behind a sheet of thick, scratched perspex. The manager pointed. 'There, in the corner. Her and her brothers and a few kids.'

Tankard drove slowly through the park. Sutton sensed his restless, swivelling eyes. To be that obsessed would be to invite an ulcer, he thought. He pointed. 'There.'

Sofia and a small naked girl were sitting on frayed nylon folding chairs under a canvas awning at the side of a dirty white Holden Jackaroo that had been converted into a small mobile home. There was a matching Jackaroo behind it and a caravan behind that. There was no vehicle coupled to the caravan but a rugged, snouty-looking Land Cruiser was parked under a nearby tree. Sutton saw three men watching from a cement bench-seat and table in the shade of a leaning wattle. The ground was bare and hard. Sutton had an impression of untidiness, even though Sofia and the men were neatly dressed and there was no sign of litter at the site.

Perhaps it was the dog, a skinny, threadbare blue heeler. It was lying in the dirt, paws on what Sutton realised had recently been a good-quality leather backpack, the fine black leather now torn and chewed.

The three men watched him get out of the Commodore. As he closed the door, one got to his feet and sauntered away. Before Sutton had reached Sofia and the child, a second man strolled off, his hands in his pockets. Then the third. What flashed into Sutton's mind then was the fact of the four-wheel-drive vehicles with rear compartments. Then he thought of Sofia and the reason for his visit, and realised that, with the men gone, John Tankard could aim his camera without being spotted.

'Remember me, Sofia?'

She watched him. There was no humour or animation in her face. 'Your little girl is happier.'

'That's because the creche is closed from now until the end of January. My wife—'

'She needs time to adjust.'

Sutton supposed that Sofia meant his daughter, not his wife, and wondered if she were being clairvoyant now or simply expressing an obvious truth.

'Two things, Sofia. Number one. You came to us saying you knew where Jane Gideon was. Have you thought any more about that? Was this a feeling you had, did someone tell you where she was, did you actually see her? I might have been a bit offhand the other day,' he concluded hastily.

'Not offhand. Disbelieving. You disbelieved me.'

'Well, it's not every day—'

'You found her near water, didn't you, just as I said you would.'

'Perhaps your brothers—'

'They don't know anything.'

105

'Fine. So you *felt* that Jane Gideon was dead, is that what you're saying? You had no direct knowledge?'

'If you want to put it that way. What's the second matter you want to talk about?'

Sutton looked at the dog. It had fallen asleep with its jaw on the backpack. 'Sofia, in your role as clairvoyant—'

'Seer.'

'—seer, do you sometimes bless people? Their homes or their possessions, I mean. Tell them their worldly goods will multiply, that kind of thing?'

Sofia seemed to draw upon her reserves of dignity. 'I'm not a magician. I don't conjure up things that aren't there to begin with.'

'Fine, fine.'

'There are charlatans who say they can do these things.'

'You wouldn't know of any of them? Where I can find them?'

At that point, a small brown snake began to cross the space between the rotting nylon chairs and the caravan. Neither Sutton nor Sofia said anything, but Sofia gently stepped over to the child in the second chair and lifted her free of it. The snake glided, unconcerned, beneath the caravan.

'You learn to live with them,' Sofia said.

There was a special article about him in the main Saturday paper. It said he'd 'snatched' both women. What a laugh; they both got willingly into the passenger seat. Number three, now, she was snatched, good and proper.

He hadn't been prowling when he saw her the first time. It had been dawn, first light, and he'd been on his way to work. He saw her jogging, slim legs pounding, elbows pumping, shoulderblades flexing beneath the narrow straps of a singlet top. Sweatband to hold her hair back. His headlights in the uncertain dawn picking up the reflective strips on the heels of her running shoes. The air was cool. It would be hot later, and she probably had a job to go to, so that's why she was running at dawn. He veered wide around her, went on down the Old Peninsula Highway, thinking it through.

That had been several days ago. Each morning after that, the pattern had been repeated.

This morning he'd left half an hour earlier, pulled over on to the dirt at the side of the road, raised the passenger-side

106

rear wheel with a quick-release hydraulic jack, removed the hubcap and one wheel nut, and waited.

When she came upon him he was walking around in small circles at the back wheel, bent over, his hands clasped behind his back. Her feet pounded, coming closer, and began to falter.

'Lost something?'

He looked up at her with relief, flashing a smile. 'Blasted wheel nut. The light's not good enough and I haven't got a torch.'

Half-bent, he continued to search near the jack. She joined him. In these conditions—dawn, air quite still—he'd have plenty of warning if another vehicle were coming. He and number three walked around like that for a short time, then, when she widened the search to take in the area near the exhaust pipe, and crouched to peer beneath the rear axle, he took her.

Now, that *was* a snatch.

TEN

'Bye-bye, Sprog,' Scobie Sutton said.

'Not Sprog. Roslyn. Ros . . . lyn.'

'Roslyn.'

Her little arms shot up, there at the back door. 'Daddy, you hold me.'

'I have to go to work now, sweetie.'

'You take me? Please?'

'Maybe another day.'

'Scobie, love, you'll give her false hope.'

It was often like this. You really had to think hard before you said or did anything around a three-year-old, for if they got the wrong message about something, a lot of the groundwork could go out the window.

He said, 'Kiss Daddy goodbye. We'll have a barbecue tonight, how would that be?'

'Shotchidge?'

'Shotchidge on bread with lots of sauce.'

'*Two* shotchidge?'

'As many as you like.'

Through the kisses goodbye, he heard his wife say, 'I'm so lucky, I can't believe it.'

'I'll try to get home early.'

'It *is* Christmas Eve, my love.'

*

Pam Murphy went surfing early that morning, hoping to stumble upon Ginger with a class, but he wasn't there. Sunday, Christmas Eve, she should have expected it. The day stretched ahead of her. She rang her parents.

Ninety minutes later she was getting off the Melbourne train and on to the Kew tram. Her parents lived in a turn-of-the-century house set in an overgrown garden on a hill overlooking Studley Park. Visiting them was something she did from time to time, not only because they were her parents, and getting on in years, but because, just once, she'd like them to express approval of the life she'd made for herself.

And today she wanted to put Tankard, Kellock and McQuarrie out of her mind, and give her parents their Christmas presents, and get some presents from them, and generally put her police life out of her mind for a few hours before she had to report for duty again at 4 p.m..

The house was in bad shape, rotting window frames, peeling paint and wallpaper, salt damp in the walls, leaking roof, even if it did sit on half an acre of prime real estate.

She had her own key.

'That you, dear?'

Who else? Pam thought. 'Me, mum.'

Kerlunk, kerlunk, and then a scrape as her mother's walking frame manoeuvred through the sitting-room door, and more kerlunking as the old woman made her way along the hallway. It was dark inside the house, despite the dazzling sun outside. It beat against the heavy front door and barely lit up the stained glass.

Pam kissed her mother. 'How's Dad?'

A considering frown: 'Let's say he's had a so-so day.'

'Typing?'

'Yes.'

Pam rubbed the palms of her hands together, gearing up for the long walk past her mother and down the dim, dampish hallway to the back room, where her father lived now, surrounded by his books. Dr Murphy didn't seem to sleep. He spent all of his time propped up by pillows, a portable typewriter on his lap.

Pam hesitated. 'How's it going?'

'We spent the morning squabbling about the use of a hyphen,' her mother replied. 'He insisted that it should be oil hyphen painting, I said that once upon a time it would have been, but that two single words was acceptable nowadays.'

There were three PhDs in the family. Pam's father, and both of her brothers, who were several years older than her. The brothers were teaching at universities in the United States and were never coming back. That left Pam, who'd still been a child, an afterthought, when her brothers left home to live in university colleges. Some of the family's intellectual sparkle seemed to go with them, and Pam grew up in the belief that her own development hadn't mattered as much to her parents, that the family's brains hadn't been passed on to her. And so she made it clear that she was happy to swim and cycle and play tennis and go cross-country skiing. Solitary sports, mostly. But she made an interesting discovery: these sports taught her to think well, for they encouraged problem solving, solitude and reflection, so that she no longer believed that she wasn't clever. When she graduated from the Police Academy, she was ranked third in her class.

Not that the family registered that fact.

'Hi, Dad.'

'What is this "hi" business? Should I now respond "low"?'

'Hello, Dad, Father, Pater, O Kingly One.'

Her father grinned. The room smelt musty, a smell composed of old flesh and old furnishings and books. Pam crossed to the window.

'Leave it!' her father said.

'As you wish.'

'Sit, sweetie. What are the lawless up to?'

And Pam told him, embellishing, watching her father's avid face. It was more than a simple desire for salacious detail. Pam suspected that he took a certain eugenicist position on crime.

'And what did this fellow look like?'

'Oh, pretty average,' Pam said. 'How's the book going?'

Dr Murphy had been a lecturer in mathematics. He'd led an uneventful life, but was trying to screw an autobiography out of it.

'At the rate I'm writing,' he said sourly, 'I'm likely to die before I've been conceived.'

*

110

That afternoon, van Alphen wondered about the relationship between sexual desire and cocaine. Clearly Clara wanted him, but he didn't know how to read it. Simple desire, for him as an individual? Gratitude for his being there when she needed him after the fire? Or was it chemical, the cocaine itself acting on her, and nothing to do with him as a person?

She was discreet. He'd never seen her take the stuff. She'd hidden it away without taking any the night he delivered it, and when he'd called around yesterday it was clear that she'd already had some. No way did he want to see her take it, and she was protecting him, insisting that he always contact her before he called in to see her.

Whatever, she was always ready for him. But did she need to get stoked first? Did she see him as no more than her supplier, who had to be kept sweet, because he didn't want payment in cash but in sex?

He was a long way in, now. He'd given her grams and grams of the stuff. 'Clara, don't be offended, you're not going to sell the stuff on, are you?'

She was shocked, genuinely outraged. 'Van, I told you, it's for my nerves.'

'I know.'

'You can *see* it's helping, can't you? I mean, do I seem as jumpy to you any more?'

'I guess not.'

'No. So don't ask me that. I feel ashamed enough as it is.'

'Okay.'

'It's not as if I'm a junkie or anything.'

There were old scars, scarcely visible. Maybe she had been, once upon a time. 'Forget I said it, Clara, okay?'

'All right,' she said grudgingly, then stretched out fully against his flank. 'God you're good for me.'

She'd drawn the curtains. Incense was burning. In the perfumed dimness he turned and kissed her. She broke away. 'We're forgetting *you*, Van. You seem edgy.'

'Ahhh,' he said, rolling on to his back and flinging an arm across his eyes, 'it's been a hell of a couple of days. Two of my constables arrested some rich prat two nights ago, now the mother's making waves, complaining to the superintendent.'

'Plus that girl being found murdered.'

111

'Plus that.'

They fell silent, began to caress each other. Afterwards, heartbeat and blood flow ebbing pleasantly, he propped himself on one elbow and with the tips of his fingers began to trace her breasts and stomach and the glorious hollows inside her thighs. 'Incredible skin,' he said. 'You wouldn't be part Maori, would you?'

Her body seemed to alter under his gaze, recoiling, shutting him out. 'Here we go,' she said. 'It had to come, sooner or later.'

'What?'

'Does it make a difference who or what I am?'

'Of course not. I just asked—'

'You like a bit of black meat, is that it? Or maybe you're disgusted but can't help yourself? Or are you trying to break it off with me?'

'I only said—'

'Just you remember where the coke came from, big boy. Hurt me again, insult me, get me into trouble, and I'll spill everything so fast you won't know what hit you. "Cop steals drugs for girlfriend," I can see it now.'

'Jesus, I only said—'

'I'm flesh and blood, aren't I, like you? I got feelings?'

'Of course.'

'I deserve respect.'

'I respect you.'

'Well don't say anything insulting to me again. Don't even *think* it. I especially don't want to hear anything about Maoris or New Zealand or anything about my past, okay?'

'Sure.'

She pushed down on his head. 'Do me with your tongue. That's it . . . that's it . . .'

She was slippery ground, but sex was firm ground, and van Alphen threw himself into it. He heard, through the dampish slap of her inner thighs against his ears, a sound like pleasure and pain.

At four o'clock, just as John Tankard was finishing a cup of tea in the staff canteen before going on patrol with Pam Murphy, someone called, 'Hey, Tank, bad luck, mate.'

'Yeah, thanks.'

'Dropping the charges, what bastards.'

'Yeah, I know.'

'So, did you get to screw old Cindy, or what?'

John Tankard propelled the other man across the room, forearm to the throat, flattening him against the wall. 'You arsehole.'

'Chill out, Tank. He was only joking.'

'Yeah, let him go, Tank. Look, we're all on your side. They think if they've got money they can get away with anything. It's not right. We're on your side. So let him go.'

Tankard released his colleague. It wasn't often—ever?—that the others were on his side.

Challis picked up the phone and heard Tessa Kane say, 'Hal, I thought I'd ring now to wish you Merry Christmas. I'll be with my family all day tomorrow.'

There was a touch of desolation in her voice. Was her life like his? He breathed out heavily. 'Have a happy day.'

'Thank you.'

Then her voice dropped, taking on slow, lonely tones. 'You should have called.'

Challis waited, then said carefully, 'I was going to.'

'I wish you hadn't left like that.'

They were silent. Eventually Challis said softly, 'I'd better go. I'd like to see you again soon.'

'Wait! I heard you arrested—'

Challis put the phone down. Arrested Lady Bastian's son, she was going to say, and apparently there were questions all over the arrest, but that wasn't his problem.

He glanced at his watch. Six-thirty. He decided against going home and then coming back again, and walked down High Street to the Fish Bar, a bistro between the shire offices and the jetty. From the window he could see the open ground that the town had set aside for fairs and carnivals. Tonight: Carols by Candlelight. Late January: the Westernport Festival. Anzac Day: dawn service.

He liked eating alone. He often had no choice but to eat alone, but he did like it, most of the time. Tonight it would have been better to have dined with someone, for he felt peaceful and relaxed for the first time in a while—which owed a lot to the fact that it was Christmas Eve and the town—even the police station all that day—was in a slowed-down mood, everyone benign and full of good intentions.

At eight o'clock he paid his bill, and as he was standing, waiting, folding his credit card receipt into his pocket, he saw Scobie Sutton's car draw into the kerb on the other side of the road. The grassy area near the little bandstand was filling rapidly. Sutton and his wife and daughter got out of the car, carrying blankets and hymn books. The child was sleepy. Challis watched them join the crowd. Someone gave them candles from a cardboard box, and they settled on to their blankets. But Challis didn't join them when the carol singing began. He might have, and been welcomed, but he found a corner of the crowd where he could sing and not be expected to talk.

ELEVEN

Challis woke at six on Christmas morning and desolation flooded him. He hadn't expected to feel this way. He'd thought he was above all that. He remembered what he'd read somewhere—if you're depressed, go for a long walk—and swung immediately out of bed and hunted for his Nike gardening shoes, a T-shirt and an old pair of shorts.

He walked for an hour. As the bad feeling lifted, he found himself listening to the birds. He could swear he was hearing bellbirds, the first in his five years on the Peninsula. The world was still and silent, and he was alone and light-footed in it, this morning. He took deep breaths. Yellow-breasted robins watched him and a thrush sang high in the canopy of branches above his head. There were creatures scratching in the bracken. Only a plastic shopping bag caught in a blackberry cane spoiled the morning for him—that, and the realisation that he'd been depressed but wasn't now, yet might be again as the day developed.

At nine-thirty he left the house. Ellen Destry and her husband and daughter lived in a cedar house on stilts in an airless pocket between ti-trees and a small, humped hill at Penzance Beach. The house looked like—and had been, before the Destrys bought it—someone's holiday house. And nothing—not even the new shrubs and herbs and fruit trees, or the fresh paint job and the hanging plants—would alter that. Three cars in the driveway, three out on the street. Challis groaned. He wasn't ready for a crowd. He mostly preferred solitariness yet worked in an occupation that demanded permanent sociality.

Alan Destry came to the door. 'Hal. Come in, come in, Merry Christmas.'

Ellen's husband wore an air of grievance. He was a constable, attached to the Traffic Division in the Outer Eastern zone, married to a fast-tracking CIB detective. That's how Ellen had explained it to Challis once, at the pub, when she wanted to stay and drink and not go home. 'Merry Christmas yourself,' Challis said, offering his hand.

At that moment a light plane passed overhead, following the shoreline. Distracted, Challis looked up. Twin-engined Cessna. He didn't recognise it.

'Some people have their feet on the ground,' Alan Destry said.

It was a clumsy insult, delivered with a grin of Christmas cheer. Challis wanted to say that some people had all the luck, but let it go. People underestimated him, he knew that, and didn't care. They thought that a policeman who liked to restore old aeroplanes and had a wife who'd tried to have him shot was a man who would allow things to happen to him. A man destined to remain stuck where he was in the force, detective inspector, no higher.

He proffered a terracotta pot wrapped in green and red Christmas paper. There was a clump of lobelia spilling over the edges. 'Good of you,' Destry said, looking about for a flat surface and deciding on the verandah floor, beside the door.

They went through to the sitting room. The windows were open, admitting gusts of warm, dusty air. It was an oppressive room. No wonder Ellen intended to have air-conditioning installed. She wasn't in the room. Nor was Scobie Sutton. But the other CIB officers were, and a couple of Alan Destry's colleagues, together with spouses and children. The Destrys' daughter, Larrayne, scowled in a corner, trying to ward off the imploring fingers of a small boy.

'Ellen not here?'

'Ah, mate, a sudden death. A kid.'

Challis felt sick. To lose a child on Christmas Day.

He forced down a glass of beer and absently palmed toffeed

116

nuts into his mouth from a bowl on the television set. There were cards on the sideboard and on a loop of string across the far wall. Mistletoe. Parcels heaped at the foot of a tired, tinselly pine-tree branch that was shedding needles. As he watched, a bauble fell to the carpet. The small boy rushed to it, kicked it in his haste, and Challis saw it smash against the skirting board.

The Destrys' daughter looked so miserable and put-upon that Challis crossed the room to her, greeting people as he went. Larrayne saw him coming. She stared fixedly at the floor, as if to hide or appear too negligible to be bothered with. She wore a short denim skirt, a Savage Garden T-shirt and sandals. She'd painted her nails. Her legs, knees together and inclined to one side, seemed too long for her slight frame. Wings of hair furled down about her young round face. She was fifteen but looked at once ten and twenty.

'Hello, Larrayne.'

She was low in an uncomfortable chair and Challis towered above her. She was forced to stretch her neck to see his face, and that strangled her voice. 'Hello.' She said it quickly and looked away again.

Challis crouched beside her. 'Merry Christmas.'

She muttered a reply, leaning her knees away from him.

'It's a pity your poor mum had to go out on a call.'

Larrayne shrugged, then said, 'Me and Dad had to do everything, as per usual. She invites people over, then goes out, leaving us to do everything.'

Challis knee-creaked until he was standing again. He couldn't be bothered with the Destrys' daughter. He wandered across to the main window.

When Alan Destry came by with a bowl of nuts, Challis said, 'Did Scobie go with Ellie?'

'Yep.'

'Do we know what happened?'

'Cot death.'

A cot death. Challis wondered how secure he really was in life. His eyes pricked. He felt very alone again, and welcomed the despatcher's call when it came.

TWELVE

They were country people: decent, bewildered, fearing the worst. They'd been expecting Trina to arrive some time on Christmas Eve. It's a long drive from Frankston to Shepparton, so, although they'd been worried when their daughter hadn't arrived, they'd told themselves to expect her after they'd gone to bed, or Christmas morning at the latest, though they'd have been cross with her if she *had* left it that late. She'd always been a bit wilful and inconsiderate. Not malicious, mind you, just always went her own way. But when she hadn't arrived by ten o'clock, they'd phoned. No answer. Then, remembering that two girls had been abducted and murdered, they'd phoned the police in Frankston, who sent a divisional van to their daughter's address.

Trina Unger lived in a small, worn-looking home unit. The doors were locked, the blinds drawn. The police had broken in eventually, but the place was empty. Trina Unger's bed was unmade. A half-packed weekender bag sat on the end of the bed. The other bedroom had been hastily tidied. There was a flatmate, according to the Ungers. They didn't know where she was. At her parents' for Christmas?—as Trina should have been.

Then at lunchtime Trina Unger's car was found on a lonely stretch of the Old Peninsula Highway, just ten kilometres from Frankston. All of the windows had been smashed in.

Now it was three in the afternoon. The parents had arrived from Shepparton, and Challis and Sutton were interviewing them in their daughter's sitting room. The walls were close and faintly grubby, the ceiling too low, and the overstuffed, mismatched op-shop armchairs crowded the small, tufted orange carpet. The place smelt damp, despite the heat of summer.

'The second bedroom?' Challis said.

'That would be Den's,' Mrs Unger said. 'Denise.'

'Do you know where we can contact her?'

'Afraid not.'

Challis nodded to Sutton, who stood and made for the bedroom. All of the detective constable's movements were slow and automatic, his bony face drawn, his eyes ready to brim, as though he could not get the image of the cot-death baby out of his head.

Challis turned to the Ungers again. 'We found your daughter's car.'

Kurt Unger was sitting upright, his fists bunched neatly on his large knees. The words wouldn't come clearly, so he coughed and tried again. 'Yes.'

'On the Old Peninsula Highway,' Challis continued. 'That's in the opposite direction from Shepparton. And she'd started packing, but hadn't finished. Have you any idea where she might have been going?'

'None,' Freda Unger said.

'Does she have a boyfriend? Could he have called her?'

Freda Unger made a wide gesture with both arms. 'Who knows? We never met any, if she did have boyfriends. But she was young still.'

'Twenty?'

'Twenty-one in March.'

Kurt Unger coughed. He said, 'I overheard a policeman say the windows were broken on her car.'

Challis cursed under his breath. 'Yes.'

'She locked her doors but he broke her windows with a rock and dragged her out,' Kurt Unger said fixedly. Nothing moved, only his bottom jaw.

His wife crumpled. 'Oh, Kurt, don't.'

'We don't know what happened,' Challis said. 'My feeling is, it's not related to her disappearance. All of the windows

119

were smashed, suggesting vandals, and the radio had been ripped out and the boot forced open. Someone saw her car there and decided on the spur of the moment to break in.'

'But what was she doing there?'

'It's possible your daughter's flatmate will know,' Challis said. 'We're tracking her down now.'

As he spoke, Scobie Sutton entered, holding an envelope in his long fingers. The flap was open; there was a letter inside. 'It's from this Denise character's mother,' he said. 'There's a return address on the back, somewhere in East Bentleigh. Do you know where the phone is, Mrs Unger?'

'The kitchen.'

'Right.'

'Excuse me,' Challis said, and he joined Sutton in the kitchen nook. 'Scobie,' he muttered, 'if the girl's there, ask her what Trina's car was doing on the highway.'

Sutton looked as though he'd just remembered his manners. He held out the handset. 'You want to make the call, boss?'

'No, I didn't mean that. Ask her the obvious questions, Trina's movements over the past couple of days, any boyfriend, was she aware Trina was missing, that kind of thing, but we must know about the car.'

Challis returned to the sitting room. The parents were whispering to each other. Reluctant to intrude, he crossed the room to the front door, stepped outside, and wandered across to the police car that had been parked in the driveway for most of the morning. A uniformed constable sat in the driver's seat with the door open, eating a sandwich. She swallowed hurriedly. 'Do you need me inside again, sir?'

'Not just yet. They're holding up for the moment.'

'Sir, we just got word a walkman and a sweatband have been found near the car.'

'How near?'

'A few hundred metres away.'

Jogging, Challis thought. That's what she was doing there. But when? Yesterday? The day before? Why hadn't the flat-mate noticed her missing?

Sutton joined him. He tried for some humour. 'Denise has been hitting the Christmas champagne pretty hard. Hard to get any sense out of her. But she said Trina Unger likes to go jogging on the highway. Used to jog around the park, but got

120

scared off by a flasher a few months ago, and now jogs on the highway because it's quiet.'

'What time of day?'

'Early morning. Daybreak.'

'Never in the evening?'

'Not according to Denise.'

'When did she last see Trina?'

'Friday night. On Saturday she went to stay with her parents in East Bentleigh to help her mother get ready for Christmas. She noticed that Trina hadn't come back from her run, but didn't think any more about it.'

'Boyfriend?'

'She didn't know of one.'

Challis stared unseeingly over the rooftops. Young men and women left home to lead their separate, secret lives, and some of them didn't make it. 'Scobie, go home, spend some time with your wife and kid. I'll see you tomorrow.'

THIRTEEN

On Boxing Day the *Age* and the *Herald Sun* carried stories about the missing girl. At 8 a.m., Tessa Kane came to the station and told Challis that she was bringing out an issue between Christmas and the New Year after all. 'We received another letter. It was hand-delivered to the box we have next to the main entrance.'

Challis spread it out inside its clear plastic slip case and read: *Like you, my eyes are everywhere. But mine know what to look for. Do yours?*

'Fancies himself,' Challis said. 'Well, that's true to form.' He sighed. 'You've taken a copy?'

'Yes.'

'I'll send this to the lab.'

'We go to press tomorrow night.'

'Tess, you're inflaming the situation.'

'Try and stop me, Hal. I've had legal advice.'

'That's not the point,' Challis said. 'You're scaring people, and in danger of attracting crackpots, not to mention copy-cats.'

'That doesn't negate the fact that there's been two murders and a possible third.'

'At this stage it's an abduction.'

'Hal, come on.'

Challis said, 'I'd prefer it if you didn't publish, that's all.'

Ellen parked her car. Rhys was waiting for her again. Working on Boxing Day? Talk about keen. He crossed to where she was standing and handed her an envelope. 'Your quote.'

She opened it, saying, 'Rhys, this is the season to be jolly. It's also the season to get the phone bill, the gas bill, the electricity bill . . .'

She said it with a grin, but there was a flash of irritation and he said, 'I thought you were serious. I kept the costs down as much as possible.' He turned toward the shrubbery border to cross into the grounds of the courthouse.

'Rhys, wait.'

She caught up to him and said, 'Look, I didn't mean to offend you. You must be wondering what you've got yourself into with my family.'

He was still prickly. 'I got the distinct impression the other day that your husband doesn't want aircon fitted.'

Ellen said, keeping it light, 'Oh, he'll come around eventually.'

'He didn't seem to like me much. That I can do without.'

There was no point in avoiding what had happened. Rhys had stayed for a barbecue lunch, but it had been a disaster. 'Alan gets like that sometimes. It's not a pleasant job he's got, he sees terrible road accidents.' She grinned. 'But yeah, I don't think another barbecue is a good idea just now.'

She saw the tightness go out of him a little. He looked at his watch. 'I'd better get back to work. Why don't you look over the quote and I'll catch up with you later in the week.'

She said, 'A drink would be nice.'

He hesitated. She seemed to wait for a long time for him to smile and say, 'Good idea.'

Challis briefed them at eight-thirty, saying: 'Unger, curiously, was snatched at dawn, when she'd gone for an early morning jog. But what does that tell us? Not much. Does our man prowl up and down the highway for hours every night, to see what he can find? Was he coming home when he saw Unger, or on his way somewhere, to work perhaps? Was it opportunistic, or had he seen her jogging before?

'Which brings us to his psychological make-up. A loner,

123

according to one of our shrinks. Probably smart, in his thirties, a normally functioning citizen on the surface. You'd live next door to him for years and not know he liked to rape and kill young women. Probably some trouble in his childhood. Drunken, abusive father, unhealthy attachment to his mother. Unable now to relate easily to women, beyond surface pleasantries. We've heard it all before, there's no point knowing these things unless to have them proven *after* the fact. The point is, he looks, and behaves, like the man next door, he has no work, family or other link to his victims, and so we'll simply have to rely on luck and chance along with good old-fashioned detective work.

'I won't kid you, things have stalled. Not much forensic joy from the bodies, and nothing on the letter sent to the *Progress*. The paper comes from laser printer paper available at any newsagent and many supermarkets. The printer was a Canon, and they're a dime a dozen, found in businesses and homes all over the country. The envelope was post office issue. There are prints on the envelope, but they're smudged and likely to be from mail-sorters and posties. We're checking that now.'

He paused. 'Since then, another letter has come.'

'Any more on the vehicle, boss?'

It was one of the Rosebud detectives. So far there was no sign that Ellen Destry's crew, or the reinforcements arranged by McQuarrie, were losing faith in him. 'No. And once you ask yourself who on the Peninsula uses a four-wheel drive, you want to have a Bex and a good lie down.'

He started numbering his fingers. 'First, any farmer, orchardist, winegrower or stock breeder. Then we have your ordinary suburban cowboy, who's never taken his pride and joy off the sealed roads. After that, your average house painter, electrician and handyman.' He stopped numbering. 'Not to mention mobile mechanics, courier drivers, shire council workers, power-line inspectors, food transporters.'

He gazed at them. 'The link we need could come by accident. We have to be alert, and read the daily crime reports. Maybe our man is known to us, or will become known to us, for a quite different offence. Maybe his vehicle's been involved in something—Yes, Scobie?'

Scobie Sutton was half way out of his chair. 'Boss, while we're on that subject, I've got one possibility.'

'Go on.'

'On Saturday I went out to Tidal River to question a gypsy woman for theft. She was camped there with three blokes and at least one kid. Two camper homes, one caravan, a couple of Holden Jackaroos. The thing is, she came to the station last week more or less saying she'd had a vision of where we could find the body. Near water, she said. I thought she was a crank. Sorry, boss.'

Challis was angry but tried not to show it. 'You'd better get out there straight away.'

'Yes, boss.'

Kees van Alphen delivered a second freezer bag. 'You're really getting through this stuff, Clara. Hadn't you better cut down a bit?'

He felt her arms go around his neck. 'Gives me an appetite. Haven't you noticed?'

'I'll say.'

'Then what's your problem?'

'Supply, that's my problem. Getting found out. Going to gaol. How's that for starters?'

'Then you'd better bust a few dealers, hadn't you? Restock the evidence cupboard and deal direct.'

He'd thought of that. He could do it, but didn't feel good about it.

Afterwards, on her patterned carpet, lit by the curtained window light, he traced her nipple and said, 'I have to go.'

'So soon?'

'The neighbours are going to wonder why there's always a police car in your driveway.'

'Them? They scarcely know I exist.'

Scobie Sutton asked for two vans, a police car and two probationary constables. Pam found herself driving him. She'd had a call earlier to say that her mother had fallen, not badly, but enough to bruise her poor, ropey arm. Pam had been ironing her uniform when the call came, listening to a new CD, a compilation of '60s surfing songs: 'Wipeout', 'Pipeline', 'Apache', a couple of Beach Boys hits. Ginger had once told her you could hear, in the beat and the guitar of '60s surfing instrumentals, the shudder in the wall of a breaking wave, so she'd been listening hard, as she ironed her uniform shirt and longed for him.

Sutton broke in. 'You know how my kid pronounces "quickly"? "Trickly." To get her to go to the loo when she wakes in the morning we have to pretend her teddy needs a wee. So she rushes off to the loo on her little legs, saying, "Trickly, Blue Ted, trickly, hold it in, hold it in."'

His bony face was wreathed in smiles. 'Huh,' Pam said, trying to work up some good humour.

'And vegemite sandwiches? She calls them sammymites.'

'Cute.'

She sensed that Sutton had turned his protuberant eyes upon her, gauging her remark. After a while, he looked away again.

Five days until New Year's Eve. She had time off, and thought about Ginger and the parties he was bound to be going to.

They entered the Tidal River caravan park, skirted the central reserve, and made their way to a dismal, unsheltered corner by the main road.

Sutton groaned. 'They've legged it.'

Hard-baked, grassless earth, spotted with oil, but no sign of any gypsies. Pam watched Sutton get out of the Commodore and peer at the ground, as if searching for tyre tracks. He looked livid. Then he crossed to a rubbish bin and began hauling out food scraps, takeaway containers and bottles. At the bottom was what looked to Pam like a wad of black cloth. Then Sutton shook it out, and she saw straps and buckles, and realised that he was looking at a backpack. It was a mess. Sutton shoved it back into the bin.

FOURTEEN

On Wednesday 27 December, dark cloud masses rolled in from the west and banked up in huge thunderheads above the bay. By lunchtime an electrical storm had brewed. It lurked and muttered through the afternoon, approaching the Peninsula, building with gusting winds into a cloudburst at four o'clock. Challis, in the incident room at Waterloo, wondered how clogged his gutters were. He couldn't afford to have rainwater overflowing the gutters before it reached the downpipes that took it to his underground tank. Ellen Destry, also in the incident room, thought of her house, shut up all day in the heat. Would Larrayne have had the sense to open the windows? She glanced out across the car park to the courthouse. Rhys Hartnett, stripped to the waist, was snipping tin vents in the rain. His body glistened. He seemed to sense her there; straightening, lifting his streaming head to the rain, he shook the water from his thick hair. John Tankard, out in the divisional van, switched on the wipers and pulled in to the rear of the Fiddlers Creek Hotel, opened his window, snatched the sixpack of Crown Lager from the manager, and slipped away again, stopping by his flat on the way back to the station. Meanwhile the ground under Clara's mailbox had turned to blackish mud. Kees van Alphen, exhausted in his bed at home, heard nothing of the storm. Four days had passed since Trina Unger's abduction. Her body had not been found. Life went on.

On Thursday the Waterloo *Progress* came out in a small special edition. There was little advertising and only a handful of news items and a page of sports results. The front page was devoted to the second letter, under the banner: KILLER MOCKS POLICE. There was also a sidebar speculating that a four-wheel-drive vehicle had been used for the abductions. And, at the bottom, an item headlined 'Charges Dropped':

'Police this week announced the dropping of charges against Mr Julian Bastian, 21-year-old playboy son of Melbourne and Portsea society matron, Lady Susan Bastian.

'Mr Bastian was facing charges of driving while intoxicated. When arrested, his companion, Miss Cindy Price, 19, of Mount Eliza, was in the driver's seat of his BMW sportscar. Arresting police alleged that Bastian persuaded Miss Price to say that she was the driver.

'Senior Sergeant Kellock of the Waterloo police station said: "There were procedural errors in the arrest."

'Lady Bastian's late husband, Sir Edgar Bastian, was the moving force behind the White Sands Golf Course. Members include Superintendent Mark McQuarrie, of the Victoria Police.

'Superintendent McQuarrie is superintendent of Peninsula District.'

On Friday, Pam Murphy and John Tankard were back on the day shift, making their regular sweep of the town and the side roads.

'See the paper yesterday, Murph?'

Pam's mother had been treated for a blood clot. The treatment was plenty of rest and pills to dissolve the clot, but was she going to get much rest? Not likely, not with the old man the way he was.

'You see it?'

Pam looked through the windscreen, the side window, alert for kids on bikes and skateboards. 'See what?'

'The article about that Bastian prick.'

'I saw it.'

'Pretty good, eh?'

'In what way?'

'Well, it raises doubts, doesn't it? If I can get some senior officers to swing behind this, maybe the charges will be reinstated.'

'And pigs might fly.'

'You're a negative bitch, you know that?'

And Tankard folded his arms and leaned, tired and depressed, against the passenger door with his eyes closed.

On Saturday morning Challis noted that the road outside of his front gate was dry and dusty again, almost as if there hadn't been rain earlier in the week. He made for the Old Peninsula Highway, as he always did. But this week he'd been braking slowly when he reached the Foursquare Produce barn and pulling on to the gravel forecourt. As usual today there were two cars parked hard against the building itself—employees' vehicles. The main door was open. He could see them, two women, one building a pyramid of apples, the other preparing price labels with a black marker pen. They recognised him and waved. He wondered what they thought of the occupant of the third car, which was parked next to the phone box. Pity? And embarrassment, for when we see such naked grief and desperation we turn away from it.

He got out. As he approached the car, the driver's door opened and a woman eased out from behind the wheel. 'Inspector Challis.'

'Hello, Mrs Gideon.'

There were posters as large as television screens over the rear windows: *Did you see who took our daughter?* A blurred photograph, Jane Gideon clipped from a group of friends, smiling a little crookedly, a little drunkenly, for the camera. There was a tangle of streamers behind her, the edge of one or two balloons, and a man's shoulder tucked into hers. A few lines of description under the photograph, and the circumstances of her abduction. *If this jogs your memory, please call the police on*, and a direct number to the incident room.

There were smaller copies pasted on to the nearby power poles and to the sides of the phone box. Mrs Gideon also kept a bundle in her car and patiently through the long days she handed them to anyone who stopped at Foursquare.

Challis asked what he'd asked every day since Boxing Day: 'Any nibbles?'

Mrs Gideon smiled tiredly. She hadn't washed her hair. She was overweight, a heavy breather, which seemed to intensify the desperation that she was showing to the world. 'People are very kind. They always look closely, and they listen, but they always shake their heads.'

'You're doing your best.'

'But are the police, Mr Challis?' she chided gently. 'It strikes me as unusual that there have been no developments.'

'It's baffling,' Challis said. He never liked to hedge or lie. By telling Mrs Gideon that the police were baffled, he was stressing their commonality with her and the man and woman in the street.

FIFTEEN

At midday that same day, Danny Holsinger and Boyd Jolic were in a stolen Fairmont, approaching a secluded dirt road behind the Waterloo racecourse. Quiet Saturday lunchtime, no-one around, everyone on holiday.

'Here we are,' Jolic said.

A big house set back from the road. Plenty of trees, acres of close-cropped lawns, white railing fences for hundreds of metres, holding yards in the same white railing, a stable block, sheds, dam, fruit trees. A 'forthcoming auction' sign had been bolted next to the driveway entrance. It all spelt money. Well, so it should. Last year's Caulfield Cup winner had been bred and trained there.

But as Jolic slowed to turn in, the engine cut out. 'Fuel's vaporising,' he'd said, the first time it had happened, and now here it was, happening again. 'Piece of shit,' he said, grinding the starter, pumping the pedal. The Fairmont coughed and shook and they steered their shuddering way up a clean white gravelled drive to the side of the house.

And just as they were getting out, a woman stepped through a screen door and said, 'Are you the new farrier?'

Unoccupied, Jolic had said. He had a plan of the house and assurances that the owners were holidaying in Bali until mid-January. A manager to feed and water the horses and a

131

gardener two or three times a week, but that's all, and no-one around on a Saturday afternoon.

So, who the fuck was this? Danny turned to Jolic, 'Jesus, Joll,' and Jolic elbowed him hard, in the chest. 'Want to give the bitch our fucking names?'

Next thing, Jolic was out of the car and running straight at the woman, one arm concealing his face from her, reaching her and spinning her around and clamping a hand over her mouth. 'Shut up and you won't get hurt.'

He caught Danny's eye, jerked it at the screen door. Danny, also concealing his face, ran with a crush and scrape across the gravel and opened the door.

They bundled the woman inside. They were in the kitchen: copper pots on hooks, a huge Aga oven, a bench as long and broad as a couple of single beds end to end, stained wooden floors and inbuilt cupboards. Searching frantically, Jolic snatched a cast-iron frying pan from a wall hook and slammed it against the side of the woman's head.

She dropped like a stone.

They were panting. Danny thought they might have been yelling.

Who else was on the property?

Had he said it aloud? Yes, he was shouting it, and it was accusatory, telling Jolic he was acting on piss-poor information, doing over an 'empty' house. Now it was an aggravated burglary, and, for all Danny knew, from the way the woman had fallen and now just lay there like a rag doll, murder.

'You arsehole, who else is here?'

He'd never called Jolic that before, not to his face.

'Well why don't you go and fucking look, Dan.'

'Not me.'

'We'll both do it.'

They ran through the house, room to room, and saw no-one. So they calmed a little. Jolic bent over the woman, removed the plain gold necklace from around her neck, gave it to Danny. 'Sorry, mate. Give this to your sheila.'

Mollified, Danny said, 'Ta.'

Jolic took out his floorplan. He'd marked it with red crosses—a crystal cabinet here, solid silver cutlery there; here an antique clock, there some china figurines and a top-of-the-range sound system. They wrapped the delicate stuff in bubble wrap and stuffed everything into garbage bags.

There was a man in the kitchen corridor. He had his back to them and had clearly just stepped in from working outside: dusty, sweaty, smelling of horses, a weary hand in the small of his back. Water darkened his hair and collar, as though he'd come in via the laundry, freshening himself up a little first. Late lunch, Danny thought. Just fucking bloody perfect.

Yelling, charging like he was playing American football, Jolic took the man down in a low tackle. The man flipped back at the waist and Danny saw his head smack the wall before he crumpled to the floor.

Two down. How many more to go?

Jolic was like a cornered tiger now, stepping from foot to foot and swinging his head about, searching for his pursuers. Danny saw why some women might be attracted to him. He was fierce, reckless, arrogant, quick and light on his feet, his eyes alight. But he was also mad and dangerous, and snarled at Danny, 'Help me get 'em out.'

'Out?'

'Out on the fucking lawn, dickbrain. Now.'

The woman, then the man, letting their heads bump like potatoes in a sack down the back step and over a border of white-painted stones and on to the cool cropped grass.

'Well away from the house,' Jolic said.

'What for?'

'We've left evidence behind, moron.'

The woman coming out of the house like that had distracted them. They'd failed to remember the latex gloves in their pockets. It meant going through and wiping everything. Unless . . .

'Joll, no, you're—' what was the word? '—escalating it.'

'Escalating my arse,' and Danny trailed behind him, into the workshop, where there was plenty in the way of rags and tins marked 'flammable'. Then back to the kitchen and the other rooms, splashing it about, chucking matches as they retreated, kitchen last, then out the side door and into the Fairmont.

Which wouldn't start. They heard it grinding away, tireder and tireder. 'Fuck!' Jolic slammed his palms on the wheel.

'Jol, look.'

A Falcon ute, hot lilac paint job, chrome roll bar, fat tyres, smoky glass all round, towing a covered trailer in the same paint job, marked *Steve Pickhaven, Farrier*. By now there was smoke leaking from the house, and flames behind the glass as the curtains went up. They saw the guy get out, his bottom jaw dropping in disbelief as he put two and two together. Then he was digging in his top pocket for a mobile phone and punching at the keys.

Jolic was calm now, thinking, a dangerous condition in him. 'Got a hankie? Quick wipe of the car, dashboard, door handle, window, everything. Forget the stereo, we'll take the smaller stuff with us.'

'On foot?'

'Got a better idea?'

Within one minute they were through the railing fence and cutting across a paddock, past a horse trough and skirting a dam and losing themselves in a small wooded area on top of a rise. Here they had a view of the approach roads. Danny groaned. He went behind a tree and lowered his jeans and jockeys and felt it slide out of him, quick, soothing and perfectly formed. He fastened his jeans again, spat on his hands and rubbed them on his shirt, and felt unclean, the stink of defeat sticking to him.

But Jolic was more intent on their predicament. 'Didn't take the bastards long. Look.'

Pursuit cars, red and blue lights flashing, a distant wail of sirens. They were coming in on the house from both directions. And now a fire engine. It was doubtful, Danny thought, that he and Jolic would have made it even if the Fairmont hadn't given up the ghost. Roadblocks, the police helicopter, they'd have been caught like rats in a trap.

Jolic watched avidly. He looks like he wants to be there, Danny thought, fighting the fire from the back of the Waterloo CFA truck. After a while, Jolic backed away, turned, began to cut through the trees, the garbage bag of stolen items bouncing over his shoulder. He didn't say anything to Danny. What was Danny supposed to do? What was their plan? Was Jolic abandoning him? He ran, hard at Jolic's heels.

'Where we going?'

Jolic panted, 'We pinch a car, right?'

Around the edge of the Waterloo racecourse, to a round-about, then along the side of a housing estate, new houses cheek to jowl behind a high wooden fence. In at the first entrance, then along a couple of winding side streets, to a maroon Mitsubishi Pajero, sitting in the driveway of a house, dripping water on to the forecourt, keys in the ignition.

Sirens in the distance.

There had been a flurry when Jane Gideon's body was found, but the investigation had stalled, so an aggravated burglary was good for sweeping the cobwebs away.

Ellen Destry parked the white Commodore off the gravel drive. The ambulance and the fire trucks and most of the police cars had come and gone. It was up to CIB now, and the fire inspectors, and the forensic crew dusting the Fairmont for traces of the burglars.

According to the farrier, the owners of the property had been called back early from holidaying in Bali. The stud manager had been worried about the condition of a pair of three-year-old mares, potential champions, particularly given that a January heatwave was expected.

The wife: severe concussion. The husband: groggy, but able to say that two men were involved, which was backed up by the farrier. Basically, they were looking for a small skinny guy and a tall, athletic guy.

Ellen wandered through the house. An odour of wet ash and dampened carpets, scorch marks on the walls and ceilings, some quite major fire damage in the front room, a sitting room, which had been torched first. 'Check it out,' Challis had said. 'We haven't got the resources for a major investigation. Bring in the arson squad if it looks big.'

Big meant over two hundred grand's worth of damage, and this wasn't two hundred grand's worth. But it was messy. Arson, aggravated burglary, theft of a motor vehicle—*two* motor vehicles, if the Pajero reported stolen over in the housing estate was involved, and Scobie Sutton and Pam Murphy had been sent to investigate that. Ellen pulled on latex gloves and began to go through the house room by room.

She was standing in the study, doing what Challis often suggested, thinking her way into the case, when she saw a heat-buckled cashbox in the charred remains of the desk. She poked at the lid with a ballpoint pen. Five hundred dollars, in a paper band from the Commonwealth Bank, and it fitted as slim as a wallet into the inside pocket of her jacket.

At the same time, but some distance away, a horn sounded behind Stella Riggs again, but she refused to slow down, accelerate or pull over. Really, Coolart Road was the worst road on the Peninsula for incidents of bad driving: cutting in, overtaking on blind stretches, tailgating, speeding, impertinence and just plain anger. And a worse class of driver in respects other than manners. They were rougher to look at. They drove wrecks. And the number of times she'd had to brake for the oncoming garbage truck as it veered across in front of her, collecting the rubbish from both sides of the road. Why couldn't it simply go up one side of Coolart and back down the other? Because those men wanted to work the shortest day possible for the same wage, that's why. Rough, blue-singleted, jeering men.

She glanced again in the rear-view mirror. That idiot was still trying to pass, sitting just metres from her rear bumper, and she was going a hundred! What if she had to brake suddenly? The fellow was a fool. Look at him, darting out, seeing that it wasn't clear, darting back again.

She began to organise her thoughts, to write a report in her head, if ever one was needed. The incident had begun where Coolart Road crosses the Waterloo Road. She'd been driving home in her Mercedes, turning left into Coolart, and a Mitsubishi Pajero had approached the intersection at the same time, from the direction of Waterloo. The time had been two o'clock in the afternoon. She had the right of way, and had begun her turn when she noticed that the Pajero was also turning, no indicators on, threatening to cut her off. On snap consideration, she had accelerated, so as to complete the turn first. She had the right of way, after all, not the other fellow, and that needed to be demonstrated clearly to him. Besides, there were other cars behind her. It would have caused unnecessary alarm if she'd braked suddenly. So, she sailed through, completing her turn with inches to spare.

The look on that man's face!

Description. More of an impression, really, for the side glass was tinted. He looked lean and tough, with close-cropped hair and the suggestion of tattoos. Aged in his late twenties? The other fellow, the passenger, well, he looked to be full of alarm. He was much smaller in build, with quite long fair hair. Also in his twenties. Neither man looked to be particularly intelligent. Blue collar, she'd say.

Odd that they should be driving a Pajero rather than a more common sort of car.

Anyhow, after the incident at the corner they had tailgated her Mercedes as if they wanted to run her off the road. She could see a fist shaking at her. Horn blaring. Right down the length of Coolart Road. At Chicory Kiln Road she turned right, and—and this was something she'd not tell the police, if she ever reported the incident—extended her arm out of the side window and stuck her index finger into the air as she turned, making sure they saw her do it.

And now . . . ?

Stella swallows. The Pajero has overshot the corner, but now it's backing up and turning into Chicory Kiln Road and coming up hard behind her. She can't drive any faster, for Chicory Kiln Road is in a terrible state of repair, soft and treacherous at the edges, badly corrugated in the middle. And dusty! She has no hope of shaking the men off—all they have to do is follow her dust.

Which they do, as she turns into Quarterhorse Lane.

Snap decision. If they follow her to her door, they might attack her.

She remembers that before Christmas there'd been a bit of drama at the other end of the lane, near where it meets the Old Peninsula Highway. Clara, that was her name. Someone had set fire to her mailbox. Since then Clara had been having pretty frequent visits from a policeman—almost daily.

Boyfriend?

So Stella doesn't drive the Mercedes home. She turns right, noting the charred mailbox, into Clara's driveway, hoping, as she follows the curving gravel, that the police car is there.

It isn't.

Behind her, the Pajero brakes, but doesn't turn in. It waits, dark and malevolent looking, its engine ticking over. Then it reverses into the driveway before accelerating away again, back the way it had come.

Her breathing is ragged now. Her hands are trembling. But then a curtain twitches at a front window of the house, so she drives the Mercedes out of that driveway as hard as she can, up the road to her own house before those men come back and spot where she's gone.

Tomorrow she's flying to Sydney for a few days, friends on the North Shore, and, frankly, tomorrow can't come soon enough.

The numberplate? A vanity plate, LANCEL, whatever that meant.

Pam Murphy had her notebook open. 'You didn't see them steal it?'

'No, I'm telling you,' the woman said, 'I just stepped inside for a minute to wash the dirt off the chamois.'

'That's when you heard the engine start?'

'Yes. Thought at first it was the people next door.'

They were standing in the hallway of a house in Seaview Estate, Scobie Sutton just behind Pam, letting her ask the questions. She took it as a vote of confidence. Meanwhile the Pajero's owner, Vicki Mudge, was in a curious state, angry because her vehicle had been stolen from under her nose, but with an edginess under that, as if she didn't want the police involved at all.

'We'll talk to your neighbours in a minute,' Pam said. 'Meanwhile, I'll need some details about the vehicle itself. Mitsubishi Pajero,' she said, scribbling in her notebook. 'Colour?'

'Maroon.'

'Year?'

'Er, not sure.'

'All right. Petrol? Diesel?'

'Petrol. I think.'

'Registration number?'

Here the woman's face seemed to close down. Pam couldn't read outrage or anxiety or any other useful emotion in it.

'Look, if it turns up, it turns up. Probably kids out for a joyride. If it gets damaged, insurance will cover it.'

'We still need the registration number, Mrs Mudge.'

Vicki Mudge folded her arms and stared at the carpet and said woodenly, 'Personalised plate. Lancel.'

Pam asked for the spelling. Then suspicion hardened in her.

She was suddenly very alert. 'Mrs Mudge, are you employed at the moment?'

'What are you getting at? What's that got to do with the price of eggs?'

'I have to ask you this: did you arrange to have the Pajero stolen?'

The woman snarled, 'By Jesus, you've got a nerve.'

Sutton cleared his throat. 'Who else lives here, Mrs Mudge?'

'My husband. He's in Thailand on business.'

'You *do* want your vehicle back again, I take it?' Pam said.

Vicki Mudge shot a look past her ear. 'Yeah, sure, it's insured.'

There's something there, Pam thought. A suggestion that she'd be uncomfortable if the Pajero turned up.

When van Alphen found Clara she was trembling, sitting in curtained gloom, a kitchen knife in her hands. No incense this time.

'Clara?'

'I've been trying to reach you all day!'

'We had a suspicious fire.'

'They were here!'

'Who were?'

'The people who want me dead.'

He crossed to her, thinking that he couldn't keep up with her and she was bad news, but he was in too deep to let her go. She bewildered him. She'd be lucid, calm and funny, her head firmly on her shoulders, then a little sultry and uninhibited when it was time for sex, then strangely hyper and funny but also easy in her head whenever she'd done a line of coke—and then she could be like this, freaked out and making no sense. He couldn't avoid thinking that she'd never been a casual user in the past, but an addict, and it had fried her brain, only she was good at hiding the fact. And now she was on the stuff again, courtesy of him, and the madness was showing.

He thought all of these things even as he hugged her tight and stroked her temples and wanted her so badly that he slipped his hands under her T-shirt, to where her flesh was hot and pliant.

139

She erupted, shoving, screaming at him. 'Didn't you hear what I said? They were here!'

'Clara, who were?'

'I told you, the people who want me dead.'

'Who wants you dead?'

'People from my past. It doesn't matter. The thing is, I need protection.'

'What did they look like?'

'I didn't see them.'

'Then how—'

'I saw their car.'

'Where?'

'It came right into my driveway, sat there, then went away again.'

'Ah,' van Alphen said. Maybe she wasn't losing her marbles. 'Can you describe it?'

'It was a white Mercedes.'

'You're sure?'

'I had one like it once, in the good old, bad old days.'

See? Sharp and self-mocking again.

'Okay, white Mercedes. Did you—'

'I had the impression,' Clara said, concentrating, 'that there was another car out on the road, a big dark one. It slowed as it went past the gate, but by then I was paying more attention to the white one in the driveway.'

'Did you get the registration?'

'Forgot. I was too scared.'

'That's okay, most people forget.'

'What will you do?'

'Stay the night, for a start.'

She hugged her upper arms, sat rocking, her knees together. 'I'm really strung out, Van.'

'I'll give you a massage.'

She rounded on him, shouting, 'I don't want a fucking massage. I need you to get me some more blow.'

'Clara, lay off that stuff. You've had a shitload since I met you.'

She was scornful, looking him up and down. 'You want me, right? My cunt?'

'Clara, I—'

140

'If you want me you're going to have to pay for it, like any punter. Do I owe you special privileges? I don't think so.'

He was dismayed to find himself so hurt and so floundering. 'I thought—'

'You thought this was special? Uh, uh. *I'm* special. You want me, lover boy, you pay for me. What's wrong? Shocked, are we? Thought I was a little angel, did you?'

'I looked after you.'

'Then fucking continue looking after me. Get me some more stuff, or fork out a hundred bucks a time to see me naked.'

She lifted her T-shirt, waggled her torso briefly, covered herself again. Something fractured a little further in van Alphen then. That life boiled down to supply and demand, rather than values, was the position he'd reached after a working life doing this shitty job.

Saturday night, about eleven o'clock, and Challis was alone in the incident room, logging on to the database to see what the analysts had found. He was looking for a similar pattern of abductions and rape-murders in other parts of the country, with cross-references to mini-vans, four-wheel drives and other rear-compartment vehicles.

When the call came, a Mitsubishi Pajero found abandoned and torched at the side of a dirt road near the Old Peninsula Highway, his first thought was: *Maybe our man's panicking, getting rid of evidence.*

But within an hour he'd established that the Pajero had been stolen earlier in the day, probably by two men fleeing from an aggravated burglary, and, disappointed, he logged off and left the building.

He got home just as one day drifted into the next and it was New Year's Eve.

Sixteen

Sutton was in the Displan room telephoning Vicki Mudge with the news that her Pajero had been found. 'Unfortunately it's been destroyed. Abandoned and then burnt.'

A strange gasp in the woman's voice—almost of relief, Sutton thought—covered immediately by a cough: 'Burnt? Oh dear.'

'You might like to inform your insurance company. Meanwhile we'll be investigating this pretty thoroughly. We think the men who stole your Pajero yesterday were responsible for a pretty vicious aggravated burglary earlier.'

And that's how he learned that Vicki Mudge was not the owner of the Pajero but the sister of the owner. The owner's name was Lance Ledwich and he lived on the other side of the Seaview Estate. Cosy, Sutton thought.

When Challis came in, he said, 'Boss, we need to take another look at Ledwich.'

'Convince me.'

'He lied to us. He owns a Mitsubishi Pajero, only he kept it at his sister's house, not all that far from where he lives.'

'Why didn't your DMV check turn it up?'

'Registration had lapsed, boss.'

'Go on.'

'It's the Pajero stolen after that ag burg yesterday. The one that was torched last night.'

'You think he arranged to have it destroyed?'

'It's possible, but I think it was just bad luck.'

'Good luck for us, perhaps, except that as evidence it's worthless now that it's been destroyed. What about the sister?'

'Name's Vicki Mudge.'

'She known to us?'

'Her husband is, Paddy, sexual assault.'

Challis went very still and alert suddenly. 'They're working together.'

Sutton shook his head. 'Paddy's been in Thailand since late November.'

'Check it out.'

'I will,' Sutton said. 'The thing is, boss, yesterday when I questioned Vicki Mudge she seemed pretty edgy, and just now, when I said the Pajero had been burnt, she sounded relieved, then edgy again when I said there'd be a thorough investigation. That's when she came clean about who owned the Pajero.'

'She knows something's up, and she's protecting her own skin.'

'Could be.'

'All right, talk to Ledwich again.'

'I'd like to take that new female constable with me.'

'Why?'

'She's cluey.'

'Fine,' Challis said.

Pam Murphy's shift didn't start until midday, but Detective Constable Sutton came looking for her in the canteen and said, 'You're coming with me. I've talked to your boss.'

She drove, Sutton talked.

'Everything's dragons and monsters at the moment. Maybe she's picking up vibes. When the wife heard about Trina Unger, she said, "The man's a monster," and Ros said, "Where's the monster? Is there a dragon, too?"'

'Really?'

'Plus it's become a battle of wills. She plays the wife and I off against each other, refuses to go to bed, kicks up a stink when it's bathtime, won't eat what's put in front of her.'

'Sounds typical,' Pam said.

'Typical, sure,' Scobie Sutton said, 'but until you've encountered it yourself you don't realise what strong wills they've got. I mean, my daughter, three years old, could teach a tribe of Hell's Angels how not to back down in the face of authority.'

Pam fingered her jaw. It hurt. She'd been struck by her board in the surf during the morning's lesson with Ginger and ever since then she'd been exploring the bruise with her fingers, aggravating it, but unable to leave it alone. 'Sir, where are we going?'

'No need to call me "sir". "Scobie" will do. Inspector Challis wants us to have a word with a man called Lance Ledwich.'

'Why me, sir?'

'I watched you yesterday. Your instincts told you there was something off about Vicki Mudge. Well, she's Ledwich's sister, and had been looking after the Pajero for him.'

Pam mused on that. 'Is Ledwich a suspect in the highway killings?'

'He was, then he wasn't, and now he is again.'

'How come?'

'One, he's on the sex offenders list. Two, his alibis are weak. Three, thanks to our burglars we now know that he owns a four-wheel drive—or did, until they torched it for him.'

'Pity about that. Now you can't check it for forensic evidence.'

'I told Challis you were on the ball.'

Pam rolled her jaw a little. 'Thank you, sir.'

'Something wrong with your mouth? Toothache? Take it from me, don't leave it and hope it'll go away. See a dentist straight away. I had a bad toothache once, I was in court all week, couldn't do a thing about it except stuff myself with painkillers. When I was finally called to give evidence, the defence walked all over me. Couldn't think straight.'

'I got clipped by a surfboard, sir.'

He stared at her. 'You're kidding me. You surf?'

'Learning to.'

'Huh.'

They found Ledwich on a stepladder, erecting a sensor light on the corner of his lockup garage. He climbed down, wiping his hands on an oily rag. 'You can't be too careful.'

144

'Can't you?' Pam said.

If she disliked the look of a man, she'd stare disbelievingly, to rattle him. She saw it work on Ledwich. There was something oily about him.

'We were wondering, Lance,' Sutton said, taking out his notebook, 'whether you wouldn't mind reconsidering one of the answers you gave me the other day.'

'Which one?'

'The one that went: No, I don't own another motor vehicle.'

Ledwich flushed sullenly. 'My sister. Stupid bitch.'

'Why should she get into trouble over you, Lance?'

'Look, it was unregistered, I'm not allowed to drive for another twelve months, she's got a good garage, so I thought, why not store it at her place.'

'Your heart must really be broken.'

'Why?'

'Your pride and joy, stolen and trashed like that.'

'Oh, yeah,' Ledwich said, as though he'd just remembered to grieve for it.

'You don't *seem* too upset, sir,' Pam said.

'Well, you know, insurance'll cover it.'

'Are you sure about that?'

Ledwich faltered. 'Won't they?'

Sutton said, 'Did you pay someone to do it for you, Lance?'

'Do what?'

'Steal and burn your Pajero.'

'Christ no.'

'It's a fair assumption.'

'I don't follow.'

'Fibres from the dead girls inside the Pajero, the police checking tyres, only a matter of time before you got caught out. You must've been panicking, needed to get rid of the evidence in a hurry.'

'You're clutching at straws, mate.'

He was too cocky, as though some of his cares had been laid to rest recently. Pam found the nerve to say, 'Let's assume you're the victim here, Mr Ledwich. Was there anything in particular about your Pajero that might explain why it was stolen, or anything that might help us identify who took it? Accessories, CD player, items left inside it, that kind of thing?'

Ledwich wiped his palms again. 'No. I got nothing to hide.'

Now, that was an odd response. Pam pushed it: 'No-one suggested you had, Mr Ledwich.'

'You lot are acting like you're more interested in my car than who took it. I mean, Jesus.'

'He's wound up,' Pam said later.

'Definitely hiding something.'

They questioned the neighbours, then drove to the scene of the aggravated burglary. The Fairmont—traced to an elderly widower in Waterloo—had been towed away. Fire and insurance investigators were there, but not the owners, who were still resting in hospital. Pam walked through the house while Sutton talked to one of the stable hands. The damage was minimal, she realised, some scorching and a patina of soot and smoke, so that, with imagination, she was able to picture the rooms as they'd been before the fire. A vulgar hand had decorated the place. It was as if she were looking at an interior design magazine in a doctor's waiting room, one fussy room blending into another, so that they seemed oddly familiar to her.

Ellen got in late after a fruitless morning interviewing other names on the sex offenders list. She was surprised to see Rhys Hartnett's Jeep at the courthouse, and after locking her car, crossed the driveway to find him. He was unloading wall vents. 'Hi,' she said, startling him.

'Hi.'

'We'll have to stop meeting like this.'

He frowned and rolled his shoulders, as though she'd come too close and should back off.

'You should give yourself some time off, Rhys,' she said.

He shrugged. 'If I don't get this job done I'll miss out on other contracts.'

Ellen realised that she hadn't accounted for his finishing at the courthouse and going elsewhere. It would leave a hole in her life. She hadn't discussed the matter further with Alan and Larrayne, but she found herself saying, 'Speaking of which, I've decided to accept your quote.'

He stopped what he was doing and looked at her carefully. 'That's okay with your husband?'

'It's my money.'

'Just out of interest, what did the other companies quote?'

She looked down briefly and toed the gravel with her shoe. 'I didn't actually approach anyone else.'

'To set your mind at rest,' he said, 'the reason why I've always got work is because I quote low.'

'I can give you a cash deposit,' she said. 'Would that help?'

'Help me with the tax man.' He held up both hands. 'Whoops, forget I said that.'

'We all have hassles with the tax man, Rhys.'

'Yep. Look, a deposit won't be necessary. Pay me at the end.'

Ellen thought: What a stupid conversation. He must think I'm stupid. It's because we don't know each other. We stand here out in the open when we should be in a quiet corner somewhere.

'What do you say to lunch in the pub?' she said, careful to keep it light.

He looked at her for a long moment, then glanced at the ground. 'Now?'

'Give me ten minutes.'

'See you then,' he said.

Pam Murphy came back with Scobie Sutton to find John Tankard waiting for her in the passenger seat of the divisional van.

'Sucking up to CIB, Pammy?'

She ignored him and drove the van to the Sunday market in the car park opposite the Waterloo tennis courts. There had never been reports of stolen goods on sale, but still the police were obliged to make a walk-through of the market. Pam parked the van under a gum tree and got out, leaving Tankard sprawled in the passenger seat. In the old days, before the leaflet campaign, he would have been in the car park measuring tyre-tread thicknesses, slapping roadworthy infringement notices on windscreens, generally hassling the natives. Not now. Too much palpable hatred in the air whenever he showed his face in public.

She saw Danny Holsinger and edged toward him. Danny and his mother operated a stall every Sunday, selling crocheted shawls and doilies, woven string holders for hanging plants, slip-on covers for hot-water bottles, teapot cosies and other fussy pink things that no-one had much use for, certainly not on a hot Sunday morning.

When the mother was out of earshot, Pam said, 'Happy new year for tomorrow, Danny.'

Surprised, he said, 'Yeah.'

'There was an ag burg near the racecourse yesterday. Rather a nasty one. What's the word?'

Danny looked edgy. Then again, he'd always looked edgy around teachers, policemen, priests, anyone with any authority over him. 'I'm not into that.'

'I didn't say you were. You're a loner, Danny. But have you heard any whispers around the place? We're looking for two men, one big, the other about your size. They stole a Pajero. Torched it some time last night, over by the highway.'

'Wasn't me.'

'Danny, relax. Just keep your ear to the ground, okay?'

Then the mother returned with an armful of fussy cot blankets from the boot of her car, so Pam wandered through to the organic produce stall, thinking she might buy some tomatoes. Next to it was a donut van. She stopped, bought a couple for John Tankard.

She returned to the divisional van, winding her way among the remaining stalls. Where did they get their stuff, all that junk, half of it old, half of it brand new and made of cheap metal and plastic in China somewhere? Toys. Tools. Household gadgets. She couldn't see anyone in Waterloo arranging a buying trip to China. So it had to be bankrupt stock, sold at auction, except the handmade stuff, the jams and doilies and coloured bead jewellery.

Tankard hadn't moved. 'Hungry?'

He opened his eyes. 'Murph. You're a doll.'

Pam belted herself in, started the engine, eyeing him sadly. 'That is not a pleasant sight.'

His mouth full, sugar on his chin, he asked, 'Where to now?'

'That Pajero,' Pam said.

'What the fuck for? Leave it to CIB.'

'CIB think something smells wrong.'

'Big-deal detective, on the case.'

Pam ignored him. Ginger had been so sweet this morning. He'd taken her back to his house and gently massaged a strange, foul-smelling cream into her jaw. Said it was pawpaw extract and would work wonders. She was still waiting.

They rode in silence, until Tankard stiffened like a hunting dog. 'Check that. Broken tail light.'

That was pretty typical, Pam thought. Lonely road, solitary, vulnerable motorist. 'Leave it, Tank.'

'Yeah, well, we all know about you, soft on the locals.'

Pam ignored him. Tankard went on: 'You know what your problem is? You're a snob.'

'First I'm soft on the locals, now I'm a snob. Which is it?'

'Never see you down the pub. You don't mix. What are ya?'

'I'm not *you*, Tank, that's all that matters. You want the world to be like you, and frankly that is a terrible thought.'

The Pajero site was easy to find, a smallish patch of blackened grass and scorched trees and fence posts. A farmer coming home from the pub after a cricket match late the previous night had seen the blaze and put it out with the fire extinguisher he kept in his car.

There was a white sedan parked nearby. A man in a short-sleeved shirt was taking photographs. Pam approached him, saying, 'May I ask what you're doing, sir?'

The man straightened. He was about forty, calm and unhurried-looking. 'Insurance,' he said.

Pam nodded, then looked at the burnt grass. 'Where's the vehicle?'

'Carted off to the police garage about—' the man looked at his watch '—half an hour ago. I'd given it the once-over. Now I'm checking the scene.'

They stood together musingly. Bracken, blackberry thickets, rye grass and gum trees hugged both sides of the road, but here there was only an area of ash the size of a room, dotted with lumps of molten glass and plastic, some remnants of the electrical circuitry and four fine wire sculptures that were all that remained of the tyres. Scattered around the perimeter were bottles, drink cans and cigarette packets, as though whoever had torched the Pajero had stood there gloating.

'We get a couple of these a month,' the insurance investigator said. 'It's become a copycat thing.'

'And a summer thing,' Pam said.

'Yeah, the general madness.'

On an impulse, Pam collected the newer-looking cans,

bottles and cigarette packets, picking them up with the end of her pen and stuffing them into a large plastic evidence sack. She paused. Was that the guts of a car phone?

'You're fucking mad,' John Tankard said when Pam was behind the wheel again. 'You want to give yourself a rest or you'll get a promotion.'

Danny discovered, as the day progressed, that his fingers were all thumbs. He dropped coins, couldn't open paper bags, spilt the thermos coffee over one of his mother's tea cosies, there on the trestle table, just as someone was about to buy it.

'What the hell's got into you?'

'Sorry, Mum.'

'Look, take yourself off for a walk, get out of me hair.'

'Sorry, Mum.'

He took her advice and walked along the bicycle path. The truth was, his nerves were shot to pieces. That stunt of Jolic's yesterday, bashing those people, then following that sheila in her Mercedes just because she gave him the finger. The way he kept shouting, 'I'll *kill* the cunt, I'll *kill* the cunt,' spit flying around inside the Pajero. The way he just drove and drove after that, for hours, risking discovery but not giving a damn, he was so worked up.

Culminating in Jolic parking on a back road and using the Pajero's car phone to call one of his heavy mates to come and fetch them.

Danny hadn't understood. They'd waited there on that dirt road, Jolic a massive dark shape in the dim light of the moon, and he'd asked, 'Why can't we just dump it near home and walk the rest of the way?'

'Because,' Jolic had said.

Danny soon understood. When the mate, Craig Oliver, arrived in his panel van with a few tinnies from the pub, Jolic torched the Pajero. They stood there, the three of them, watching it burn.

And now that young copper, turning up like she knew something.

No wonder his nerves were shot.

McQuarrie came by at five o'clock, bidding them a happy new year and suggesting a brief brainstorming of the case. More of a brainbashing than a brainstorming, Challis thought, as the clock on the wall showed five-thirty, six, six-thirty. Sunday evening, New Year's Eve, he could see how thoroughly demoralised everyone was. As soon as McQuarrie had left the room, he tiptoed comically to the door, stuck his head into the corridor, looked left and right, pulled back into the room and shut the door, his face a pantomime of subversive intent. Good, they were laughing, relaxing.

'I know you've all got families to go to,' he said, 'but if anyone wants to stay on for a quick meal, pasta, a glass or two of red, it's my shout.'

He watched them uncoil. All but a couple reached for the phones to call home, some of them arguing, others pleading and apologetic. By seven o'clock they were seated in the bistro overlooking the marina. They were noisy, their way of shaking off McQuarrie and cruel deaths and life's mischances. Challis felt some of his tightness relax. He knew that at the end of it his detectives would be a little more united and work together a little better. There was also the reminder that they were not so very different from other wage-earners, entitled to a night out with one another and the boss.

At one point, Ellen Destry roared in his ear, 'When are you taking me flying again?'

'Any time you like.'

'I was not popular at home afterwards.'

'Why?'

'Alan thinks he's losing me.'

'Losing you to me?'

'Losing me in general,' Ellen said.

After a silence, she said, leaning close to his ear, 'Hal, did you ever cheat on your wife?'

Challis swung away from her, hooking one eyebrow. 'Ellie, I seem to recall it was the other way around.'

Too late, she realised what she'd said. 'Good one, Ellen. Hypothetically speaking, Hal—' that rolled nicely off the tongue '—speaking hypothetically now, do you think in most couples there is a temptation to stray?' She shook herself, attempting to focus on him. 'Hypothetically speaking.'

'You're pissed, Ellie.'

She swayed back. 'So what if I am? I'm entitled.'

'Of course you are.'

'I started at lunchtime.' She poked his chest. 'One day we'll see *you* sozzled.'

'How about now?' Challis said, and felt himself grin and slide down in his chair.

Pam Murphy felt herself snap awake with the answer there clearly before her. She'd not been reminded of magazine photographs when she toured the burnt house, but of *actual* photographs, laid out on a shop counter. She closed her eyes again, mentally putting a case together. She'd take it to Sergeant Destry; with any luck she'd be allowed in on the arrest. Sleep didn't come again. When the dawn light began to leak into her room, she left the house and walked down through the dunes to the beach, where the water and the wide world were still, and she felt herself tingling, like a hunter.

SEVENTEEN

Monday, 1 January. When Pam Murphy came on duty, she went straight to Sergeant Destry with the crime-scene photos and said, 'Sarge, I think Marion Nunn was behind that aggravated burglary.'

Destry stared at her for a long, half-amused moment. 'There's nothing I'd like better than to put Marion Nunn away, but you're going to have to convince me first.'

'Well, the other day John Tankard and I were called to a photo developing shop because the manager was worried about some photos he'd just developed. They were interior and exterior shots of a house, and the customer was Marion Nunn. Later when I walked through the ag burg house, it seemed somehow familiar. Last night, I twigged.'

'What's Marion Nunn got to do with the house?'

'Her firm's selling it, Sarge. There's an auction sign on the front fence. No-one's going to question it if her firm's selling their place for them and she's there taking photos that they think will be used in advertising.'

'If they're not used for advertising, what are they used for?'

'I think Marion Nunn has an accomplice. She gives him the photographs, and he uses them to plan how he'll commit the burglary.'

'What did the photos look like?'

'Not the kind you'd normally take if you were trying to sell a house. There were shots of the back door, the windows, interior shots of glass cabinets with her reflection in the glass, the alarm system, etcetera, etcetera.'

'Maybe a junior in her office took them, that's why they looked amateurish.'

'Marion Nunn dropped them off for developing, Sarge.'

'But it's not proof that she took them. And wouldn't the owners have been suspicious of the sorts of shots she was taking?'

'I checked the date in my notebook. When the photographs were dropped off for developing, the owners had already been in Bali for four days. If she was selling the house for them, she'd have had a key.'

'Okay, let's say for argument's sake that Marion Nunn *was* behind it. Who does she give the photos to?'

'Someone she's defended in the past.'

'Maybe. Let me do some checking, talk it over with Inspector Challis.'

'So you think I've got something, Sarge?'

'It's as good a theory as any I've heard recently.'

And so the next morning Pam was called to Sergeant Destry's office and told, 'Since you're so keen, I've arranged for you to do some legwork for CIB on this aggravated burglary. I'm told you found the remains of a car phone where the Pajero was burnt?'

'Yes, I—'

'Contact Ledwich, get the number of the car phone, see what calls were made on it between, say, early afternoon and midnight on Saturday.'

She was okay, Destry, but, like anyone with rank, a bit short on pleasantries. Already she was turning away to open one of the files on her desk. If Pam didn't turn and leave now, Destry would likely look up and ask, 'Was there anything else?'

There was something else, Marion Nunn and the photographs, but Pam stepped out into the corridor and went in search of an unoccupied desk phone.

Lance Ledwich wasn't overjoyed to hear from her. 'The number? Why? I've seen what's left of my vehicle—sweet bugger-all. What good's the phone number to you?'

'Mr Ledwich, whoever stole it may have used the car-phone to call someone.'

'I don't like this. I don't see that it's necessary.'

'Mr Ledwich, who are you fooling? You used to drive the Pajero despite being banned, is that it? Right now I don't care about that and I can't prove it. I just want the carphone number. We're hoping that whoever stole your car made some calls.'

Ledwich thought about it for a long time. Perhaps he doesn't want us to find out who *he* had been calling, she thought. Finally he said, 'Fair enough,' and after a minute's rummaging came back on line to recite the number. 'Got that?'

'Got it.'

'It'll all be straightforward, won't it?'

'How do you mean, sir?'

'The insurance and that. The vehicle was stolen from me fair dinkum. I mean, I don't know who, or why.'

'We're looking into it, sir,' was all the satisfaction that Pam felt inclined to give him. If the job developed instincts, then hers were setting off bells.

But she put that aside and called the phone company. By lunchtime she'd ascertained that three calls had been made on Ledwich's car phone before midnight on Saturday. The first two, made between 9 a.m. and midday, were to small video libraries. Pam dialled the third number. It rang for some time. The voice that answered was surly, hurried, bitten off, and Pam asked it to repeat itself.

'Refinery Hotel, I said. Look, *you* called *me*, remember?'

Pam explained who she was and said, 'I wonder if you can help me with a call that was made to this number late Saturday evening.'

The man laughed. 'You must be joking. This is the main bar. You know how many calls we get here?'

'Were you working the bar on Saturday, sir?'

'Me? No way. Right now it's morning, right? Well, I work mornings.'

'Could you tell me who was working the bar that night?'

'Hang on, hang on,' and Pam flinched as the handset at the other end clattered on to a hard surface, probably the bar.

She waited for several minutes. The man came back with the names of two women and one man.

155

'Do you have home phone numbers for them, sir?'

'Can't help you, sorry. Try the book, but bear in mind they were working last night, so they'll be asleep now.'

Pam matched names and phone numbers with the phone book listings and found addresses for all three. She waited until early afternoon before knocking on doors.

At the first address, a ground-floor flat in a small block behind the shopping centre in Waterloo, a cheerful-looking woman told her, 'Love, we're generally too busy to pay attention. Sure, sometimes someone wants to speak to one of the regulars.'

'Do you recall if any of your regulars took a call that night?'

'No.'

At the next address, a weatherboard house set in weeds behind the Waterloo aerodrome, she learned even less. 'Wouldn't know, sorry,' the barman said.

'This would be late evening, around eleven.'

The barman yawned and scratched his belly. 'I always let someone else answer it.'

'A man—probably a man—wanting to talk to one of your regulars.'

'Look, try the girls working with me. Maybe one of them took it, Liz or Rina.'

'I've talked to Rina. No go.'

The door began to shut. 'Try Liz.'

Pam put her foot in the gap. 'Did *you* receive a personal call, sir?'

'Me? Nobody'd call me.'

And the door shut and Pam looked at the weeds and thought that the barman was probably right.

Liz, at the front door of her house in the Seaview Estate, said, 'Late evening?'

'Four past eleven.'

'We don't get that many calls. Let's see . . .'

'A call either to hotel staff or to one of your patrons,' Pam said. 'More than likely a man.'

'There were two or three like that.'

'To your patrons?'

'Yes.'

'Can you remember who?'

Liz laughed. 'On a Saturday night we get the hard-core

regulars, holiday people, locals out for a meal and a drink, plus visiting tennis and cricket teams. Give me a day or two. It'll come to me.'

As Pam turned away, Liz said, 'Those other two have quietened down a lot.'

Confused, Pam stopped and said, 'The people you work with?'

'No, no, those two coppers, Tankard and that other one. They've been keeping their heads down.'

Pam didn't want her offside, but a cosy chat about van Alphen and Tankard would amount to a betrayal of the line she'd drawn when she was posted to Waterloo, so she said nothing, just nodded and smiled non-committally, and walked to the van.

'It's good knowing you're around, Pam,' the woman shouted after her.

Pam didn't remember ever seeing her before.

The telephone rarely rang at the Holsingers', and so when it rang on Tuesday morning, Danny told his mother: 'If that's Joll, tell him I'm not here. Tell him I've gone off for a few days.'

'That moron,' his mother said.

She picked up the phone. Danny waited, stepping from foot to foot in the kitchen. The way his mother glanced at him then, he knew that it *was* Jolic on the line. 'Not here,' his mother said. 'Don't know when he'll be back. The foreman gave him the rest of the week off, so he's gone to stay with his auntie up in Sydney. Tell him yourself,' she said finally, and put down the receiver.

'You want your head read, hanging around with that moron.'

'Mum, I'm going around to Megan's.'

'Another moron.'

Megan was alone. Danny said, 'Why don't we go off together, somewhere new.'

'What do you mean?'

'Up Cairns way,' Danny said. 'Surfers Paradise. One of them.'

'Just like that. Dump my job, my mum, my friends, and just take off.'

'Not forever, just, you know, for a while.'

157

Megan stared at him suspiciously. 'You in trouble or something?'

'Me? Nah.'

'You could have fooled me. Something's going on and I want to know what.'

'Nothing, I tell ya.'

'Is it Boyd Jolic? I bet it is. What's he got you into?'

Danny chewed his bottom lip. 'I tell ya, Meeg, he's mad.'

'Tell me something I don't know. What's he made you do now?'

'Nothing. But he's a mad bugger. He's *fire* mad for a start.'

Megan's fingers went to the thin strand of gold at her throat. Danny had given it to her last Sunday. Plain, elegant, classy, except now it felt heavy and grubby, like she had a dog chain around her neck. She took it off. 'Where did you get this?'

'Bought it in Myers,' Danny said, quick as a flash. 'Look, if he comes looking for me, tell him you haven't seen me. Tell him I've gone off somewhere.'

She stared at him. 'Like where?'

'Give us a break, Meeg. I'm scared of the bastard. I want to stay clear of him for a while.'

'I don't like this.'

'So, what do you reckon? Cairns? Noosa? Surfers?'

'Danny, I'm not leaving. You go, if you want.'

Danny chewed on his lip again. When he put his arm around her, she pushed it away.

'Come on, Meeg, just a quick one, before your Mum comes home.'

'That's all I'm good for, right?'

'I tell you what, I got this video we can watch, get us in the mood.'

She frowned. 'What kind of video?'

'You'll see.'

After a few minutes, she pulled away from him and scrabbled for the remote control. 'That's disgusting. It's *sick*. How could you? How could you think I'd be turned on by stuff like that? God, Danny.'

Even Danny seemed stunned by what he'd seen.

That afternoon, van Alphen told Clara, 'That's it, finished. Santa isn't coming any more.'

The look she gave him told him that he'd just shown his true colours, and as she twisted out of his arms he found himself in a foolish tussle with her, made up of an attempt to embrace and console her on his part, and fury on hers. He wanted her to want him as much as he wanted her. He wanted her to listen to stern reason, give up the cocaine, and find her lifeline in him.

But she shook him off finally and yelled at him, bent forward at the waist, thrusting her hate-filled face at him. 'You think you're here to save me, right? Think I'll melt in your arms. I'd have to be fucking hard up, mate, I can tell you. As a root you're less than average. So if you can't get me any more blow, I'm going elsewhere.'

She walked to the curtains and jerked them open. Then she extinguished the incense stick in the dregs of her gin and tonic. The light through the window was harsh on her face, the room; a harsh judgment on what van Alphen had got himself into with her.

He could see the irony. He'd just spent a few days of his spare time in shadowing a local dealer, finally getting lucky when he searched an empty flat the guy had visited twice in a row. He'd found a stash of cocaine and amphetamines hidden above a ceiling batten in the bathroom. He'd flushed away most of it, bagging just enough to replace what he'd removed from the evidence safe. He'd nearly been caught, but the point was he hadn't been caught, and he'd walked coolly back into that old feeling of being able to take on the world and win.

The chink in the armour was Clara.

'You don't need the stuff any more. You need to get straightened out.'

'What are you, my father? My brother? Both of them fucked me, so what's the difference?'

He found himself snapping, 'Grow up.'

'Oh, that's a good one. Look who's talking.'

He struck her, a quick hard cheek slap that rocked back her head and shocked her. She was livid. 'Just for that, I'm dobbing you in.'

She'd said it before, as if it were a hold she had over him. 'Yeah, sure.'

'You're piss weak. No wonder your wife walked out.'

159

They were snapping off the insults now. Van Alphen felt pressure building inside his skull. 'I could kill you,' he said.

'You wouldn't have the guts.'

Boyd Jolic was grabbing some shut-eye when the phone rang. He stumbled through to the kitchen and snatched it up, but the ringing continued and he stared blearily at the handset before he located the source.

His mobile was on the table, next to a greasy plate, a stripped-down Holley carburettor and an oily rag. All of his old practised motions seemed to desert him as he fumbled to find the right button. 'Yeah?'

'I need to see you.'

'Oh, it's you,' he muttered.

'And lovely to hear your voice, too, Boyd. Just what a girl needs after a hard day.'

A long time since you were a girl, Jolic thought, as he scratched his stomach, his back. He began to contort, his fingers searching under his T-shirt, reaching high, between the shoulderblades. 'When do you want to see me?'

'Now. Tonight. Whenever.'

The itch relieved, he looked across the room at a Country Fire Authority poster on the wall above his sofa: WILDFIRES: WILL YOU SURVIVE? 'Can't tonight,' he said.

'Why, have you had a better offer?'

'Unfinished business,' Jolic said, but told her later in the week, and cut her off.

He liked to keep her eager.

It was four o'clock in the afternoon. He might as well stay up, now that he was up. Work out a plan of action, given that he'd be on his own tonight, that little prick Danny wimping out on him.

Tessa Kane was out all day, and didn't open her office mail until five o'clock. There was only one item. She knew at once who it was from: the same block capitals, the same kind of envelope.

She weighed the envelope down with a stapler while she opened the flap with a letter opener. Then, pinching the envelope by one corner, she teased the letter out with the blade,

160

and found that she was thinking of Challis. She was doing this for Challis, keeping her prints off.

The letter read:

Hit a brick wall, have you? Put me in the too hard basket?
Big mistake, fuckers.
Am I resting—or am I feeling the itch again?
That's what you should be asking yourselfs. People don't care about burglars or the spoilt rich. They want to know if it's safe for their daughters to go out alone.

Tessa laughed. She'd put his nose out of joint. He wanted to be back on page one.

She lifted the phone.

Damn. Challis had left, according to the receptionist. Wouldn't be in again until the morning. She looked up his home number, made to dial, and hovered.

The phone was ringing when Challis got in that evening.

'Hal.'

'Hello, Ange,' he said.

He looked at his watch. Seven. Surely they should all be in their cells by now?

'Hal, I had to hear your voice.'

'How are you, Ange?'

'Don't be like that.'

'Like what?'

'Standoffish. Shutting me out.'

'Look, Ange, I'm tired, I've only just this minute stepped in the door. I'm talking on the hall phone, briefcase in one hand. Let me take this call in the kitchen, okay?'

'You're always just walking in the door.'

'Ange—'

'I wish I could see your place. I keep trying to visualise it. I—'

Challis went to the kitchen. He tried to spin out the fixing of a drink and a sandwich, but she was still there when he lifted the handset from the cradle above the cutting bench.

'I'm back.'

'It hasn't been a good day for me.'

'I didn't expect to hear from you at this hour, Ange.'

His wife replied brightly, like a child just home from school: 'I'm in the play! We've been rehearsing this evening.'

She told him about it. He thought about his killer on the Old Peninsula Highway, and he thought about Tessa Kane. He'd hoped it might be her, when he'd heard the phone, ringing to repair the damage.

Or was that up to him?

Either way, he wanted to hear her low growl in his ear.

Clara had driven to Frankston after van Alphen left her, where she scored a small amount of coke from an islander kid who called her 'sister'. The quantity was small but the price was high, and he'd offered her a better deal on heroin, said it was pure and there was plenty of it around, but she told him she wasn't touching that stuff. Then two cops on bicycle patrol, looking like jet-streamed insects, had come pedalling down the mall, and the islander kid had scarpered and she'd turned on her heel and ducked into the closest shop. It had NEW YEAR SPECIALS! pasted across the window and sold computers. She'd never been in a computer shop in her life before. She said, 'Just browsing,' and when she looked at the equipment and the vividly coloured boxes on the shelves, she felt scared, ignorant, ignored, left behind in life, and couldn't wait to get out of there. She went straight to her car and did three lines of coke, and felt so high she didn't want to risk driving home but took a taxi instead. The good thing about Witness Protection, there was a little money there from time to time if she ever needed it.

So now she had a pleasant buzz on, but it would wear off pretty soon. She knew she'd want to score again, but she could hardly go back to Frankston at this hour of the night, one-thirty in the morning. Besides, she'd left her car there.

Then the background sounds of the night seemed to alter in her consciousness and one of them clarified as a tyre crush on gravel outside of her window. She was just formulating an adage from her old days, 'Never get involved with a copper,' when glass smashed somewhere at the rear of the house.

Eighteen

It was a night of hot northerlies, hotter where they passed over the flaming roof timbers. Sparks streamed from the burning house, and some alighted here and there in long grass that had not been slashed despite a request from the shire inspectors. The small fierce firefronts became one, consuming the grass, and then treetops caught, and one eucalyptus after another exploded in the nature reserve between the burning house and the orchard, which bordered the winery on the northern boundary fence and a horse stud at the rear. The orchardist heard his dogs before he was fully awake and able to separate the smell of the smoke from his dreams and the fact that his dogs were agitated. In the stables beyond his eastern boundary fence, horses were panicking, waking the stud manager and his wife. They stepped outside and saw the firefront, rolling as hungrily as a tidal wave upon a sleeping coastline. Evacuate. Evacuate.

It was too hot to sleep. And too noisy. Penzance Beach had swelled by the hundreds, it seemed—families who'd come to their beach shacks for four weeks, people camping, people looking for parties to crash. Pam found herself thinking of Ginger. If she had the nerve, if he lived just down the street instead of farther around the coast, she'd sneak down and tap on his bedroom window. She stood on the decking of her rented house, sniffing the wind.

Smoke.

The phone rang.

'Pam? Ellen Destry. I'll collect you in five minutes.'

Tessa Kane was in Challis's bed this time, and she couldn't sleep and wanted to go home. Now she knew what it had been like for him, that first time, when he'd tried to slip away from her bed. She glanced at him. He was wide awake, too. They didn't want to make love again. They disliked each other, just at that moment. They didn't want to be together. They wanted daylight and to be alone. These were temporary feelings, and would pass, but right now they were crippling.

'Go, if you want to.'

'I think I might.' She began to dress.

'I'll make you a cup of tea.'

'Hal, it's two o'clock in the morning.'

'You've a thirty minute drive ahead of you.'

'No tea, thanks. Thanks for the thought.'

As she dressed, he said, 'No more letters from our man?'

She looked for an earring. 'I'd tell you if there were.'

He nodded. 'What about Julian Bastian? Has there been any pressure on you to drop the story?'

'Pressure from whom?'

'Lady Bastian. Her friends in high places.'

She paused to stare at him. 'Like McQuarrie? Are you siding with him now?'

'Christ no,' he said. 'I think the charges should be reinstated against the little prick.'

She laughed. 'Can I quote you?'

First his mobile rang, then hers.

A fire.

Jolic swooned to see the flames. His skin tingled. He was breathless. A strange pleasurable electric heat started in his groin and spread upwards to his throat. He wanted badly to rut. Holding the hose on the CFA firetruck, Jolic was a vengeful rutting king.

John Tankard was on Myers Road, his patrol car parked

164

crosswise, emergency lights flashing in the darkness. There was not much normal traffic at this time of night, but an increase in the ghouls and gawkers, attracted by the sirens, the Emergency Services helicopter, the evacuation warning for householders south of Myers Road. A Triumph came barrelling toward him. He waved his torch and held his gloved hand high to stop it, indicating Quarterhorse Lane, the detour that would take all traffic away from the fire. But it was bloody Challis. He had Tessa Kane with him.

'Sorry, Inspector. Go on through.'

'Thanks, constable.'

The editor leaned across Challis. 'How bad is it, John?'

'One house destroyed—that's where it started. It spread quickly, jumped the road into the nature reserve.' He looked up, into the red-glow sky. 'This wind doesn't help.'

'Any casualties?'

'Some horses had to be moved.'

'Whose house got destroyed?'

Tankard looked to Challis for guidance. Challis said, 'It's all right. She has to know sometime, and so do I.'

'We don't know who lives there, sir. A woman by herself, according to the neighbours.'

'Is she all right?'

'No sign of her, sir.'

The wind seemed to shift then, and shift again. It was hot on their faces and heavy with smoke. Ash alighted on the back of Tankard's glove. He brushed it away, smearing the white leather. Funny, he could *hear* the danger—the wind, the flames?—but he couldn't see anything but a glow in the distance.

'Sir, I don't know how dangerous it is in there. We're directing traffic along the lane here. That's where the fire started, but it's safe there now.'

Challis pulled the automatic stick into Drive. 'We need to go in, John.'

Tankard thought: Don't call me John, you prick.

A part of Ellen Destry felt betrayed by the sense of exhilaration and competence-edged-with-risk that the fire seemed to engender in everyone. They were all equals, men and women, cops and civilians. They worked well together. They faced the flames

165

and beat them back. They communicated efficiently. There were no shirkers. The lights, the trucks, the dirty men and women in their yellow emergency gear, the roaring hot wind, the red coals and leaping flames. Once or twice gum trees exploded above their heads. She found herself helping Pam Murphy to pass out cups of tea, bind a couple of burnt hands, move vehicles and stock away from the path of the fire, fetch an old woman's cat. A part of her could understand the sentimentality of newspaper accounts of community disasters, when firefighters, policemen, ambulance workers and ordinary civilians pulled together.

But another side of her recognised that it was also essentially a blokey bonding exercise. Men embraced men and the women were honorary mates.

Then she learned that she had detective work to do.

Challis left Tessa Kane at the community refuge, where one of her photographers and two of her journos were already interviewing people, then drove carefully along Quarterhorse Lane to the house where the fire had started. The air was smoky and hot. Smouldering fence posts marked a route between an untouched orchard on one side of the road and ashy black earth on the other. He passed beneath a burning tree. The odd thing was, as he was turning into the driveway of the destroyed house, he saw signs of an earlier fire: a scorched pine tree. He looked closer. A small, newish, metal mailbox on a length of iron pipe.

He drove in. Ellen Destry was already there, staring at what had once been a weatherboard farmhouse and was now a flattened patch of charred wood and twisted, blackened roofing iron. A chimney stood forlornly at one end of the ruin. It was apparent to Challis that the fire had started at the house. The wind had then carried sparks to the grassy hill beyond it, and a firefront had developed, sweeping south toward the roadside gums on Myers Road, leaping it and taking hold in the nature reserve. Well, there wasn't much nature there any more, but the fire had been contained before it reached the dozen or so houses south of the reserve.

Suddenly Ellen was doubled over, coughing and spitting. 'You okay?'

166

She wiped the back of her hand across her mouth. 'I've been breathing thick smoke for the past two hours.'

A length of roof crashed behind them. Kees van Alphen, kicking and tugging.

'Leave it, Van. Wait for the fire inspector.'

'A woman lived here, sir.'

'If she was home, she didn't survive this,' Challis said.

Van Alphen was there when they found her body—or what remained of it. The ruin bewildered him. All of his senses were turned around. Only the blackened refrigerator and the stainless steel kitchen sink told him exactly where her body lay in relation to the rest of the house.

And the flames had got her. It wasn't smoke inhalation. If it had been smoke inhalation he might have touched her, kissed her, even, for she'd have been recognisable, but he wasn't saying goodbye to this fire-wracked, shrivelled twist of charred meat.

NINETEEN

Daybreak, Wednesday, 3 January. Challis hadn't been long at the burnt house before the fire inspector arrived and talked him through it.

'It's my belief the seat of the fire is here, at the kitchen stove. A hot, dry night, hot northerly wind outside, plenty of natural accelerants like cooking oil, cardboard food packets, wooden wall cabinets. Then weatherboard external walls, wooden roofing beams.'

He pointed. 'See that? Open window, creating a draught.'

Challis said, 'How do you know it's the stove?'

'Look.'

Challis looked. The stove top was as black and twisted as anything else in the ruin.

'See that? That's the remains of a saucepan, a chip fryer. That's the seat of your fire.'

Challis went away wondering why the victim had been cooking on such a hot night, and why she'd been cooking so late at night.

Ellen Destry made it a point always to switch off when she was at work. Switch off the things that had happened earlier, at home, in the bedroom or around the kitchen table.

She rang the post office. The dead woman was called Clara

Macris. Originally from New Zealand, the postmaster thought, judging by the accent.

That's as far as Ellen got. She could feel the badness creeping up on her: the abductions, the woman burning to death. She looked out of the incident room window and there was Rhys Hartnett, effortlessly lifting and measuring, whistling even, as he worked, while at home she had a husband who was getting fat because he drank and sat in a Traffic Division car all day, jealous because he sensed that she felt something for Rhys, who'd been around to the house three times now, measuring and planning, and resentful because she earned more than he did.

She'd said, as she'd headed out to her car after breakfast, 'I'll be late tonight. I'll get myself something to eat.'

The kitchen door opened on to the carport. In the early days, Alan would have walked her to it and kissed her good-bye. Now he couldn't even be bothered to look up at her. 'Whatever.'

Morning light streamed into the kitchen, giving the room a falsely homely look. Larrayne was still in bed. Alan was reading the *Herald Sun* and forking eggs and bacon into his mouth. His moustache glistened. After each mouthful he patted it dry. Ellen stood in the doorway, watching for a moment, jingling her keys. 'What's that supposed to mean?'

He looked up. 'What's what supposed to mean?'

'You said "whatever". What do you mean by that?'

He shrugged, went back to his breakfast. 'Doesn't mean anything. You'll be late tonight, you'll get yourself something to eat, me and Larrayne will have to fare for ourselves again, so what's new? The story of this marriage.'

She almost went back to the chair opposite his. 'The story of every police marriage. We knew that when we started. Mature adults know how to work around that.'

He belched, a deliberate liquid sound of contempt. 'Mature? What a joke.'

'What's that supposed to mean?'

'You go around this house like you're on heat, like you're a teenager whose tits have been squeezed for the first time.'

'Well, if someone's squeezing them, it sure as hell isn't you,' she'd said, and she'd slammed out of the house.

Now she picked up the phone. A long shot, but she was

calling the New Zealand police. It would be different if Alan had something concrete to be jealous about, but her lunch with Rhys Hartnett hadn't developed into anything. Rhys himself had seemed—not evasive, exactly, but conscious of the proprieties of getting involved with a married woman, especially one who was a cop. The dial tone went on and on. As for Larrayne, her judgment of Rhys was brief and to the point. 'He's a creep, mum, and a sleazebag.'

'Hal, I'm cutting at eleven,' the pathologist said.
    'Beautifully put, Freya.'
    'You know me.'
    'Eleven o'clock. I'll be there.'
The region's autopsies were carried out in a small room attached to Peninsula General Hospital in Mornington. When Challis arrived, Freya Berg had a student with her in the autopsy room, a young woman. Challis stood back, a handkerchief smeared with Vicks under his nose, and observed.

White tiles, pipes, hoses, a constant trickle of water. The pathologist and her assistant wore green rubber aprons and overshoes, and goggles waiting around their necks to protect their eyes against the bone chips and blood thrown up by the electric saw. The table had a perforated, channelled stainless-steel top, pipes at each corner running down to drains in the industrial-grade linoleum floor. A hose dribbled water as Freya Berg cut into the body. Above her, dazzle-free lamps. Extractor fans hummed in the ceiling, ready to take away the stupefying odour of the stomach contents and internal organs.

Freya said:
'Most fire victims die of smoke inhalation. Their bodies will be intact and recognisable, although some may reveal surface burns, particularly to the hands and face. In these instances the evidence is all there in the lungs. If there is little smoke residue in the lungs, then look for another obvious cause, such as failure of the heart. The most surprising subjects may succumb to heart failure under extreme stress. But this—this one's, shall we say, been cooked.'

Together Freya and her assistant began to turn the body on the cutting table. Two patches of oily white colour in the blackness of the upper arm and the hip stopped them.

The assistant photographed the black flank of the body, and

then Freya teased the fabric away with tweezers. 'Ah. Cotton, I believe. A nightdress? T-shirt? She was lying on her side when the flames finally reached her.'

They completed turning the body over. Freya began to cut.

The student assistant grew agitated. 'Epidural haemorrhage, Dr Berg,' she said. 'Bone fractures. Like she's been beaten up.'

The pathologist smiled tolerantly. 'Looks like it, doesn't it? But don't jump to conclusions. Haemorrhaging and bone fractures are one result of extreme heat.'

Challis stepped forward, still holding the Vicks under his nose. 'So you're saying she simply burnt to death.'

'Preliminary finding only, Hal. I haven't finished yet.'

'I have,' Challis said, and he pushed through the door to where the air was breathable.

Boyd had come to her in the early hours of the morning, smelling of soot and sweat and smoke, with a kind of snarling hunger for her body. 'We fucked like rabbits.' It was a phrase from twenty years ago, when she was a student, and each new affair started like that, hot and greedy, so you barely paused for breath. She hadn't thought she'd ever find that level of intensity again.

But now it was lunchtime and she had clients to see. Boyd lay sprawled on his stomach. He looked beautiful—if streaked with soot. A nice neat backside, nice legs and a tapering back, but God, the smell—stale sweat, smoke and cum and her own contribution. She'd had to scrub herself in the shower. He'd be gone when she got back tonight. She'd have to wash the sheets and pillowcases and air the house. She had a beautiful house, and the clash between it and what Boyd Jolic represented never failed to puzzle and excite her.

Pam Murphy found the Tank in the canteen. 'I've just seen van Alphen. He wants us to doorknock Quarterhorse Lane. Seems no-one knows anything about the woman who got burnt last night.'

Tankard forked rice into his mouth and chewed consideringly. 'But Van knows her.'

'Does he?'

'Yeah. He went round there a few times. Her mailbox got burnt. He knows her.'

171

'There's knowing and there's knowing.'

'Oh, very deep, Murph. You must come from a family of brains or something.'

'Look, the fact that van Alphen saw her when her mailbox got burnt doesn't mean he knows where she came from or who her family is. That's what we have to find out.'

Tankard scraped up the dregs from his plate. 'I'm sure you're right.'

Pam drove. Beside her, Tankard was racked with yawns.

'I was directing traffic last night. Didn't even go home. Showered and changed at the station. God I'm buggered.'

And I'm not, Pam thought. I worked through the night too, but that doesn't count. 'What do you think?' she asked. 'Was it accidental?'

Tankard shrugged. 'Couldn't say. They reckon it started in the kitchen.'

A short time later, as they turned into Quarterhorse Lane, Pam leaned forward to stare and said, 'What's going on?'

At least a dozen cars were parked along the fenceline on both sides of Quarterhorse Lane, restricting traffic to one narrow strip of corrugated, potholed dirt.

'Gawkers,' said Tankard contemptuously. 'Ghouls.'

As they approached the ruin, they saw people with cameras. Twice, at least, Pam thought, their van was photographed as it passed along the avenue of cars and turned into the driveway of the burnt house. Tankard wound down his window and shouted, 'Haven't you people got anything better to do?'

'It's a free country.'

Pam wound down her window. 'Move along please, or you'll be arrested for obstruction.'

'Police harassment.'

'Yeah, I love you too,' Pam muttered, following the driveway between small scorched cypress bushes. 'God, they're in here, too.'

Two women were aiming their cameras at a CFA volunteer, who was wearing his full fire-fighting kit. He was grinning, his overalls a streak of vivid yellow against the charred beams and blackened roofing iron.

A man wearing fireproof boots, grey trousers, a white shirt and a hardhat stepped out of the ruin. He was carrying a clipboard. 'It's like the Bourke Street Mall here.' He cast a contemptuous look at the CFA volunteer. 'Bloody cowboys.'

Pam read the ID clipped to the man's belt. He was a fire brigade inspector. 'We'll clear everyone away, sir.'

'Thanks. I actually caught someone nicking souvenirs earlier. This woman, could be your old granny, nicking ceramic dolls from out of the ashes.'

'Sir, did you find anything to tell us who the victim was? Any papers, deed box, wall safe, anything at all?'

'Not a thing,' the fire inspector said.

Going home from work on his trailbike, bumping down Quarterhorse Lane at two o'clock in the arvo for a quick gawk at the house that got burnt, gave Danny an idea. All those cars, all those people with nothing better to do, people he knew . . . Well, if they were here, looking at the burnt house, they weren't home in their own houses, now, were they?

'Was that young Danny Holsinger?'

'It was.'

'Up to no good.'

'Bet on it,' Pam said.

'I'll radio it in, ask the others to keep an eye open.'

Pam turned right, away from the cars of the gawkers, and drove for one third of a kilometre to the next driveway, which took them to a large wooden structure shaped like a pergola. A sign said, 'Tasting Room.'

'Good wine here,' Tankard said.

Pam stared at him. Had he liked the wine or had he simply liked the drinking? A woman came around the side of the building. She wore overalls and carried a small stepladder.

'You've come about the fire?'

'Yes.'

'There's not much I can tell you. We decided to evacuate, just in case. Didn't come back till this morning.'

'Actually, we're after information about the householder,' Pam said.

'You mean Clara?'

'Yes.'

'Poor woman. What a dreadful thing. Was it an accident?'

'We believe so. What can you tell us about her?'

'Not much. In her late twenties, New Zealander. I don't think I ever knew what her surname was, or I've forgotten it if I did know.'

'Friends? Relatives? Anything like that?'

'Can't help you, sorry. She kept to herself.'

The next driveway, at the top of the hill, took them to a large house with a view across Waterloo to the refinery point on the bay. The curtains were drawn in all of the windows and no-one answered when they knocked at the front and back doors. Pam peered through a gap in the lockup garage and saw a newish-looking Mercedes.

Then they heard a tin clatter in the gardening shed and came upon an elderly man pouring petrol into a ride-on mower.

'God, you nearly gave me a heart attack.'

'Do you live here, sir?'

'Me? No. I pop in now and then, do the mowing, watering, check on things. Why? What's up?'

Pam got out her notebook. 'Can you tell me who does live here?'

'Stella Riggs. She's away for a few days.'

Pam noted the details, including a reminder to come back and question Riggs. 'Sir, do you know anything about the fire down the road?'

'Me? Nothing. Should I?'

'A woman called Clara died in it. We're anxious to trace her relatives.'

'Don't know a thing about her.'

'Do you live locally, sir?'

'No.'

Pam looked around pointedly. 'I don't see a vehicle.'

The old man indicated a rusty bicycle. 'What do you think that is?'

Danny had been seen going over the fence. He was also seen coming back, this time by Sergeant van Alphen and a constable in a divisional van.

'Danny, my son.'

'Shit.'

'Now look what you've gone and done. Perfectly good VCR, and you have to drop it in the dirt.'

'I can explain. The heads need cleaning and I was just taking it around to—'

Van Alphen punched him, not hard, but enough to make him reconsider his position. 'What was that, Danny? I didn't quite catch that.'

Tears came unbidden to Danny's eyes and he saw it was true, what they said about van Alphen. 'Don't hit me no more. I want to see Constable Murphy.'

'What do you want to see her for?'

'She'll give me immunity.'

'That's a big word for a squidgy little shit like you. And I doubt it, somehow.'

They took Danny to the station and charged him. But the Pam Murphy chick wasn't in the station, so Danny said, 'I want to call my lawyer.'

Nunn was quick off the mark. There in ten minutes. Danny couldn't believe it. She demanded time alone with him, and as soon as the door was shut she said, 'You're a fuckup, aren't you, Danny, eh?'

'What's that supposed to mean?'

Danny looked at her hotly. Thinks she's so good, all dolled up in her tight skirt and jacket, briefcase, hair looking like its been washed and brushed for hours, smelling like a bottle of perfume's fallen all over her, nasty superior look on her face. 'You got no right to call me names.'

'I've got every right. As your lawyer, I've got every right. What did you think you were doing? Broad daylight. You've got a good job. Can't you be satisfied with that? I can't go spending all my time bailing you out of trouble.'

Fucking stuck-up bitch. Who did she think she was? 'So, am I getting out or aren't I?'

'Mate,' Marion Nunn said, 'quite frankly I can't get you out of here quick enough. You can't be trusted to keep your gob shut.'

Now, what was that supposed to mean? Still, better out than in.

Challis picked up the ringing phone and snapped off his name. It was six o'clock and he wanted to go home. 'Challis.'

'It's Freya. Got a minute?'

Challis sat back in his office chair and stared at the ceiling. 'This sounds like bad news.'

'It is.'

'I'm all ears.'

'The lungs. Fresh and pink inside.'

Challis put his feet up on the edge of his desk. 'You're saying she'd stopped breathing before the fire started.'

'I am.'

'Heart?'

'The heart was fine. But you know those bone fractures, and the bleeding?'

'How will I ever forget.'

'Well, most were due to the extreme heat, but not all. She'd been bashed around first. Beaten to death, in other words.'

Challis said goodbye and stared at the wall. After a while, he called the *Progress* and told Tessa Kane, 'You might want to stop the presses.'

And wondered at his motives.

TWENTY

Ellen was late on Thursday morning. Challis's Triumph was already in the car park, Scobie Sutton's station wagon, cars she recognised as belonging to the seconded officers from Rosebud and Mornington.

She found Rhys slicing open the tape around a small box with a pocket knife. He smiled, then immediately sobered and touched her forearm. 'Are you all right?'

She'd been crying for half of the night. 'Just tired.'

'Tell me.'

His big hands were on her shoulders. She looked away, blinking hard. 'It's nothing, Rhys. I'm okay.'

She felt his fingers relax and finally release her. He turned away. 'Fair enough. None of my business.'

In a way, it was. She tugged him back and searched his face. She wanted to be able to say that she'd had the most godawful row with her husband, that her husband felt scared and threatened, and had accused her of being fast-tracked because she was a woman, of splashing her money about on air-conditioning just to show him up, and of fucking the man she'd hired to install it. But all she said to Rhys Hartnett was, 'Things are a bit tense at home, that's all.' She paused. 'Look, Rhys, I don't know how to say this—I'm sorry, but we won't be having aircon fitted after all. It's . . . the time's not right.'

He jerked away from her. 'I didn't like being the focus of your husband's dislike anyway. Or your daughter's.'

'Oh, Rhys, it's not that, it's—'

'I'm not stupid.'

She watched his face, then said, as firmly as she could, 'I'm very sorry.'

He looked away and stood there, stiff and chafing. 'It happens.'

'You won't be out of pocket?'

'It's summer. People always want aircon.'

'That's good.'

His shapely fingers took a small calibrated instrument from the box. 'I'll be finished here this morning. Just have to mount a few of these thermostats and I'm done.'

They gazed at the courthouse. 'I'll miss seeing you around the place,' she said.

'Yeah, well . . . ,' he said.

'Look, I feel terrible.' She fished in her wallet. 'Here's a hundred dollars. You spent hours measuring up the house, doing costings, all for nothing. Call it a kill fee.'

He stared at the money. She knew at once that she'd been graceless, and wanted the ground to swallow her up.

Challis nodded at Ellen Destry and waited for her to sit down. He'd called an emergency briefing, and the incident room was crowded with his CIB officers and all available uniformed sergeants and senior constables.

He stood. 'We're not downgrading the abduction inquiry, but, until further evidence or leads come in, we can't do much more than follow through on what we already have. Meanwhile, our fire in Quarterhorse Lane. As you know, it's now officially a murder investigation.'

He pointed to a photograph pinned to the wall; the body was revealed as a glistening smudge. 'The victim was one Clara Macris. It appears that she was bashed to death before the fire started. As for the fire, it was intentional but constructed to appear accidental, by someone who knew what he was doing. Was he trying to conceal the fact that it was a murder? Was he getting a kick out of lighting the fire? In any event, we'll have to follow up the suggestion in today's *Progress* that we have a firebug on our hands.'

178

Challis saw amused and knowing grins. They know about me and Tessa Kane, he thought. He went on:

'I want you to look again at any fire we've had recently. That rash of mailboxes, for example; that Pajero, the attempted torching of that house over near the racecourse. Is our firebug also a burglar? Is he escalating? Are there any nutters fighting fires in the local CFA units? Check with the Arson Squad. Have any known pyromaniacs settled in the district? Sergeant Destry will brief you further on who will do what.

'Now, the dead woman. Clara Macris. That's about all we know about her. Her neighbours say she kept to herself. We've still to talk to shopkeepers, bank tellers, anyone else who may have come into contact with her. Apparently she had a New Zealand accent, but we don't know how long she'd been in this country. It may have been years. New Zealand police have been contacted to see whether or not she had a record. We do know she moved into the area about eighteen months ago. Was she renting, or did she buy? I want someone to check that out. Did she go to the pub regularly? Play sport? Travel? Check the local travel agents. Someone else can look at her mail as it comes in.

'Meanwhile, her car is missing. See if it's been reported stolen, found abandoned, impounded or taken somewhere to be repaired.

'See if she ever took taxis anywhere.

'All of this is necessary because we don't know who she is, and the fire destroyed any personal papers that might have told us.

'Now, let's keep an open mind on this. Maybe our firebug isn't responsible. Someone else, someone she knew, was let in—or broke in, it's impossible to tell, given that the house was destroyed—and killed her. Why did he kill her?—assuming it was a man, and I don't want you necessarily making that assumption. Was he a burglar, caught in the act? In which case, this incident relates closely to our latest aggravated burglary—except that Clara Macris clearly wasn't wealthy and this one happened at night.

'Or was it someone she knew, friend, relative or lover, and they had a disagreement over something? We badly need to know something about her personal life. Van, you were investigating officer when her mailbox was burnt. Can you tell us anything?'

The question, the way it was posed, the switch from the general to the particular, seemed to silence the room and draw everyone's attention on to Kees van Alphen. His lean, pale face coloured. He opened and closed his mouth, then coughed, then recovered completely and said, 'She was pretty close-lipped, Inspector.'

'You didn't meet anyone else there? She didn't talk about herself?'

'Not to me.'

'Your officers have been questioning the neighbours. Have they turned up anything?'

'Nothing. One neighbour, a Stella Riggs, is still away, returning tomorrow.'

'We'll need to speak to her. We need to cover a lot of ground very quickly, so I want you to go out in pairs, one uniform, one CIB, asking questions wherever Clara Macris might have gone.

'Now, let's brainstorm a little. Let's say the killer wasn't a family member or an intimate, and wasn't our firebug. We have a house on a quiet back road. Who and what, in terms of people and vehicles, might we expect to see on it? Scobie, do the honours.'

Hands went up, and Scobie Sutton, his eyes wide and self-conscious, made a list on the whiteboard: neighbours, mailman, newspaper delivery, garbage truck, recycle truck, LPG gas truck, meter reader, council grader, power company linesman, taxi, courier, surveyors, council weed-control and fire-control inspectors, rates assessor, take-away food delivery.

Challis said, 'I live on a similar road. I've seen sewage carters, blackberry sprayers, water carriers, repairmen of all kinds. Men delivering firewood—though not in this weather. A man comes with a portable machine to shear my neighbour's half-dozen sheep. Another slashes grass with his tractor. Young people work in the vineyards. Maybe we're looking at a contract gardener. Anything else?'

'Jehovah's Witnesses.'

Sutton wrote it down on the board. The men and women in the room sank a little deeper into their chairs.

*

In the canteen John Tankard said, 'You little ripper.'

He was across the table from her, stretched back in his chair, the newspaper open and concealing his head and trunk, which suited Pam just fine. There was a headline about a firebug, which apparently was causing senior officers in CIB to get very pissed off. She sipped her tea, thought of Ginger.

But the newspaper shook. 'Listen to this, Murph. "According to police reports, Superintendent Mark McQuarrie of Peninsula District rang the arresting officers on behalf of the Bastian family and charges against Julian Bastian and his girlfriend were withdrawn on the authority of another officer, Senior Sergeant Vincent Kellock."'

'We know that,' Pam said.

'But listen to this. "Sources also report that the charges against Mr Bastian had been dropped after his family agreed to drop charges of wrongful arrest and harassment against police."'

Pam leaned forward. 'They did a deal? The bastards.'

Tankard was still behind the paper. 'Yep.'

'I thought it was simply a case of, he's got rich and powerful mates so you can't touch him.'

'Nup.'

They fell silent. Pam stared across the table at the newspaper. The *Progress* seemed to like causes of one kind or another. According to canteen gossip, the editor was having it off with Challis.

Tankard cleared his throat. '"Arresting police are reportedly furious."'

'It says that?'

'Yep.'

'I'm furious, you're furious, but how does the *Progress* know we're furious?'

Tankard reached around the corner of his newspaper for the half-consumed donut that sat like a fat worm on his plate. His mouth full, he said, 'You know, sources and that.'

'Yeah, sure, Tank,' Pam said.

You had to laugh. Before Christmas, Tankard was no better than a Nazi stormtrooper. Now he stood for justice in a world ruled by cronyism.

Suddenly van Alphen was there, as silent as a cat, looming over them. 'You two, come with me, please.'

They followed him to his office. It was like the man: tidy, underfurnished, an area of plain surfaces. 'All hell's broken loose,' he said. 'You'll be working on that fire for the time being. Forget any minor infringements that come your way. We simply haven't got the time or the manpower.'

'Okay, Sarge.'

'You'll each be paired with an officer in plain-clothes, door-knocking, talking to shopkeepers, talking to the neighbours again. We need to know Clara Macris's habits, who knew her, who was seen with her. The usual.'

He pushed a sheet of paper across the desk. Pam scanned it. She was paired with Scobie Sutton.

Tankard, next to her, twisted in his chair to ease the ache in his lower back. 'What was she like, Sarge?'

He sounded genuinely curious, but Pam saw van Alphen's face grow closed and wary. 'What do you mean, what was she like? How the hell should I know?'

'No offence, Sarge. I mean, was she a bit iffy? You know, a junkie. Friends in low places.'

Pam said, 'Tank, that's what we're being sent to find out.'

'Fair enough. Just asking.'

Van Alphen gave her a curious look of gratitude. It was there and gone in an eyeblink. Then she saw him slide a manila folder shyly across the desk toward them.

'Meanwhile, I've written a report for the District Commander.'

She picked it up. 'On what, Sarge?'

'Read it.'

Tankard pulled his chair next to hers. He gave off enormous heat; she could *hear* his body. Then she heard his voice, reading aloud, as she leaned away from him and read to herself:

'The dropping of charges against Mr Julian Bastian on the day of the listed court date in the Waterloo Magistrates' Court causes grave concern to myself and the arresting officers, Constables John Tankard and Pamela Murphy.

'The allegation my officers lied and contrived an arrest situation is false. I have every faith in their ability and judgment. All the evidence supports their charges against Bastian.

'The situation is potentially damaging to the Force. Already allegations of favouritism, corruption and intervention at the highest levels have been made by the local press, which could soon become state wide.'

Pam found her heart lifting. Beside her, John Tankard was saying, 'Good one, Sarge.'

Van Alphen murmured, 'Something had to be done.'

He looked tired, the flesh tight on his skull. Tired, and almost, Pam thought, stricken with a strong emotion, like sadness, heartache.

The briefing over, Challis made his call. He had the *Progress* on the desk in front of him. The first page asked *Is There a Firebug at Work?* and went on to outline what Tessa Kane called 'a rash of deliberate fires in the district'. Twelve mailboxes set alight, one memorable night before Christmas (including the victim of this latest tragedy . . . Had she seen something? Was this a payback?). A stolen four-wheel drive torched on Chicory Kiln Road. An attempt by burglars to burn down a house near the racecourse.

She also offered a psychological profile of the typical firebug:

'He betrays the symptoms of an anti-social personality— another name for a psychopath—from an early age, including bed-wetting, cruelty to animals, anger at the world, a tendency to get into fights, a history of lighting fires and then fighting them or standing back to watch others fight them.

'He often uses fire to express his anger, to avenge himself on individuals and institutions that he feels have wronged him. Fear eases his anger. Its destructive capacity fascinates him. He feels powerful.

'The association of fire and sex in pyromaniacs is well known. Fire seems to heighten the desire for sexual release.'

When she came on the line, Challis said, 'What the hell are you doing?'

'Lovely to hear your voice, too, Hal.'

'There may be no connection between any of those fires.'

'Hal, come on, there has to be a connection between some of them. Face it, there's a firebug at work.'

'Far from being community-minded, you keep trying to scare everyone. Flash headlines, some psychological garbage that you probably cobbled together from some cheap magazine.'

'I resent that.'

'Tess, it was irresponsible.'

Ellen walked down High Street to the bank and withdrew four hundred dollars to add to the one hundred that she'd tried to give Rhys Hartnett. She had to wait in a slow queue, everyone wanting to talk about the fire and where they had been in relation to the danger it posed. Everyone was excited and laying claim to lucky escapes and fear and leapfrogging statistics. When she got back to the station, she stuffed the five hundred into the poor box in the foyer. When she was growing up, her mother had always referred to the 'mission box', meaning unwanted clothes that she put aside for the Inland Mission. Every Christmas Day, she would put an empty envelope on the table and tell the family shyly, 'Perhaps you would like to give to the mission.' Ellen wondered if people still did that, and wondered how far she had changed since her childhood, and how far she had drifted from her mother.

Their easy way with labels: 'Killer Highway.' 'Highway Killer.' Did they think he could be defined by a label? What were they going to call him now that he was in amongst them, prowling where they wheeled their prams and washed their cars and chinwagged with their neighbours?

They'd find something to call him, something inane, convinced that they'd pinned him down according to pattern. And when they did, he'd alter the pattern again.

But not the killing.

Other men dreamed. He made it happen. The slavering dream, followed by the shuddering release. The snarling hunger of it, like a meal savoured and devoured.

This next one was a real slag. He was going to enjoy this one. Doing her was going to really hit home, right where they'd feel it. Snatch her tomorrow morning, in broad daylight, between the milkbar and the church, right from under their noses.

Linger over this one.

Kind of like revenge. Sweet, juicy revenge.

TWENTY-ONE

At nine the next morning, Scobie Sutton said, 'Mrs Stella Riggs?'

She had her back to him, checking that she'd locked her front door. 'Yes?'

'I'm Detective Constable Sutton. I need to ask you a few questions regarding the fire at your neighbour's house.'

He watched her turn from the door and step on to the path as if to brush him aside. 'I'm afraid I can't tell you anything.'

'According to my notes, you've been on holiday?'

She was almost past him, following a line of roses away from her front door. 'If you know that, then you know I couldn't possibly know anything about the fire. And she's scarcely my neighbour. There is another property separating hers from mine.'

'I understand that,' Sutton said, hurrying along beside her. He didn't like the woman. Clipped voice, born-to-rule manner, an air of impatience and indifference. 'But I do need to ask you how well you knew Clara Macris.'

'I didn't know her at all.'

'You never talked to her? Visited her?'

'Certainly not.'

'Did she ever visit you?'

'Good heavens, no. Look, all of my mail is being held for

me at the post office. I got in late last night and have a lot to do. If you don't mind, I'd like—'

'Do you know who her friends were?'

Sutton was asking questions on the run, now, following Stella Riggs around to the side of the house, where she pointed a remote control at the lock-up garage. The door slid open, revealing a white Mercedes.

'How should I know who her friends were? Nothing to do with me.'

'Recent visitors, regular visitors, strangers, nothing like that?'

'There's her boyfriend. At least, I'm assuming it was her boyfriend. His car was always there.'

'Boyfriend,' Sutton said.

'One of your lot. A policeman. In a police car. Always there. Tall, gloomy-looking fellow. Now, if you'll excuse me, I have a lot to do.'

Sutton returned to the car. He muttered, as Pam Murphy started the engine, 'There's a prize cow.'

'Sit down, Sergeant,' Challis said, one hour later.

But van Alphen continued to stand, and first he gazed grimly at Challis, then at Scobie Sutton, and finally at Senior Sergeant Kellock. He pointed at Kellock. 'What's he doing here?'

Kellock cleared his throat. 'I'm representing the interests of the uniformed branch, Sergeant.'

'Bullshit. You're here because you're pissed off that I questioned your decision on Bastian, you and McQuarrie, and you're hoping to see me sink.'

Sutton said, 'Van, why don't you just sit?'

Fatigue had sharpened the planes of van Alphen's face. Not for the first time, Sutton was struck by van Alphen's resemblance to Challis. They were lean, hard-working men driven by private demons. As though aware that the greater challenge came from Challis, van Alphen sat, finally, and squarely faced the inspector across the desk.

Challis said, 'You claimed just now that the Senior Sergeant hoped to see you sink. Are you expecting to sink? Is there anything you wish to tell us?'

'I'm not stupid, sir.'

'Nobody suggested you were.'

'I'm as tuned in to canteen gossip as anyone, even when it's about me. You think I killed Clara Macris.'

Challis said, 'Do we?'

Van Alphen folded his arms. He sat rock still and apparently filled with contempt. It was contempt for a police force that didn't protect its own, Sutton decided, and not aimed at Challis in particular. 'Van, we need to know more about your relationship with the dead woman,' he said.

Van Alphen's narrow head swung slowly around until they were staring at each other. No wonder the locals hate him, Sutton thought.

'What relationship, *Constable*?'

Fine, Sutton thought, if that's the way you want to play it, I'll drop 'Van' and call you by your name and rank. 'Sergeant van Alphen, we have a witness who saw a police car at Clara Macris's house on a number of occasions. We've checked the vehicle logs and duty rosters. You often signed a car out.'

'Really. Is that a fact?'

Challis stepped in. 'You investigated the woman's mailbox fire, is that correct?'

'Yes.'

'You made follow-up visits to her?'

'I may have done.'

'Either you did or you didn't. It wasn't that long ago.'

'She was badly shaken up.'

'And you went around and gave her a cuddle, hoping she'd come across for you,' Kellock put in.

Challis darkened. 'Senior Sergeant, please leave the room.'

'I have a right to be here, Inspector.'

Challis was clipped and dismissive. 'No you don't. This is a murder investigation. Constable Sutton and I investigate murders. You don't.'

'This is my station.'

Challis slapped his hand on the desk and shouted, 'And this is my investigation. Now get out.'

Kellock stood slowly, massively, and with feigned good grace left the room.

Challis grinned. After a while, van Alphen allowed himself a wintry smile.

'Clara Macris was a user,' Challis said. 'According to the toxicology report on her body.'

'I thought she might have been.'

Challis nodded. 'But that's all we know about her. And it's one aspect of her that must have led her into contact with other people.'

Van Alphen shrugged. 'I guess so.'

'Do *you* know who was supplying her?'

'No.'

'What did she tell you about herself?'

'Nothing much.'

'Did you like her?' Sutton asked suddenly.

Van Alphen blinked. 'Yes.'

'Is that why you kept going back to see her?'

Van Alphen said irritably, 'I didn't *keep* going back to see her at all. I may have dropped in a couple of times.'

'Did you have sex with her?'

'No.'

'Did you want to?'

'Oh, so that's why I killed her. I wanted a fuck, she didn't, so I killed her.'

'Well, is that what happened?'

'No. I mean, no, I didn't kill her.'

Challis had been watching this, leaning back, his right foot resting on his left knee, tapping a pen against his teeth. He straightened again. 'What did you talk about?'

'Nothing much.'

'She didn't tell you about her private life?'

'No.'

'What about your old cases, Van?'

Van Alphen frowned. 'My what?'

'You're not very popular. Has anyone threatened you? Been following you? Could someone have wanted to kill your girlfriend to get back at you?'

'She wasn't my girlfriend. No-one was following me.'

'Come on, Sergeant, we're offering you a lifeline here. You were sleeping with her, weren't you?'

'No.'

'Were you supplying her with drugs?'

'Was I what?'

'You heard. She had a habit. She told you she'd sleep with you if you supplied her with drugs.'

'I can't believe I'm hearing this.'

188

Now, you shouldn't have chosen those words, Sutton said to himself. They don't ring true. He decided to push it. 'Where did you get the drugs? The evidence locker?'

'It seems,' van Alphen said, looking at the ceiling, 'that I should have a lawyer present.'

'Or did you rip off a dealer? Is that how you kept her supplied?'

'You're making an awfully big leap from my visiting her a couple of times on official business to my supplying her with drugs in order to sleep with her.'

'More than a couple of visits,' Challis snapped. 'Your car was seen there several times, by several of the residents of Quarterhorse Lane.'

Van Alphen muttered something sullenly.

'Speak up, Van.'

'I said, she thought someone was after her.'

The tension ebbed from the room. Challis said gently, 'Were you sleeping with her?'

'Yes.'

'What did she tell you about herself?'

'Almost nothing. She came from New Zealand, I suspected she was a user, and that's about it.'

'Who did she think was after her?'

'She didn't, wouldn't, say.'

'What led her to think someone was after her?'

'She thought the mailbox business was a warning.'

'You told her about the other mailboxes?'

'Yes. I think I convinced her, but in general she was pretty agitated. The abductions didn't help. She told me she thought it was a smokescreen, that she was the intended victim and it was just a matter of time.'

'You must have formed an opinion of her, Van,' Sutton said. 'Who she was, whether or not she was hiding anything.'

Van Alphen looked at the ceiling again. 'I formed the belief that she was running away from something.'

'Like what?'

'Some heavy people. A vicious husband or boyfriend. Someone she owed money to. Someone she ripped off. Something along those lines.'

'But she didn't say?'

'No.'

'Running away from trouble in New Zealand, do you think?'

'I've no idea.'

'But you think they found her?'

Van Alphen looked at Sutton and said carefully, '*She* thought they'd found her. But she was generally predisposed to think that. She was scared. If anything out of the ordinary happened, she misconstrued it, thought it applied to her alone.'

'Except,' Challis said, 'this time she didn't misconstrue it.'

'I guess so.'

'You're not making this up?'

'There were firemen there with me the night her mailbox got burnt. They'll tell you, she was scared out of her brain, when anyone else would've simply been pissed off.'

Sutton nodded. They'd already talked to the firemen.

'So, where does that leave me?' van Alphen said, challenging them.

Challis said, 'Senior Sergeant Kellock wants you suspended.'

'I bet he does, the prick.'

'But we're not going to suspend you,' Challis went on. 'However, I don't want you on outside duties while we continue our investigation. I don't want you talking to anyone. I want you indoors, making a list of anyone you've helped put away, or anyone with a grudge against you for anything at all.'

Van Alphen sneered. 'Feels like a kind of suspension to me.'

'And you feel like a not-quite-so-straight copper to me,' Challis snarled. 'That's all. You can go.'

Challis bounced at a clip down the stairs. He sounded almost breezy.

'How's your daughter, Scobie?'

Sutton hurried to draw alongside him. Was Challis really interested, or going through the motions? 'A handful now that she's home all day long.'

'Will you send her back to the childcare place when it reopens?'

'Probably. See how it goes.'

'Good.'

Maybe Challis had wanted kids, before things blew up on

him. They reached the ground floor and Sutton changed the subject. 'Boss, you don't think Van killed her, do you?'

Challis pushed through the rear door into the car park. The heat hit them. 'I doubt it. But he was more than just a concerned copper to her. That's why I want to have a talk to Stella Riggs. She seems to be the only independent witness.'

'I don't know what else she can tell you, boss. Wasted trip.'

'Scobie, I'm not questioning your interview with her. I just want to be on firmer ground before we start digging any deeper into van Alphen.'

Scobie snorted. 'She won't thank you.'

'Won't she?'

'She's a stuck-up bitch.'

'Then I'll have to unstick her. Any luck with the gypsies?'

'None.'

'They could be in New South Wales by now.'

They had reached the Commodore. Pam Murphy, lounging on the grass beneath the line of gums that separated the police station from the courthouse, brushed leaves from her uniform and hurried toward them. Challis leaned on the roof of the car. 'What about Ledwich? Still think there's something iffy about him?'

'Boss, we've checked him pretty thoroughly. His alibis aren't crash hot, but we can't prove that he *wasn't* at work each of the times we're interested in. The Pajero business is a fizzer. The registration had elapsed and he'd lost his licence, yet was still driving around in it, and was scared the police and the insurance company would find out, that's how I read it.'

'You think that's why he was so edgy? Trying to avoid discovery?'

Sutton shrugged. 'It's one explanation.'

They drove out of the car park. 'Back to Quarterhorse Lane, Constable,' Challis said.

Stella Riggs showed them into a broad, gleaming room with polished floorboards, a vast open fireplace, several roomy leather armchairs and twin matching sofas, an antique drinks cabinet, and windows that offered a view across vineyards and orchards to Westernport Bay in the hazy distance. Around to the right, the ground was scorched bare.

'As I told your man here, Inspector, I didn't know the woman.'

Sutton bridled. She wasn't British, but sounded it, in voice and attitude. Before he could respond, Challis said, 'Yet you knew something of her movements.'

'All I *knew*, Inspector Challis, was that she was often visited by a policeman in a police car. On two occasions I actually saw him. I gave your fellow a description.' She turned to Sutton. 'I trust you passed my information on. It wouldn't surprise me if—'

Challis said, 'You never visited her?'

'No.'

'Never saw anyone else visit her?'

'No.'

'Never saw any person or vehicle in Quarterhorse Lane that shouldn't have been there?'

'No. Or rather—'

'Yes?'

'I was once followed by someone.'

'Go on.'

'You must know about it. It's been in the papers.'

Sutton frowned. What was the stupid cow on about? 'What, Mrs Riggs?'

She turned to him, her back rigid, her nose tipped back as though to avoid catching his scent. 'Road rage, of course.'

'Road rage,' Challis said.

'This fellow thought that I'd cut him off, and he followed me all the way home.'

'But what did that have to do with Miss Macris?'

'Obviously I didn't want the fellow to know where I lived.'

Scobie still didn't get it. 'So?'

But Challis did. He stared with distaste at Stella Riggs. 'You didn't drive to your own house, you drove to Clara Macris's house.'

'Yes.'

'You thought if there was going to be trouble later, then it would be *she* who copped it.'

'I must protest. It wasn't nearly so calculated as that. I—'

'Many road rage incidents involve quite considerable violence. Clara Macris may be dead because of you.'

For the first time, Stella Riggs's composure began to break. 'I didn't think—'

'No, you didn't.'

She shrieked, 'I turned into her driveway hoping the policeman would be there, or if he wasn't then he could be fetched to help me.'

Challis closed his eyes. He opened them again and said gently, 'Then what happened?'

'The man following me drove past the front gate, then turned around and drove away again, so I left.'

'You didn't see or speak to Miss Macris?'

'No.'

'What did he look like, this man?'

'Two men.'

'Two men. Would you recognise them if you saw them again?'

'The driver had short hair and wore a singlet, that's all I can tell you. He looked like a labourer. The other fellow was smaller.'

'And the vehicle?'

'It was a Mitsubishi Pajero.'

Challis sat back. 'A Pajero.'

She sounded almost proud. 'My late husband drove one for many years. That's how I know.'

Sutton said, 'What colour?'

'Maroon, from memory.'

'What more can you tell us about it?'

Stella Riggs got up and crossed the room to the mantelpiece above the fireplace. 'I jotted down the registration. Yes, here it is.'

On their way out, Sutton said, 'She killed her, didn't she?'

'As good as,' Challis said.

When Pam Murphy knocked on Challis's door, half an hour later, she was tentative, wondering if he'd be distracted and dismissive.

'Sir, I heard you talking in the car. You think whoever was driving the Pajero might have come back and killed Clara Macris.'

The inspector switched his attention fully on to her. 'It's possible. Do you have something?'

She told him about the litter that she'd bagged where the Pajero had been torched.

'You did this off your own bat?'

'Yes, sir.'

'Bottles, cans, and what else? Cigarette packets?'

'Yes, sir.'

'You didn't handle them?'

'Picked them up with my pen, sir.'

'Where are they now? Evidence locker?'

Pam squirmed. 'My own locker, sir.'

'Damn.'

'Sir?'

Challis looked up at her, faintly irritable. 'We require a clear chain of physical evidence if we're to use it in court. Anything you find at the scene of a crime must be logged in officially and immediately. If the chain is broken, the evidence, in effect, is tainted, even if it hasn't been touched by anyone else.'

'Sorry, sir.'

'What were you thinking?'

'Well, sir, I wasn't supposed to be at the scene and I felt a bit stupid, Tank—Constable Tankard, sir—slagging off at me for wasting my time. And it was near the end of the shift and we had a lot on our plate . . .'

Challis gestured. 'It's all right, Constable. At least we can see if we've got any prints worth using. If we're lucky, they'll match prints already on record. If they do, then it's a matter of leaning hard or finding other evidence we *can* use in court.'

'Yes, sir.'

'So, get it all over to the lab. I'll tell them to give it priority.'

'Thank you, sir.'

'How old was the stuff you picked up? Had it been there for long?'

'I left the really old stuff, sir.'

Tessa Kane waited at the front desk for almost an hour before Challis appeared. She saw his face shut down the moment he recognised her. He looked tired. Pushing the hair away from his forehead distractedly, he said, 'I'll see if I can find us an empty office.'

'It's all right. I'm just dropping this off.'

She handed him a letter and then an envelope, in separate freezer bags. 'It was in the box this morning. I tried to contact you earlier, but you were busy.'

He said, without looking at her, 'That's right.'

They were both looking at the letter in his hands. 'Our man sounds resentful,' Challis said.

Tessa leaned against him fleetingly. 'He wants to be on the front page again.'

After a while, Challis said, 'Thanks, Tess,' and made to go. 'Hal, can't we start again?'

Later, as Challis bumped along the narrow track to his front gate, Tessa Kane hard behind him in her Saab, he was forced to brake to avoid a massive structure ahead of him, one edge protruding a little into his path, the other filling the side gate to his neighbour's vineyard. It was a superphosphate bin, chalky white in the evening light, sitting high on metal struts. Another country lane stranger to add to his list: top-dressing contractor. He'd already thought of a further two since leaving Waterloo. Horse trainer. Red Cross collector.

He stopped thinking about it. It was all academic, anyway. They had to find who wanted Clara Macris dead, not who had a reason to be in Quarterhorse Lane.

Challis parked and opened the front door. His eyes glanced automatically at the light on his answering machine. One message. He pushed the play button, heard his wife's voice, low and choked and hectic, and immediately switched it off.

Tessa Kane entered the house behind him, carrying shopping bags. She'd bought fresh fish, a salad mix, a lemon, potatoes to make into chips. It was seven, the skyline pink as the sun settled. They cut the potatoes into chips, oiled them in a pan and placed them in the oven. They had little to say to each other and Challis wondered if he was making a mistake, even as he thought that it was nice, doing this, making a meal with an attractive woman and taking drinks out on to the decking while it cooked. He lit a citronella candle to drive away the mosquitoes and touched his glass to hers. In the half light, she looked not so hard-edged or apt to be secretive. The phone rang. Challis groaned. He knew people who could blithely ignore the phone, and people who were desperate to answer it. If he lived a normal life and wasn't a policeman, he'd be one of the former, he often thought. 'Excuse me.'

It was Scobie Sutton. 'Boss, turn to "Crime Beat", Channel 9.'

Challis's kitchen opened on to the sitting room and the little television set he kept in the corner. He found the remote control, turned the set on and returned to the phone. 'Okay.'

'Watch.'

There was an outside shot, a modest house in Dromana, then the parents of Kymbly Abbott were seated on a velour sofa that had seen better days. They were raw-looking, anxious, the victims of a poor education and a poorer diet. They seemed to sense the skin-deep sympathy and staged sentiments of the interviewer, a young woman with cropped hair, a short black dress and plum-coloured lips.

Even so, Challis thought, as the interview progressed, they're getting a kick out of being on television, and that's almost, *almost*, overriding their grief. He heard the interviewer say:

'You'd like the police to do more.'

Kymbly Abbott's father intended to do all of the talking. 'Yeah.'

'You think they should be doing what you and the parents of Jane Gideon are doing?'

'Yep.'

'Handing out photographs and talking to people.'

'Yep.'

'Are Mr and Mrs Gideon helping you?'

'We got the idea off them.'

'You think handing out your daughter's photograph will help jog someone's memory?'

'Yep.'

Then Kymbly Abbott's mother leaned forward and made the only original observation that Challis had heard so far:

'Like, the whole time, all youse reporters have done is concentrate on *us*—' she poked herself in the chest '—our *feelings*, instead of getting people to try and remember if they saw Kymbly.'

As Challis watched, the screen filled with a close-up of a leaflet, Kymbly Abbott in full colour, the words *Did you see who took our Kymbly?* across the top, a description and a phone number at the bottom.

The phone to his ear, Challis said, 'I wish they hadn't done that.'

'Boss, when they flash on that leaflet again, check out the description and the photo.'

Challis watched. Another close-up, and a voice-over, describing Kymbly Abbott the night she was abducted and murdered.

'Scobie, I'm missing something here.'

'The backpack, boss. They bloody forgot to tell us she had a backpack with her when she went missing.'

TWENTY-TWO

Saturday, 8.15 a.m., Challis standing before the whiteboard saying: 'Right, it's going to be another scorcher today, so the sooner we're not cooped up together in this place, the better.'

He leaned both hands on the back of a chair. 'Two pieces of much needed luck. One, Pam Murphy, a young uniformed constable, had the foresight to bag a few bottles and cans at the scene of the torching of Lance Ledwich's Pajero in Chicory Kiln Road.'

He indicated the location on the wall map and swung around again. 'As you know, we believe the vehicle was stolen by the two men responsible for that ag burg near the race-course. Their original getaway vehicle had stalled, and they legged it to a nearby housing estate, where they found the Pajero. According to the prints recovered from the bottles and cans, and assuming that the same men are responsible for the ag burg, and stealing and then burning the Pajero, then we're looking at Boyd Jolic, Danny Holsinger and Craig Oliver, all from Waterloo and all known to the police.'

A voice: 'I thought you said two men, boss.'

Challis nodded. 'We believe that one of the three drove out to Chicory Kiln Road to fetch the other two. A call was made on Lance Ledwich's car phone to The Refinery Hotel that same night. A barmaid has since confirmed that Craig Oliver took a call and left the bar soon afterwards. Now, it's nice to think we've got a lead on that ag burg, but we've also had a second piece of luck, a witness who can place that same Pajero in Quarterhorse Lane.'

He went on to explain Stella Riggs's road rage incident, and how her evasive tactic may have led to the murder of Clara Macris. 'Jesus Christ,' someone said. Others shook their heads.

'We've sent three teams out to arrest Jolic, Holsinger and Oliver,' Challis went on. He looked at his watch. 'They should be returning soon.'

'So Van's off the hook, boss?'

Challis gazed at the room of officers. After a while he said, 'I've heard the rumours—van Alphen was screwing Clara Macris, they had a falling out, he killed her. You all know that we questioned Sergeant van Alphen.'

He paused. He seemed pleasant, offhand, obliging, then suddenly snapped forward, both palms on the desk in front of him. 'Clara Macris was murdered. You are investigating a murder. You are police officers. That job, and your role, come before fear or favour. If a copper is implicated in a crime, however vaguely—or falsely, through someone else's agency— then we investigate that copper until we're satisfied one way or the other.'

He straightened. 'Have you all got that?'

They coughed, shuffled, murmured, wouldn't look at him or looked sourly at him.

'If it will put your minds at rest, Sergeant van Alphen is not high on my list.

'Now, another development. Some of you may have seen 'Crime Beat' on the box last night. The parents of Kymbly Abbott were on, doing a Gideon—in other words, they've been hanging around street corners near the start of the Old Peninsula Highway, handing out photos of their daughter.'

'But she's *dead*, boss.'

Challis frowned. 'Don't you think they want her killer caught? Poor sods, they hope someone may have seen her getting picked up. The point is, both the photograph and the description that they give for their daughter mention an expensive black leather backpack. I wish we'd known this before. Someone may have found the backpack near where the body was found, for example, and either kept it quiet or not realised its significance. Or maybe the killer still has it. We don't know.'

He waved a leaflet at them. 'I called on the Abbotts last night and obtained a few copies of these, so you can see for yourselves what the backpack looks like. Meanwhile Scobie wants to add something.'

Scobie Sutton stood uncomfortably and said, 'Before Christmas a gypsy woman came to me with some clairvoyant mumbo jumbo about where Jane Gideon's body could be found. Later I went to question her in relation to a series of thefts. As you know from an earlier briefing, I saw three men at her camp, and a couple of four-wheel drives. The thing is, I also saw a leather backpack. They'd all shot through when I went back to arrest her on the theft charges, and I put out a description, but the backpack makes it imperative that we find them.' He sat down, red in the face.

Challis stood. 'I agree. They must be found.'

As Ellen Destry left the room and walked down the corridor to the stairs, Challis caught up to her and murmured, 'Are you okay?'

'Fine, Hal.'

'You look ragged. Everything all right at home?'

He was someone you could confide in. His own pain made him a reliable listener. She wanted to tell him how she'd taken the safe route in her personal life, putting her husband first; about the ache she felt, driving into the car park and not seeing Rhys Hartnett at work at the courthouse next door. But time would heal that, so they could all get fucked, and all she said to Challis was, 'Boss, you look a bit ragged yourself.'

'I don't doubt it. Okay, I want your help in the interview room. I've sent Scobie back to the caravan park to see if the backpack's still there and to follow up on those gypsies.'

'That backpack's a long shot, Hal. I've seen them around myself.'

'After this much time's elapsed in a murder inquiry,' Challis said, 'everything's a long shot.'

Danny Holsinger had been taken to an interview room next to the holding cells. Boyd Jolic and Craig Oliver were also in the building, in separate interview rooms. All three men had been arrested and brought in separately. Challis pushed into the interview room, Ellen behind him.

Danny was sitting at a small table. A uniformed probationary constable had been standing guard on the door. She moved back into position as Challis sat opposite Danny. Ellen moved around until she was standing behind him. There was a smell of industrial cleaning agents in the room, and a tide mark of grime at mop-head height around the base of the glossy white walls.

Challis began by giving Danny an official caution, then said, 'Danny, this is a preliminary interview. If all goes well, we'll make a formal record of interview, with tape and video.'

'Why, what've I done?'

'Let's see—aggravated burglary, arson on a house, theft of a motor vehicle, arson of a motor vehicle, and murder.'

Danny swallowed. 'Murder?'

Ellen put her hands on Danny's shoulders and leaned her head close to the back of his neck. She breathed shallowly. Danny didn't strike her as dirty by nature, but he had been emptying recycle crates since 5 a.m. and been arrested before he could go home and shower and change. 'Murder, Danny, that's right.'

He tried to turn around to look at her, but she kept sidestepping away. He faced Challis. 'You must be mad. I got nabbed the other day for burglary. And before Christmas. That's my style, not murder. Whose murder?'

Challis put an evidence bag containing a Fosters Lager can on the table between them. 'Danny, we found your prints all over this.'

'So?'

'Right where a Mitsubishi Pajero was set alight in Chicory Kiln Road. The same vehicle was stolen earlier by two men fleeing the scene of an aggravated burglary. Perhaps you can explain your connection to the Pajero?'

'I never took it.'

'Who did? One of your mates? Boyd Jolic? Craig Oliver?'

Ellen sensed a wariness in Danny's shoulders. She leaned close to his ear again. 'They're here, Danny. They sold you out.'

'Bullshit.'

'Your mates have sold you out.'

201

'Nup, don't believe it. Sold me out about what?'

He sounded more certain than she would have liked. She looked to Challis to continue.

'So you didn't take the Pajero. Fine. But you helped to burn it.'

'Nup.'

'You were there, Danny. Your prints on this can of lager prove it.'

'Nup. I drive the recycle truck along Chicory Kiln Road once a week. I must've chucked the can out the window.'

'Your employers won't be pleased to know that you drink on the job.'

Danny tried to backpedal. 'Maybe I took a bird up there the other night. Yeah, that's it.'

Challis pushed a sheet of paper and a pen across the desk. 'Name and address.'

'What?'

'Of this bird you took to Chicory Kiln Road.'

'Can't remember. Must of been someone I picked up in the pub. Yeah, that's it, I remember now.'

Ellen said softly in his ear, 'Megan Stokes won't be very pleased.'

Danny jumped in his chair. 'How do you know about her?'

'We know everything about you, Dan old son.'

'You leave her out of this. She'll bloody kill me.'

'Like you killed Clara Macris?'

'Who?'

'You know, Danny, it's been in all the papers and on the box. The woman murdered and burnt in Quarterhorse Lane. In fact, two of our officers saw you there the next day. A killer going back to the scene of the crime, that's what it looked like.'

'No!'

'The Pajero, Danny. Tell us about it.'

'All right, all right. Me and me mates were coming back from the pub, you know, a short cut, and we saw something burning. We got closer and saw it was this four-wheel drive by the side of the road.'

'You didn't try to extinguish the fire?'

'What?'

'Put the fire out?'

'Didn't have nothing to put it out with.'

'Boyd Jolic is a volunteer with the Country Fire Authority, isn't he?'

'Yeah. So?'

'Why didn't he do something?'

'He was pretty pissed.'

'He liked watching it burn, didn't he? Did it affect you the same way? Is that why you set fire to Clara Macris's house after killing her?'

'I never. And I wouldn't know what Joll was thinking.'

'Wouldn't you?'

'No.'

'You stole the mobile phone and called Craig Oliver at the pub to come and collect you, isn't that right?'

'No. He was there with us when we found it.'

'What vehicle were you in?'

'Er, Joll's ute.'

'You're not certain?'

'That's right, it was definitely Joll's ute.'

'Was it you who threw the car phone into the flames after you called Mr Oliver to collect you?'

'I told you, he was there all the time.'

'Explain the cans, the bottles, the cigarette packets we found at the scene, covered in your prints.'

Danny uttered a bizarre, high-pitched laugh. 'We had a bit of a party.'

'It gave you a particular thrill, standing around, watching something burn?'

Danny said sourly, 'I'm not like that.'

'What are you like, Dan?' Ellen said.

He twisted around to look at her. 'It was unexpected, seeing a car burning. You know.'

'Did you see who lit the fire?'

'Didn't see no-one.'

'Did you light it, or did Boyd Jolic light it?'

'I told you, we—'

Ellen leaned into his ear again and said, 'What if I told you that we have a witness who saw a scrawny little man—namely you—and a larger man—namely Jolic—driving the Pajero a short time after an aggravated burglary was committed at a horse stud near the racecourse. This witness did something to

203

piss you off and so you followed the witness to a house in Quarterhorse Lane.'

'She's lying.'

Challis said quietly, 'Who said it was a woman, Danny?'

'Er, I mean, Sergeant Destry did.'

'No I didn't.'

Challis took over. 'You followed this witness to a house in Quarterhorse Lane. Later you went back to this house, broke in, killed the occupant, and set a fire to cover your tracks.'

'Because that's the sort of scum you are, Danny,' Ellen said. 'Someone accidentally causes you a minor upset in traffic, and it's such an insult to your feeble manhood that murder is the only revenge.'

'No. I swear.'

'What did you hit Clara Macris with?'

'I never hit her.'

'Jolic did?'

'No. I don't know.'

'You mean, he went there alone to do it?'

'I never killed nobody.'

'Funny, why should people say you did?'

'Who?'

'Do you want your lawyer, Danny?'

'That cow. She puts me down all the time.'

'So you agree to being further questioned without legal representation?'

'I'm not saying another word. I told you all I know.'

Challis pushed back in his chair. 'All right, Danny, that will be all for now.'

'I can go home?'

'You must be joking.'

Craig Oliver gave them the same story.

That left Boyd Jolic, and when Ellen Destry realised that Jolic had Marion Nunn in the interview room with him, she took Challis aside. 'Boss, I'm sorry I didn't mention this before, the Macris business got in the way, but Nunn could be the brains behind the ag burgs we've been having.' She went on to tell him about Pam Murphy and the photographs.

Challis grinned when she'd finished. 'Even if there's nothing to it, knowing there's a suspicion is going to make this interview all the more interesting.'

They went in, turned on the tape, cautioned Jolic, and started the questioning. The story Jolic gave them was essentially the same as Danny Holsinger's and Craig Oliver's. They'd been to the pub, drinking until late. When they left, Jolic said, they'd driven along Chicory Kiln Road to avoid being breathalysed. He grinned: 'Too late, you can't arrest me now.' Then they came upon the Pajero. It was already burning fiercely. Such a sight in the middle of the night and the middle of nowhere, naturally you're going to want to stop and watch it, down a few coldies by the side of the road, smoke a few fags. That's all, end of story.

'You're a CFA volunteer. Weren't you concerned there'd be a bushfire?'

'Nah. Wasn't much of a blaze.'

'Enough for a passing motorist to stop and extinguish it.'

Jolic shrugged.

'Why didn't you report the fire?'

'Mate, we were pissed as farts, I got a record, who's going to believe we didn't do it?'

Marion Nunn stirred. 'If you have no further questions for my client, may I—'

'No,' said Challis, 'you may not. Mr Jolic, earlier in the day you were seen driving the Pajero on Coolart Road.'

'That's a lie.'

'As a result of an incident at an intersection, you tailgated another car, following it all the way to an address in Quarterhorse Lane.'

'Nope.'

'Later you went back to that same address, attacked and killed the occupant, and set fire to the house.'

'Nope.'

'Inspector, really, I hope you can substantiate these claims.'

'We have a description of the vehicle, the driver and the passenger, and we have the licence plate.'

'I'm entitled to know who your witness is.'

'We'd like our witness to live long enough to make it to trial, Mrs Nunn, so for the moment I don't intend to—'

'I resent the implication of that remark. I have never—'

Ellen cut her off. 'Get off on lighting fires, do you, Boyd?'

205

'I really must protest. If you have any solid evidence, then charge my client. If not, I'm asking you to release him.'

'We have a few more hours up our sleeves before we're obliged to do that,' Challis said. 'We're about to search Mr Jolic's house. Would you care to be present?'

Marion Nunn looked at Jolic. Challis saw a curiously private expression pass across her face. She turned back and said, 'That won't be necessary. I should like to be alone with my client, and I insist on being present when and if he's questioned again.'

'Wouldn't have it any other way, Marion.'

When they were in the corridor, Challis said, 'There's something going on there. Did you see the look she gave him?'

'She's such a pain in the bum, I'd love to put her away.'

'Why would she send Jolic into an occupied house?'

'They didn't know it was occupied. The owners came back early from holidays.'

'And instead of turning around and driving away, Jolic went in and things snowballed from there. She must be panicking.'

'Meanwhile,' Ellen said, 'if we don't find some better evidence soon, we'll have to let Jolic and company go.'

It came to Challis then. 'Pam Murphy told me she met an insurance investigator poking around where the Pajero was torched. I'll see if I can track him down. He might have some evidence that we missed.'

They returned to the Displan room. Challis called Ledwich first, Ledwich saying, 'What have I done now?'

'I need the name of your insurance company, Mr Ledwich.'

'They're not forking out, the bastards.'

'Whose fault is that? The name, please.'

Ledwich gave it. Challis called the twenty-four-hour number and used his tone and rank to get an after-hours number for the investigator. 'A detective will be around to look at the evidence later today.'

On the other side of the room, a call was being put through for Ellen Destry. There was a crackle on the line. 'My name is Goodall. I'm calling from New Zealand, police headquarters in Christchurch. I understand that you're investigating the murder of a woman called Clara Macris.'

'That's right. We—'

'Clara Macris is her assumed name. Her real name doesn't matter. The point is, she was in our Witness Protection program.'

Ellen slumped in her chair. 'Witness protection.'

'I was her case officer. I helped to relocate her.'

'You think someone over there found out where she was?'

'It's possible. I don't know how, but it's possible.'

'Had she been in contact with any of her friends, her family, the people she used to hang out with?'

'I don't know,' the New Zealand officer said testily. 'However, someone spotted her when she was leaving the country.'

He related the incident at the Christchurch airport.

'And you think she was followed?'

'Don't you?'

'Why wait eighteen months?'

The New Zealand officer said, 'To lull her into a false sense of security.'

TWENTY-THREE

Pam Murphy was driving Sutton in the same white Commodore.

'Did I see you at Myers Point the other day?'

He saw her stiffen, her knuckles whitening on the wheel. 'Might have, sir.'

'Scobie, call me Scobie. You had a wetsuit on, carrying a board. I couldn't see all that clearly, so it might have been someone else.'

'I have surfing lessons there sometimes.'

'Yeah, you were with a group of others.'

He saw her relax. 'What were you doing there?'

'We took our daughter to the beach. New pink bathers to try out. Only she convinced herself there were dragons, so we never made it past the first dune.'

Murphy didn't respond. Sutton let it go. He picked up one of the leaflets that Challis had given him, then out of nowhere he wanted to cry. He'd had a perfect image of Roslyn as she might be in fifteen years' time, happy and uncomplicated and ripe for a killer. He coughed, blinked, composed himself.

They were entering the caravan park. Pam Murphy said, 'Last time we were here the manager didn't know where these gypsies had gone, so why question him again?'

'This time we question the whole camp,' Sutton told her, 'and see if the backpack's still in that rubbish bin.'

'It won't be. Even if it is, who's to say it was Kymbly Abbott's in the first place?'

'It's not your ordinary backpack. I'd like to know its history.'

'Ordinary enough,' Pam said. 'I saw one just like it before Christmas.'

The ground had shifted. Marion Nunn looked at her lover in the interview room and said, 'Did you kill her? Tell me you didn't kill her. Did you have sex with her first?'

Boyd Jolic stared at the wall, his arms folded stubbornly. 'Ah, give it a rest, fucking cow.'

'What were you thinking of,' she hissed, 'lighting all those fires?' God, she hoped there were no microphones in the interview rooms.

Jolic shrugged.

She looked around the empty walls, then touched Jolic, sliding her hand from his knee to his inner thigh. 'Boyd? What have you got yourself into?'

'Nothing. And your job is to see it stays that way.'

Stung, she rocked back in her chair, then narrowed her eyes and spat, 'Just you remember who keeps you out of jail. Who feeds you sweet jobs. Who gives you witness addresses so you can send your frighteners around.'

He twisted his mouth. 'You fell in love with my cock, admit it, you stupid cow.'

'You're pathetic. You're a psychopath.' She tapped her skull. 'You're not right in the head. A screw loose. I bet you used to pull the wings off flies when you were little. Now you like to light fires. What happens—you masturbate while you watch? That's a novel way of putting the flames out. Stupid fucking brainless moron.'

'If I go down, bitch, you go down.'

'Then let's make sure it doesn't happen, shall we? After this, you and I are through.'

He pulled his features into a heavy-handed expression of anguish. 'Oh, dear, poor little lawyer lady, in an unholy marriage with her big bad client.'

'Shut up.'

She lit a cigarette and smoked it furiously.

Challis took Ellen with him in the Triumph.

'Boss, we're barking up the wrong tree.' She couldn't help it, she was losing heart.

He came down hard on her. 'First things first. Always, in a case like this. If our killer's a Kiwi hitman, he's long gone. Meanwhile we've still got Jolic and co. in custody, and can't hold them forever, so let's see whether or not they can be tied to the Pajero before we start looking elsewhere.'

'Sorry, Hal, you're right.'

He steered through the roundabout. She noticed that the Pizza Hut was full. None of the cars looked familiar. The town had filled with strangers since Boxing Day, summer regulars returning to their beach shacks, families camping at the cara-van parks, others renting flats and houses. They stood out in the shops. They were dressed better, somehow, as though the locals were five years out of date. Despite Tessa Kane's fears, the holiday trade hadn't really suffered as a result of the highway killings.

'Is he expecting us?'

Challis nodded. 'Mornington office.'

Thirty minutes later, they were examining photographs from the insurance company's file on Lance Ledwich's Pajero. 'Need-less to say, we rejected Mr Ledwich's claim. Not only was the vehicle unregistered, he omitted to tell us that he'd lost his licence a few weeks ago but was still driving around in it.'

'He's not too happy about it,' Challis said.

'He's ropeable.'

'He's going to be more than that,' Ellen said. 'Look at this, Hal.'

It was a photograph showing the rear of the burnt-out shell of the Pajero. Just beyond the border of ash was a lighter area, the dirt road itself, and, along one edge, the shallow road drain. There, caught in the fine, mud-and-sand base of the drain, was a perfect tyre track.

She tapped it with her forefinger. 'If I'm not mistaken, a Cooper tyre left that.'

The forensic technician confirmed it, peering at the photo-graph, then at his chart of tyre patterns.

'Definitely a Cooper. You should be able to match it.'

'We can't. All four tyres were burnt.'

'Ah.'

'Can't the photo tell you anything else? The way the tread is worn, splits and gouges in the rubber, that kind of thing?'

'I'll scan and do an enhancement,' the technician said, 'and compare it with the cast found at the reservoir.'

They watched. Challis felt a curious kind of excitement. It came when the stages of the detection, the methodology, the science and the technological tools were all working together.

He saw the tread pattern enlarge on the monitor screen. The technician isolated one segment, then another, enlarging and cross-matching with the plaster cast.

Finally he said, 'It's a Cooper. I'm afraid I can't say more than that.'

'It's enough to go on with,' Challis said.

Back in the Displan room, Ellen said, 'How do we play this?'

'Very carefully. There may be an innocent explanation. It may be coincidence.'

'I don't trust coincidence.'

'Neither do I.'

'Well then . . . ,' she said.

'We need to break his alibis,' Challis said. 'Go back and question everybody he worked with, neighbours, the usual.'

Ellen said, 'Groan.'

'We also need a warrant that stipulates our right to search the house and any other building that Ledwich may own, plus his place of work and all vehicles he or any member of his family may own. And meanwhile we'll go and pick him up for questioning.'

The phone was ringing somewhere in the incident room. It was distracting. The room itself wore an air of too many dead ends, of long airless days and nights, of cooped-up tempers and hurried meals. What a mess, Ellen thought. She tilted back her head. 'Somebody answer that, please?'

But there were only three officers in the room, their sleeves rolled, hunched over the telephones or their computer screens, so she crossed to the offending telephone and snatched it up.

'Destry.'

'Ellen?'

It was her husband. 'Alan?'

'Is Larrayne with you?'

Long afterwards she would remember that her first response was one of irritation. Her husband had been falling apart for days, in a low-level way, often emotional, forgetful, apt to misjudge things. 'Alan, it's her tennis lesson.'

'I know that. I've been waiting around to take her.'

'She's probably at Kathy's. She's done this sort of thing before. Just wait for her.'

Ellen's tone was: Do I have to do everything?

Her husband said, 'I rang Kathy. She said she hasn't seen Larrayne at all today.'

Ellen felt a crawling chill on the surface of her arms. Her heart seemed to shut down. Then she was shouting:

'Why the fuck didn't you say so!'

He sounded hurt. 'It's school holidays, you cow. Why would I be worried she wasn't here? I thought I'd understood it wrong and you were taking her to tennis.'

She found herself sniping, 'Then why did you ring me?' when she should have been slamming the phone down and taking action.

'I just thought I'd double-check, that's all. More than you would do, you fucking bitch.'

This time she didn't respond. She stood there, frozen, and something in her face and manner must have alerted Challis, for his hand closed over hers and he was taking the phone from her and taking charge of her fears.

TWENTY-FOUR

'I'll kill him,' she said.

'No you won't,' Challis said.

'If he's got her and he's hurt her, I'll kill him, Hal, see if I don't.'

Two sedans and a divisional van. Three detectives, four uniforms and two forensic officers. They were converging on the housing estate where Lance Ledwich lived. Scobie Sutton had taken a fourth car to detain Ledwich at his place of work and take him to the house.

'Don't jump to conclusions,' Challis said. 'His Pajero was destroyed, remember, so how did he snatch Larrayne?'

She seemed to fill with relief, then immediately tensed again. 'His wife's got a car. A station wagon.'

'Ah.'

She pushed her hands back through her hair. 'I don't understand how it could have happened. He must have snatched her on her way to Kathy's. But how? I mean, the kid of coppers, she'd never willingly go with a stranger.'

Then she seemed to understand the implications of what she'd said and groaned and put her hands over her face.

There were other explanations, but Challis didn't offer them. Your daughter is a ratty teenager. Your daughter hates you and has run off with a boyfriend. Somehow he knew that there was only one: Your daughter was smacked over the head with a tyre iron.

'He's shifted his locus, Hal,' Ellen said, taking her hands away from her face. 'All that publicity, we've driven him away from the highway. Now he's preying where people actually live. God.'

Challis heard the rising note in her voice, the fear, outrage and hysteria. 'One thing we've got going for us, it's daylight,' he said. 'Now calm down and think like a copper.'

'Daylight? How does that help us? He snatched her in daylight and no-one noticed.'

'But he won't—'

He was about to say, won't dump her body in daylight. He said, 'Ledwich has a job. He's accountable to people during the day. He won't do anything until it's dark.'

'Keep her tied up all day? God, bad as that is, I hope so.'

They were creeping over speedbumps now. Challis pointed. 'Scobie's already here. That was quick.'

The CIB Falcon was parked across Ledwich's driveway, effectively blocking off the station wagon, which was parked at the side of the house. Ellen was peering at the figures in the Falcon. 'I don't see Ledwich anywhere. Don't tell me he's done a runner.'

Then Sutton was at Challis's window. 'He wasn't at work, boss. Called in sick yesterday.'

Ellen Destry seemed to crumple. She began to bite on her finger. 'Oh God.'

'Have you tried the house?'

'Waiting for you, boss.'

They got out and approached the house. Challis pushed a button next to the front door, which was a heavy, carven thing, varnish peeling from its daily beating from the sun. Challis itched to pick at the varnish strips. The door opened.

'Mrs Ledwich?'

'Yes?'

Challis motioned Sutton and two of the uniformed constables to make for the rear of the property, then pushed through, into the house, followed by Ellen Destry and the other officers.

'We have a warrant to search these premises and any vehicles that you may own. Is your husband here?'

Ledwich's wife looked tired and distracted. 'He's in bed. Summer flu.' Then she stared from one to the other. 'Why don't you leave him alone? He almost lost his job over you lot coming around and asking questions. Give him a break.'

'We just need to talk to him,' Challis said.

Beside him, Ellen was fuming. She pushed forward. 'Look, are you going to take us through to him or not?'

'Keep your undies on.'

The house was depressing. The ceilings and walls were designed for a small race of people. The furniture was too big for it, as if composed of intrusive angles and surfaces. Challis saw a massive television set and an exercise machine. A radio somewhere was tuned to a talkback show. They came to the bedroom. Ledwich was lumped under a sheet and a pink blanket and he looked wretched, his features red and sodden, his breathing rattling with phlegm.

'What do you bastards want?'

Challis introduced himself but knew that something was wrong. He wasn't looking at a man who'd gone out earlier that day and abducted and raped and killed or at least hidden a teenage girl.

Ellen Destry knew it, too. Challis sensed her disappointment. She said, 'Lance, where were you this morning?'

'Right here. In this bed. Been here since yesterday.'

Challis looked around at the wallpaper, the gleaming white built-in wardrobe, the lace curtains. There was an odour of illness and stale air in the little room. The bed was a costly, vulgar monstrosity, fitted with a silvery-gold vinyl headboard. Rows of brass studs dimpled the vinyl, and there was a radio and a pair of speakers set into it.

He turned to Ledwich. 'You haven't been in Penzance Beach?'

'I'm flaming crook, I tell ya.'

'Okay, let's try this. Can you account for your movements on the nights of the twelfth and the seventeenth of December, and around dawn on the twenty-third?'

'I already told this bitch here—'

Ellen stepped close to the bed and neatly clouted him at the hairline.

'Ow.' He rubbed his head.

'Answer the question, Lance.'

'Like I told you, I was at work.'

'According to the foreman, you were often liberal with your hours.'

'Yeah, but not enough to go out and grab and kill someone and stash her somewhere. And if you arseholes done your homework you'd know I started *day* shift on the twenty-third. Six a.m. start. The wife's got it written down on the calendar. I know, because I double-checked after you done me over the last time. So I couldn't of killed whoever it was that time, and I didn't kill none of the others.'

Challis nodded to Ellen, who left the room.

'Before your Pajero was stolen, had it ever been used by another person? A friend, neighbour, member of your family?'

'My sister, my brother-in-law.'

'I understand your brother-in-law's been in Thailand for the past month. Who else has had access to it?'

A blush and a twist of sullenness under the red chapped skin. 'Look, I know it wasn't registered, I know I'm not licensed at the moment, I'll cop to that, but I was desperate, I had to get to work.'

'So you stored it at your sister's house and drove it from time to time?'

'Yes. I had to get to work.'

'Couldn't your wife have taken you?'

'She's got her own work to go to.'

'You thought that if the police ever happened to check up on you here—checking you weren't driving around while unlicensed—they'd not see the Pajero, or see you coming and going in it, and they'd assume you were being a good boy.'

'Something like that.'

'Not too bright, Lance.'

Ledwich folded his arms sulkily on the bedclothes at his chest.

'I'll ask you again, did anyone else drive your Pajero?'

'No.'

'What about the station wagon?'

'The wife's car.'

'But you drive it sometimes?'

'Not often. Not while I was unlicensed. She had this thing about the police confiscating it if I drove it.'

'Did you take it out this morning?'

'The wife did. I needed painkillers. She was only gone ten minutes.'

'Getting back to the Pajero. Did you have occasion to fit another set of tyres to it before Christmas?'

'No. Why?'

'Do you own another vehicle?'

'Do I look like I can afford three?'

'I'll come clean with you, Lance,' Challis said. 'An investigator found a Cooper tyre track left by your Pajero in Chicory Kiln Road.'

'Wouldn't know what tyres I had on it. They were already on it when I bought it.'

'The vehicle we're looking for in connection with the murder of Jane Gideon was fitted with a Cooper tyre of the same size and type.'

'Bullshit.'

'Can you account for that, Lance?'

'Account for it? You're stitching me up. You're running around like headless chooks getting nowhere, so you think, hang on, let's frame old Lance.'

'A Cooper all-terrain tyre, quite uncommon, quite distinctive tread pattern.'

Challis saw Ledwich fight with the information, and then saw his face clear and heard him say, what any good defence brief would say: 'Yeah, but you're not saying my tyre's the exact same tyre that you're looking for, only that it's similar.'

'Where did you have your tyres fitted?'

'I told you, they were already on it. I didn't take much notice what they were. A tyre's a tyre to me. Anyhow, anything could have happened after it was stolen. Maybe those what took it fitted new tyres, or maybe the spare was a Cooper tyre and they had a puncture.'

All good defence brief arguments, Challis thought.

At that point, Ellen came in with the calendar. She looked drawn and pale and defeated. Challis huddled with her in the corridor, where she murmured, 'According to this, he *did* have a six o'clock start on the twenty-third.'

'That could have been written in since,' Challis said. 'But check with his employer again.'

'Meanwhile,' Ellen said, 'Lance has been in bed all day and

clearly couldn't have nabbed Larrayne. So where does that leave us?'

Outside, Challis spoke into his mobile phone. 'Sir, a request. It will need to be quick.'

'Try me,' McQuarrie said.

'I need a team of uniforms and detectives at Penzance Beach. Sergeant Destry's daughter hasn't been seen since this morning.'

Silence. Then, 'Oh, Lord.'

'It might not be related, but we have to treat it as if it is. It's panic stations here.'

'I should have been informed the minute you knew.'

'Sorry, sir.'

'Okay, you can have your extra men,' McQuarrie said. 'Do you have any leads at all?' he added peevishly.

'Some,' said Challis coldly, 'and we're about to crack that arson death.'

'Keep me informed, Hal, okay? Regularly.'

'Count on it, sir.'

Challis pocketed the phone.

'Boss?'

Scobie Sutton had been tugging uselessly on the side door of Ledwich's steel garage. 'Locked, boss.'

'Forget it. We're going back to the station.'

One of the uniformed constables drove. Challis almost sat in the back with Ellen Destry, but her anxiety was too palpable. She spent the journey talking on her mobile phone, and from his position in the passenger seat he could sense her jittery body, hear her anguish, as she made her calls.

He heard her say, 'Anything from the hospitals?'

The last three calls had been to her husband. Was this another? No . . .

'Constable, I don't want excuses. Just do it.'

She flipped the phone off, and Challis turned around, about to talk to her, distract her, when she stabbed her fingers at the call buttons again. She had her notebook open in her lap, numbers listed in the back few pages.

'This is Sergeant Destry. I'm trying to locate my daughter. No, nothing to worry about. Has she been in the shop today?

218

No? She said she might be going in some time to buy a CD. No? Okay, thank you.'

Challis faced ahead again. The calls were serving a useful function, keeping her occupied—if hyper—and, in a way, they constituted police work. Who knows, she might uncover a person or a memory that would lead them to her daughter.

TWENTY-FIVE

The woman at the front desk had a girl with her, seventeen or eighteen, hostile, sulky. Mother and daughter, the desk sergeant decided, and turned to the mother. 'Help you, madam?'

'I need to speak to someone.'

She was thin and careworn. Her hands were veined and knuckled, an old woman's hands, though she was probably no more that forty-five. 'Will I do?'

'It's about that backpack on TV.'

Orders were that anyone with information on the abductions was to be sent straight through to an interview room. 'Inspector Challis will be along to speak to you shortly,' the desk sergeant said.

They waited for five minutes. It was early evening, six o'clock. Challis was deeply fatigued. Ellen Destry had gone home to be with her husband, but he knew she'd be back again. The other detectives were occupied with the search for Larrayne Destry. So that left him to speak to the cranks and time-wasters.

'You told my sergeant that this is about a backpack, Mrs Stokes.'

'The one on TV.'

'Go on.'

'Megan—' she indicated her daughter '—well, she has a boyfriend.'

'A boyfriend. Go on.'

'He gave her a backpack.'

'Name?'

'Well, it had a brand name stamped into the leather. And a tag of some sort stitched to the lining, but someone had cut it off.'

Challis felt his skin prickle. According to Mrs Abbott, Kymbly Abbott had stitched her name to the bottom of the designer's label of her backpack. He remembered her teary face: 'I showed her how to do it, Mr Challis,' she'd said.

'We'll come back to the backpack, Mrs Stokes. I meant, the boyfriend's name.'

'Danny Holsinger.'

Challis beamed across the table at the women. 'Now, there's a coincidence. Danny is helping us with our inquiries right at this very moment.'

'I bet he is,' Mrs Stokes said.

'Why don't you all leave him alone,' the girl said. 'He hasn't done nothing.'

'Tell me about the backpack.'

'Danny killed them girls, didn't he?' Mrs Stokes said. 'He killed them and souvenired some of their things and had the nerve to give the backpack to my daughter.'

'We don't know that it's the same backpack.'

'Course it is. I had a gander at it when he gave it to Megan. This is nice, I says. Then I see the tag's been cut off. I say, what's this? He goes, Oh, I bought it at a seconds shop, that's why there's no label. But I didn't believe him.'

Challis turned to the girl. 'Megan? Did Danny say where he got the backpack?'

She looked at the floor. 'He said he bought it.'

'In your heart of hearts, do you think that was the truth?'

'No.'

'He stole it, dirty bugger. Killed that girl and stole it.'

'He never! You're always on at him.'

Mrs Stokes faced her daughter. 'So? Twice I know of he's been done for stealing.'

She fished inside her handbag and tossed a videotape across the desk at Challis. 'Plus he's a pervert. Tried to make Megan watch this, people having sex with animals. No telling what sick things he's capable of.' She turned to her daughter again. 'You want your head read, going out with a scumbag like him.'

'How would you know, you frigid cow.'

Challis slammed his hand on the desk. 'This is a murder inquiry. There's nothing more serious on this earth. Quit your arguing and answer my questions or I'll have you both in the lockup so fast for obstruction, your heads will spin.'

Mrs Stokes composed herself and said, 'Carry on. I'm ready.'

Megan stared hotly at the floor.

'For the moment, let's forget Danny.'

'Hard to forget that little bugger.'

'Mrs Stokes, I'm warning you.'

'Sorry, sorry, I'm all ears.'

'A backpack comes into your possession, Megan. Where is it now?'

'Mum let it get stolen, didn't she? Stupid cow.'

'I see. And how did that happen?'

'She let this gypsy into the house.'

Mrs Stokes opened her arms. 'How was I to know she was going to rob the place? She didn't take much. I didn't even know she took the backpack till I saw the TV. I turn to Megan and I says, "That's like yours." Then she tells me hers has been nicked. Not my fault.'

'It *is*,' Megan said.

'Shut up, both of you. Megan, listen to me, do you think it's possible that Danny stole the backpack from someone and gave it to you?'

He watched her. After a while, she began to nod her head. 'That's why I didn't report it when it got stolen from me, especially I didn't tell Mum, you can see what she's like. Danny, you know, he likes to give me things. I don't know how he can afford half the stuff he gives me, unless he nicks it first.' She looked up and said bravely, 'I want him to make a new start. He's got to stop nicking things.'

Challis encountered Ellen Destry in the corridor, carrying her car keys. She looked dishevelled, her mood distracted. He stopped and said softly, 'How's things?'

'What do you think?'

He took her arm. 'This will cheer you up.' He urged her toward the interview rooms.

She twisted away. 'Hal, I've got things to do. Phone calls. Has Scobie checked in yet? I want to keep an eye on the search. A million things.'

'We're interviewing Danny Holsinger again.'

'I'm more interested in finding Larrayne than who killed Clara Macris.'

'Bear with me. I can tie him to the backpack.'

'*A* backpack. Like I said, there must be dozens of them around.'

'He *stole* this particular one. The label had been removed, either by him or before he stole it, I've yet to discover.'

She closed her eyes. 'I pray to God this is it.'

'Danny, did you remove the label after you stole the backpack, or had it already been removed?'

'I didn't steal it, Mr Challis. Sergeant Destry here knows I didn't.'

'I know no such thing, Danny.'

'You believed me when you and that Pam Murphy had me in here.'

'I don't believe you now.'

'I bought it fair and square at one of them seconds shops.'

'Prove it. Show us the receipt.'

'Paperwork. I don't generally hang on to stuff like that.'

Challis leaned forward. 'Danny, I'm not interested in your bullshit. I'll let you in on a secret, shall I? That backpack? It belonged to Kymbly Abbott.'

'Who?'

He seemed to be genuinely puzzled. 'She was raped and murdered a couple of weeks before Christmas,' Challis said. 'Don't you read the papers, watch the news?'

'I don't know their names,' Danny muttered.

'That sounds about right,' Ellen said. 'They're just meat to you, right? You rape them, kill them, dump their bodies. Who cares what their names are?'

His voice cracked, failing on the high notes. 'I didn't kill nobody.'

'We have to solve this case, Danny,' Challis said. 'You're the best lead we've got.'

'I can prove I didn't kill them'

'Got an alibi, have you? Boyd Jolic? Who's going to believe him? Megan? She was at the front desk just now, making a statement. It starts, "Daniel Holsinger is a liar and a thief and likes to watch illegal porn," and goes downhill from there.'

Danny looked stricken. 'She never.'

'You've got no friends, Danny. No-one's going to alibi you. No-one's going to shed any tears when we shut you away. Three life terms, you're going to get.'

Ellen leaned forward and Challis saw how hard it was for her to say: '*Four* life terms. You see, Danny, my daughter's gone missing, and right now I'm as inclined to throw the book at you as at anyone else. Never hurt a copper, Danny, didn't any of your scumbag mates ever teach you that?'

He shot back in his chair. 'I never touched your kid. I swear.'

Challis said softly, 'The backpack, Danny.'

He slumped in his chair. 'It's like you said, I took it. This house up near Frankston.'

Challis stopped him. 'Danny, you're officially still under caution. I'm going to tape this, okay? Do you want a lawyer present?'

'No.'

'For the benefit of the tape, Mr Holsinger has admitted stealing a black leather backpack from a house near Frankston. Danny, to continue, did you cut the label out?'

'It was already cut out, like you see in seconds shops sometimes.'

'Did you steal anything else from this house?'

'Might of. I forget. Cash and that.'

'Where did you find the backpack?'

Danny smirked. 'Get this—behind them panel things around the bath. I was in this other house once? Accidentally kicked the bath? The side falls off and there's a couple of rifles in there. Now when I do over a house, that's the first place I look.'

'We might need the address of that particular house, Danny,' said Challis dryly. But he felt the old familiar tingle of the hunt. This *had* to be Kymbly Abbott's backpack. It was a souvenir, but not one that could be kept in plain sight.

Ellen got to her feet. 'You're going to show us where, Danny, *now*.'

Challis held up a hand. 'Just one more minute. Danny, you've been questioned about an aggravated burglary on a house near the racecourse, the subsequent theft and arson of a Mitsubishi Pajero, and the arson murder of Clara Macris in Quarterhorse Lane. You denied all knowledge of these crimes. Would you care to reconsider your position?'

Danny dropped his head. 'The ag burg was me.'

'And the other man involved?'

'Boyd Jolic.'

'What about Mr Oliver?'

'Hal, come *on*,' Ellen said. She was frantic, stepping from foot to foot.

Challis held up his hand. 'Danny?'

'Craig come and pick us up after Joll burnt the Pajero.'

'You admit to stealing it after the aggravated burglary?'

'Me and Joll. It was all Joll's idea.'

'And the pornographic video?'

'I didn't know what was on it.'

'Danny, I'm only interested in where you got it.'

'It was in the Pajero. There was this cardboard box in the back, half a dozen videos, so I pinched one.'

'Good. Now, were you also involved in a traffic incident with a white Mercedes sedan driven by a woman driver that same afternoon? On Coolart Road? Whilst in the Pajero?'

'Yes.'

'Explain what happened.'

'This bird cuts Joll off, gives him the finger. So he follows her home. He was that mad, said he was going to come back and sort her out.'

'What did you take him to mean by that?'

'I don't know. He's a mad bugger. He tried to get me to go with him.'

'To do what?'

'Sort her out.'

'Kill her? Burn her house down?'

'He didn't say. But I wasn't surprised when I heard about the fire. Look, he's bad news. Scares the shit out of me. You got to put him away.'

In the corridor, Ellen spat, 'Precious seconds, Hal, precious seconds.'

'Exactly,' Challis said.

TWENTY-SIX

Danny took them to a tract of housing that backed on to bushland between Frankston and Baxter. Challis and Ellen were in the lead car with Danny, Challis driving. Scobie Sutton and three uniformed officers were in the second car.

'Okay, Danny, show us the house.'

His pinched face screwed up in worry. 'They all look the same.'

It was true. Small brick houses with tiled roofs, all about thirty years old. Native trees lined the streets. There were no front fences. The cars in the driveways or on the nature strips indicated modest incomes and aspirations. Challis slowed the car for a knot of teenagers playing cricket. Otherwise the streets were deserted.

He turned, completing the block, and started on the next. Then another.

Finally Danny said, 'It was sort of like that one.'

'*Like* that one, or was it that one?'

'That one.'

Over-long grass and weeds, white pebble-dashed walls and glazed tiles set it apart from the other houses, but only just. 'What do you recognise about it?'

'I dunno. The walls, kind of thing. Plus that thing on the roof.'

A satellite dish.

'Okay, let's go.'

Fifteen minutes later, Challis said, 'How sure are you?'

'Fairly sure. It was night time.'

'Danny, this house is unoccupied. It's been like that for some time.'

In fact, Challis had found a To-Let sign lying in the grass.

'Wasn't when I broke in.'

'Then you must have broken into a different house.'

Challis glanced at Ellen. Her face had fallen into lines of frustration and extreme anxiety. She blinked, letting the tears splash. 'He's got a new base. He could be anywhere.'

Challis took Sutton aside. 'Check with the neighbours. And see if you can get an after-hours number for the agency handling the lease. We need to know who owns the place, who last rented it, forwarding address, etcetera.'

'Right.'

Challis looked at the sky. It was almost dark. He could see the bluish flicker of television sets in a couple of houses. There was a glow on the horizon, the lights of Melbourne.

He returned to the car. 'Okay, Danny, we're taking you home.'

'Home?'

Ellen snarled, 'Your home for the next little while, unless you get bail, you useless piece of shit.'

Danny sniffed. He sniffed all the way out of the little estate, as Challis took wrong turnings and found himself in dead-end streets and on streets that wound back on themselves like the entrails of a complicated organism. Danny might have kept on sniffing as Challis finally found a street that would take them on to the highway if he hadn't gone tense and pointed and said, 'There. That's the house.'

It was like the other in most details, except that the grass was short, and there was a signboard advertising a business name hammered into the grass, and a Jeep bearing the same sign parked in the driveway. Trees and dense shrubbery screened the house from the neighbours.

'I remember the sign,' Danny said.

Rhys Hartnett, Air-Conditioning Specialist.

Twenty-Seven

Challis parked farther along the street and radioed for Sutton and his team. When they arrived he directed one man to stand watch over the Jeep, and Sutton and the other men he directed to the yard at the rear. 'Scobie, you wait by the back door. Put one man at either corner, so he can watch for movement at any of the windows along the sides of the house. Ellen and I will take the front.'

He turned back to the car. 'Danny, give me your wrist, please. I hate to do this, but . . .'

He cuffed the thin, unresisting wrist to the roof handle above the door. 'Not too tight?'

Danny's eyes gleamed. 'You're going after him?'

'Yes, Danny, we are.'

'I'll watch.'

'You do that.'

Challis turned away. Ellen Destry was beside herself, marking time on the footpath, wanting to talk, wanting to act. She kicked the tyres on the Jeep. Even in the half-light, Challis could see that they were worn, mismatched. 'These aren't Cooper tyres.'

Ellen's face was twisted with something like shame. 'Hal, I think Hartnett saw me unloading the tyre casts we made at the reservoir. He probably replaced the Coopers with second-hand tyres later the same day.' She looked away. 'If he's killed her, I'll never forgive myself.'

There was no point in getting angry with her. Challis took her arm. 'Are you ready?'

'Am I ever.'

They approached the front door. Dogs were barking in the nearby yards. Challis slapped a mosquito away from his cheek. He could hear the irregular splash and rustle of someone hand-watering a garden bed at the house on the right. Ellen raised her knuckles and knocked.

A voice said, 'Excuse me. You're the police?'

Challis crossed swiftly to the border of trees and shrubs. 'Yes.'

'You after the air-conditioning bloke?'

'What can you tell me about him, sir?'

'We were talking just now. When he saw your car slow down, he went barging over my back fence.'

Hence the barking dogs, Challis thought. 'Can you show me where?'

The man pointed. 'I got the feeling he was heading for the reserve.'

Challis ran to the footpath. The reserve was a dark mass in the lowering light of evening. He thumbed the transmit button on his radio. 'Scobie, is the back door unlocked?'

'Yes, boss.'

'Send a man in. Tell him to open the front door for Ellen. They'll stay and search the house. You and the others come with me. He's on foot, gone into scrubland.'

Ellen made a frantic search of the house, then gathered herself and searched again. She kept bumping into the uniformed constable. It was a small house. There was nothing ostensibly wrong about the man who lived in it. He owned a television set, a stereo, a handful of books. His habits were tidy. There was nothing freakish about the lighting, the wallpaper, the items in his cupboards and drawers. There was no pornography, there were no implements of cruelty. There was no body, alive or dead, or signs that one had ever been there.

But the house spoke of an inflexible life. No clutter, no dust, no sign that an ordinary person sprawled there at the end of the day. For just a moment, Ellen caught a sense of Rhys Hartnett, his rigidity and his hatred of disorder.

And, for what it was worth, there was a computer, and a Canon printer.

She remembered the bath. She levered off the side panels. Nothing.

Only an odour of dampness.

But he'd kept one souvenir, Kymbly Abbott's backpack. Had he kept others? Or had he ceased to do that after Danny had broken in?

'The ceiling, Sarge?'

There was a manhole. They positioned the hall table under it and she watched the constable haul himself through the narrow gap. She heard the roof beams creak. She heard a sneeze.

Then his face appeared. 'Nothing, Sarge.' He sneezed again.

'Come on down. We need to know if he owns or rents another house somewhere.'

'We haven't searched the shed, Sarge. And he might own a lockup somewhere, for his equipment and that.'

Tear her hair out, that's what she wanted to do. Her hands itched to hurt her own body.

'Shed, first.'

It was a gardening and tool shed. A rake, a fork, a shovel and a small pick were propped handle-first inside a tall wooden box in one corner. Lengths of dowelling rested across the beams above their heads. Extensive shelving had been erected around three of the walls. Ellen picked up a plastic honey tub. It was full of screws. The fourth wall was hung with hammers, chisels, screwdrivers and wrenches. The spanners were in a toolbox on the floor. She guessed that there would be more tools in the Jeep.

She grabbed the constable. 'We haven't checked his van.'

It was careless of her. Hartnett might have doubled back and escaped in it. And there were good reasons why it should have been searched first.

All of the doors were locked. Ellen sent the constable to search for the keys, while she walked around and around the vehicle, tugging on handles and attempting to peer through the darkened windows. A mobile hell, she thought, and began to cry. He'd snatched Larrayne over ten hours earlier. If he was true to form, her daughter was dead by now. She had to expect that, face that. She tugged on the rear door handles again.

The Jeep seemed to give an answering shake, so minute that she almost didn't register it. She didn't trust her senses. It could have been the plates of the earth shifting a little, far away, far beneath her, registering as a tiny shake here, in this driveway.

The constable returned, waving keys. 'In a basket on the kitchen bench,' he said proudly. He stopped, looked toward the reserve. 'They've brought in the chopper.'

Ellen snatched the keys from him. She wasn't interested in anything but getting the doors open.

The rear compartment, once so familiar to her, a small, friendly, masculine place that spoke of Rhys Hartnett's clever hands and efficiency, now seemed to be composed of sharp metal corners and the coldness of metal. Shelves, brackets, tools, offcuts of aluminium, electrical flex, drawers, a large, padlocked cabinet along one side of the tray.

A muffled knock. Another hint of rocking.

They registered it together. The constable fumbled the keys out of the door and searched for the smaller keys on the ring. Ellen made to snatch the keys from him. They performed a small, foolish dance, a playground grabbing contest, before the constable relinquished the keys to her.

The cabinet door swung upwards. Larrayne lay cramped on her side and wrapped in a blanket of thin, high-density foam. Her wrists and ankles had been taped together. There was a strip of tape over her mouth. Her eyes were wide and afraid, and then they began to blink away the tears and she began to thrash her body, thrash it until they'd pulled her out and cut her free.

Challis felt his chest tighten. His mouth tasted sour and his breathing came in tight, strained shudders that barely sustained him. Asthma. He flashed on his childhood. The evenings had always been the worst time. He'd want to run and climb and charge about, anything to avoid bed, anything to fill up the minutes before he was called inside, anything to stay outside, and the attacks would come, so bad sometimes that his panicked parents had called for an ambulance. But that was childhood. He had a more recent memory, of a small town, his wife, the other constable, the affair between them burning unnoticed by him until the anonymous call that had lured him to a patch of trees along a moonless back road. The shots. He'd taken one in the arm, a sleeve-plucking flesh wound. He'd circled around and he'd shot the man who'd wanted him out of the way. Challis stopped now, one hand resting against the trunk of a tree. His breathing rattled and wheezed. So much for silence, he thought.

There were men on the way. 'Fifteen minutes,' according to the duty sergeant in Frankston. And a helicopter with a searchlight.

Hartnett had a lead of two minutes. He knew his way through the reserve, presumably. Challis hadn't sent a car around to the bottom edge of the reserve. There were simply no roads to it. So, all four of them—himself, Sutton, the two constables—were floundering in the twilight, only two torches between them.

He thumbed his radio. 'Anything?'

The replies came: 'No, boss.'

'Everyone keep still a minute, and listen.'

After a while he said, 'Anything?'

'No, boss.'

Then Challis heard it, the thud and chop of rotor blades. A voice crackled on his radio. 'Inspector Challis?'

'In the reserve. Can you see it?'

Silence, then, 'Approaching you now.'

'There are four of us,' Challis said. 'Two uniforms, two plainclothes. We're wearing white shirts.'

'How's our target dressed?'

'I don't know.'

'Roger. We'll flush him out, sweeping now.'

Suddenly light was probing the trees near Challis. It flicked like an angry finger, then began to make steady sweeps across the reserve as the helicopter moved slowly down its length.

In the mind-numbing din, Challis felt ill. He realised that he hadn't eaten for many hours. He thought about following the light, then decided to head in the opposite direction. There were men enough to grab Hartnett if the spotlight flushed him out, but what if it had passed right over him and he was *behind* the sweep now, safe in the darkness, waiting until he could slip away.

Hartnett shouldn't have moved, Challis told himself later. Hartnett should simply have waited. But he didn't wait. He burst from a thicket, screaming unnervingly, swinging a knife. Challis felt the blade slice above his nipple. There was warm wetness at first, then the pain.

He feinted, dropping to one knee with a groan. Hartnett swung around. He was still screaming, fighting the air with the knife. The danger to Challis lay not in Hartnett's skill and calculation but in that windmilling wild arm. Challis rolled on to his back, jackknifing his knees to his chest. To Hartnett, it must have signalled submission, for he ran forward, bending low, coming around on Challis's left side, still screaming.

Challis waited. He waited for the upstroke, the moonglint on the knife that told him it was about to swing down and cut him open. Propping on his forearms, he swivelled his trunk around and shot out both feet.

He caught Hartnett's knees. One smacked against the other and Challis heard the moist, muffled crack of a bone breaking. Hartnett screamed. His arms swung up and his back arched. He flopped to the ground and began to flounder. Challis felt terrible. He'd never seen so much agony in anyone and had never caused so much.

TWENTY-EIGHT

'He kept saying, "Your mother's a bitch. Stupid copper bitch. Stupid copper bitch who goes back on her word."'

'Hush, love, it's all right.'

'It was like it was personal.'

'I think it was, this time.'

'He told me I was always rude to him. Well, I *was*. I always thought he was a sleazebag. I told you I thought that. I couldn't believe you brought him into the house.'

'It's all right, sweetie. It's all right. You're safe now.'

They were in the car. Sutton was driving, with Challis next to him. The ambulance crew had cleared and dressed Challis's cut before taking Hartnett away. Larrayne Destry was in the back of the car, with her mother. She'd refused to be taken to hospital.

'You don't have to talk about it now.'

'I want to.'

'Okay, sweetie.'

'You think he raped me, don't you? Well he was going to, he said. Kept telling me all the things he was going to do to me. Told me this time was going to be different from the other times. This time he was going to draw it out for a few days.'

Challis heard the soft scrape of fabric against fabric. He didn't turn around. They were not wearing their seatbelts but

234

were huddled together, sniffing, sometimes crying, Ellen ceaselessly touching her daughter's face.

'He showed me all this stuff.'

'What stuff?'

'There was a watch, a ring, a hair clip. Little things.'

'Souvenirs.'

'Oh.'

A cloud passed across the moon. They seemed to be alone on the black road. Challis coughed, and said, over his shoulder, 'Where did you see these things, Larrayne?'

He sensed that Larrayne was leaning toward him. 'Where Mum found me, inside that cabinet thingy in his van.'

Challis nodded. 'And he talked about the other women he'd abducted?'

'Over and over. Boasting.'

Ellen said, 'I can't believe I let him see those tyre casts. He must have enjoyed himself, working next door to the police, watching them flounder. Probably couldn't believe his luck.'

Challis nodded. It would have taken a certain kind of nerve and arrogance for Hartnett to stay on at the courthouse, working, watching.

As if reading his thoughts, Ellen said, 'He was under our noses the whole time. I trusted him.'

It occurred to Challis then that his sergeant had something to hide. She was fighting unwelcome emotions and realisations. Her talkativeness—she was feeling relief, but did she also feel betrayed and embarrassed? It was as if something had happened to challenge her good judgment of herself. He remembered seeing her with Hartnett several times. How far had it gone?

'How much longer do you intend to hold my client?'

Scobie Sutton said, 'All in good time, Mrs Nunn.'

He was tired and dirty. He'd been scratched by blackberry canes at the edge of the reserve where they'd captured Hartnett. He wanted to go home. For days, it seemed, he hadn't seen his daughter, or not awake, anyway.

Challis had briefed him. He'd listened to the taped interview with Danny Holsinger. He was ready.

'Mr Jolic, you are still under caution.'

'Sure.'

'I want to inform you that one of your accomplices has given you up.'

'Doesn't surprise me.'

'Boyd, shut up,' Marion Nunn said.

'No, *you* shut up.'

Sutton went on wearily, 'You and Danny Holsinger—'

'Danny Holsinger. Habitual thief and liar. My client—'

'Mrs Nunn, please, just let me finish.'

'Yeah, let the man finish.'

'Don't you care what happens to you?'

'Shut up. You bore me.'

Sutton decided to sit back and watch. He turned to Marion Nunn, who felt his gaze and said, 'I'd like a moment alone with my client.'

'Certainly.'

'Yeah, well, I don't want a moment alone with *her*,' Jolic said.

'Boyd, I'm warning you, don't let your tongue get you into trouble.'

Sutton swung his gaze on to Jolic. Jolic looked less tough and arrogant, suddenly. He seemed to struggle to ask, 'Mr Sutton, you'd say I was pretty normal, wouldn't you?'

'Depends how you measure it, Boyd, but sure, I'd say so.'

'Not sick or twisted?'

Sutton shook his head emphatically. 'Nup.'

'Stop this! Just stop it!' Marion Nunn said. 'Constable Sutton, I'm asking you now, terminate this interview.'

'But Mr Jolic's got things to say,' Sutton said.

'If I give you certain information, it'll look good in the eyes of the DPP, right?' Jolic asked.

'A very good chance.'

'Okay. Here goes. I done the ag burg. I burnt the fucking four-wheel drive. I killed the woman. Only you got to understand—I was aggravated. She shouldn't of—'

'Boyd, shut up.'

Boyd Jolic jerked his thumb. 'This cow here? She gives me house plans, photos, whatever, and I pull jobs for her. We split it fifty-fifty.'

'Interesting.'

'Listen, goggle-eyes, don't go taking his word against mine.'

Sutton stared at her.

'She's got this empty house, Mr Sutton,' Jolic said. 'All the stuff's still there probably.' He paused. 'She shouldn't of said I was sick.'

'In you go.'

'You're not going to rough me up, Sergeant?'

'I'm in a good mood,' van Alphen said, gently pushing Marion Nunn into the cell.

The next morning, Challis said, 'Scobie, you're coming with me.'

They drove through the town, which now seemed less edgy, more benign and trusting, as though everyone had heard the news overnight and gone back to being themselves. Or is it me? Challis thought. Do I read things as they are, or as I feel? But there were more people about. More of them looked cheery in the face of the early sun.

They found Lance Ledwich in his sitting room, watching morning television, women in leotards flexing on grass, the Sydney Opera House sailing behind them. Challis could smell eucalyptus vapour and there was a hot lemon drink on the floor. He tossed the videotape that had so offended Megan Stokes on to the coffee table.

'Know what this is, Lance?'

Some of the life seemed to go out of Ledwich. 'Never seen it before.'

'Funny, it was found in your four-wheel drive.'

'Don't know nothing about it.'

'Scobie, search the kitchen, see if you can find the keys to Mr Ledwich's garage.'

Ledwich sank in his chair. A minute later, Sutton returned, holding a bunch of keys.

'Stay with him,' Challis said. 'I won't be long.'

One wall of the garage was lined with metal shelves. Challis counted a dozen professional-grade video reproduction units. There was also a colour photocopier and a stack of garish sleeves ready to be slipped into empty cassette cases. On the bench nearby was a padded postbag with US postage on it, containing the master videotape. Was the brother-in-law on a buying trip in Thailand? Was the sister involved, too? Did they have many under-the-counter customers for their videos? Did they charge much? Enough for Ledwich to afford a Pajero, Challis decided—the Pajero also part of the man's image, the cool operator.

He looked at his watch. Noon. He was giving himself the rest of the day off. Let someone else interview Rhys Hartnett. He wasn't interested in what made Hartnett tick.

The shift in the atmosphere had been clear to Pam the moment she stepped into the station at the start of her shift. Challis had made an arrest. Destry's daughter was safe. The whole station seemed happier.

She was paired with John Tankard for the day. She drove. Their first job was to investigate reports of theft from two panel vans belonging to surfers at Myers Point. She found that her heart and stomach were doing funny things. She wondered if she'd see Ginger. Just knowing he was nearby was setting her off.

John Tankard had the *Age* in his lap. 'Charges reinstated. That's what I like to hear. Whaddya reckon, Murph?'

'Blood oath,' she said, sticking her lower jaw out, deepening her voice, grabbing the wheel as if she were going into battle.

He flushed. 'Aren't you a sweetheart.'

On the other side of the Peninsula, Challis was shaping a new airframe strut. He lost himself in the crisp bite of the wood plane, Lucky Oceans on Radio National and a letter that had come from an old man in Darwin:

'With reference to your request for information regarding A33-8. This was an air force serial number, applied to non-military Dragons that were impressed into service with the RAAF during the war. I had the pleasure of flying A33-8 in early 1942, just before the fall of Java. I was stationed in Broome, and made a dozen trips in her, ferrying Dutch refugees to Port Hedland. I do know that your aeroplane started life working for the Vacuum Oil Company, flying geologists about the north-west, but what became of her after the war, I really couldn't say. If it's not too much trouble, perhaps you could send me a snap of her.'

On the five o'clock news there was a report of human remains found caught in bullrushes at the bend of a creek on the other side of the Peninsula. Challis swept his wood shavings into a bin, bundled his overalls into the Triumph and drove home over the bone-jarring back roads. He walked inside, his footsteps booming in the hollows of the house. The red light was flashing on his answering machine. Three calls. He pressed the play button. ID confirmed on the body in the creek; then his wife; and before the third caller spoke, he discovered, with a tiny shift in his equilibrium, that he was waiting for a low, slow-burning voice.

ABOUT THE AUTHOR

Garry Disher grew up in rural South Australia and now lives near the Victorian coast. In 1978 he was awarded a creative writing fellowship to Stanford University, California, where he wrote his first short-story collection. A full-time writer for many years, he is the author of novels, short story collections, writers' handbooks, the *Personal Best* anthologies, the Wyatt crime thrillers, and books for children. His novel, *The Sunken Road* (Allen & Unwin, 1996), was shortlisted for several major awards and nominated for the Booker Prize by his English publisher.